FROM UNDER
THE BED

Fiona McClean

ROMAN *Books*
www.roman-books.co.uk

ISBN 978-93-80905-37-2

Typeset in Adobe Garamond Pro

First published in 2011
Paperback Edition 2012

1 3 5 7 9 8 6 4 2

British Library Cataloguing in Publication Data.
A catalogue record for this book is available from the British Library.

ROMAN *Books*
26 York Street, London W1U 6PZ, United Kingdom
2nd Floor, 38/3, Andul Road, Howrah 711109, WB, India
www.roman-books.co.uk | www.roman-books.co.in

Printed and bound in India by
Roman Printers Private Limited
www.romanprinters.com

FROM UNDER
THE BED

FROM UNDER THE BED

Fiona McClean was born in Dusseldorf, Germany as the daughter of an army family. After studying Fine Arts at the University of Wales, Newport, she now lives the life of an accomplished painter in South France. Fiona loves to spend her time writing and painting, walking and horse riding. *From Under the Bed* is her debut novel.

1

French Fancies from Whitsons

Every evening after work I walk along this grey, narrow street, telling myself: 'No'.

I can see my favourite shop, Whitsons. It is about twenty feet away next to Simpsons and Son. My toes and fingers scrunch up. I walk with tense footsteps and as if on a tightrope.

The sun reflects on the swinging glass doors, pushed open by the huge bottom of a woman carrying bags. The smell of fresh baked bread, and the sight of a bar of Cadbury's chocolate weaken my will, so strong in me a few minutes ago. It is as if someone has put ice in my blood. I can feel my form changing. My shoulders hunch and bend forwards and I pull the flaps of my coat around my face trying to make my head disappear. If only I had a hat.

Into the warmth I walk, up the aisle of confectionery. I know all the shelves better than the way home. Amongst the rows of cakes flash *Lyon's French Fancies*. I take six boxes into my furtive hands, leaving an almost empty shelf. Next to the counter, silver packets of chewing gum gleam at me, I manage to take one whilst balancing the teetering cakes and show it to the cashier, smiling at her.

'Anything else?'

'No, nothing.'

'The cakes?'

'I've already paid for those.' I lie.

She looks to the busy queue trailing behind me and to the

next customer, a short man with a trolley full of beer and crisps. He's in a rush, slaps the cans on the conveyer belt.

'In a hurry Jack?'

'Yeah, parked on a yellow line.'

On the way out I walk with slow certain steps before speeding up around the corner of a street bustling with people. My trench coat becomes heavier, a sack of sand, weighing me down. My sweaty hair clings like seaweed.

Leaning against a wall I rest my head back and close my eyes. A million years pass by.

Feeling something tap my shoulder, I jump in fear. A woman with a pillbox police-hat stands beside me, uniform black and demonic.

'Don't panic, just wondering if you are okay, love? You don't look well.'

She ignores my boxes of French Fancies. My head sinks to avoid her eyes.

'Have you been taking drugs? Heroin?'

'No, no.'

This morning a shop mirror glared back at me reflecting the dark shadows circling my glazed eyes. This is who she sees.

I am fragile, afraid and about to crack. A voice in me pleads: *Please go away.* But, something lilting in her speech makes me long to look at her. She leaves with an anxious expression. 'I'd go home if I were you, and get some sleep.'

Sleep? I'm too frightened to sleep. I'm frightened to stay awake. The French Fancies gnaw away at me from inside their boxes sending their delicate perfume out to me.

Highbury and Islington tube station is next. Down the concrete stairs crumpled like a paper bag by thighs and arms whooshing by. The boxes tower like high-rise flats, blocking my view of the escalator. I make a guess and jump on. The teeth of the moving steps almost catch my toes.

Twenty minutes later and I'm in front of the turquoise door to home, hand trembling, key in lock, certain that I have been followed.

The door is on a slant and closes with a quick, light click. Edging through the full-of-bikes corridor, I can spy all of my housemates through the crack of the sitting room door. Joe, a sunken black shadow, sits in an armchair which has fat sausage arms and a floral cover. Its seat, pressed by so many bottoms, is a large dimple. His left arm, the only part of him I can see, blotchy and swollen, supports his head. Emma sits cross-legged, smoking.

'Remember how we used to be: kissing in loos, swimming nude, smoking joints in Mulberry Gardens?' She flicks her hair and looks over at Nick.

Long legged Nick chuckles, his bottom hangs off the end of the chair. He has the face of a fourteen year old with a showering of freckles, satin blonde hair and he makes a noise so like a sniffle. When he talks my head tingles.

'Hey, has anyone seen Alice?' Nick asks, sitting up.

'Alice? Yeah, she's gone shopping.'

I stiffen upon hearing my name.

Emma is my only and perfect friend because her beauty sparkles and she has a great laugh that fills the room. She wears bright multi-coloured, floral dresses with neon pink flat shoes. Her auburn hair cut to a bob and her lips a lush pink.

Laughing into her cigarette smoke, Emma says: 'Sssh it's the 6'o'clock News, the weather forecast is on.' They turn to the small, noisy, black and white television like butterflies to nectar.

Tiptoeing, I tread the stairs to my small bedroom. Violet painted walls and grey carpet coat me in a still, cool peace. The south facing window overlooking the washing line, floods the room with light. Clothes clutter everywhere, but I spy a clearing near the bed for the French Fancies.

Heart beating against my ribs and hands shaking I scrunch the cellophane away from the first pink box and open it. A moment hangs in the air before dream after dream enters my mouth. Rich sponge cubes with hats of sweet smelling fondant cream and coats of lemon, chocolate or pink icing melt on my tongue. The crisp pages of my book, *Modern Art* stolen from the library, spread a gallery of paintings before me, 'The Bedroom,' by Van Gogh; Bonnard, landscapes, portraits, Matisse. The yellows calling out like ballerinas. The reds, sharp as stones. The colours make a tapestry in my mind. I start to imagine it's me painting the fields and the trees and I am filled with shame. Moist crumbs land on the pages. Frightened I will spoil it, I shut the book.

Fifty-four iced dreams wrestle for space, heaving inside my tummy, screaming to get out. They have rounded my stomach into a pumpkin and set up a battle with my skirt. Easing down the zip I walk to the pink linoleum floored loo. It's a space capsule, my body bumping and turning to fit in.

The more I make myself ill, the more I shrink. My pumpkin disappears.

Fourteen feet separate the loo from my bedroom. The blue carpet stretches between the two. Tired, my legs travel the distance. The last step lands where no floorboards whine and groan with the weight of my heavy feet.

Locking myself in, I lie down on the carpeted floor, dragging and wriggling bits of my body, which have come apart. I put them back together again under the bed. My nose almost touches the underneath. Dust makes me sneeze. I pull down the green candlewick bedspread and am in total black. Folding my arms I lie there, a mummy still and blind though my eyes are wide open, my body beginning to feel beaten and my mouth dry, I shiver and sweat. My stomach plunges into the usual dull aching pain. *I think this time is one of the worst, Alice.* I whisper. I remember the policewoman and her questions. I cannot face another day.

I was young—fourteen, when I first saw a doctor. I came home from school, my coat bulging with French Fancies nicked from Eric's grocery store. I stole so many cakes my coat started to change shape. My mother, Diana, with her smoker's breath and Lily of the Valley perfume took me to see Doctor Fall, because I ate three boxes of French Fancies and Stuart's supper. Stuart, my father shouted at Diana. Diana had had enough.

'You have Anorexia Nervosa. You are dangerously underweight,' said Doctor Fall, his glasses half way down his nose. He took my pulse. It was very low. He told me to eat more, (but not cakes) to put on 2lbs before the next visit. That was the last memory of Doctor Fall. After that came other doctors.

Closing my eyes, I can feel moisture on my cheeks, a falling tear. A silence envelopes me like a duvet, until thoughts—intruders—nag and pull at me.

French Fancies! That's all you think about. You've forgotten how to paint haven't you. When was the last time you picked up a brush? You're useless!

It's true I put almost all my paintings away. It hurt too much to see them. Only a picture of two mackerel, in rich greens and shades of rose hangs on the wall over the bed.

Look at you! Too weak to carry a canvas!

I recall trying to run, my straw legs unable to take me far.

I will get strong and paint by the end of this year, I say out loud, gulping a mouthful of dust.

2

Turning Stone Steps

Today we'll have a perfect breakfast. Birds are singing. The sky is blue with a rippling of white. Emma is up dressed in her red satin slippers from Hong Kong and blue cotton dressing gown. I'm wearing my pretty turquoise robe nicked from Littlewoods.

My lips paint a great big morning smile for Emma. She has a thin red lizard's tail of a smile for me. A mime artist, still and stony, whose sudden move frightens, she thrusts the big, brown paper bag of organic muesli in front of my nose.

A memory rushes in like an ambulance, urgent, carrying the truth. It hadn't been a dream. Me, waking up, still under the bed and surrounded by boxes. My bleary eyes looking at the clock, seeing the small hand near the three and the big hand hovering near the twelve, I had sneaked downstairs in the dark. The scrunch of the stiff brown paper and the chomping of my teeth nibbling hazelnuts, brazil-nuts and almonds sounding like distant thunder in the sleeping house.

'There are none left! Why Alice? Why can't you be normal? Why can't you stop?'

Her bright red lips are foaming criticisms and my Emma, with her quiet voice and gentle grey-green eyes, disappears into an old woman with no teeth and a crooked nose.

When I drag my eyes up from the source of my sin, they meet hers. They are softening and her half-smiling lips touch my memory. I think of when mornings had us both devouring steaming porridge, hands holding mugs of strong PG Tips tea and we talked to the bone about life. Now we have nut-less muesli and shouting.

'Look love, I can't take this anymore. You've got to do something. You're ill, you've eaten ALL the nuts. That's not bloody normal! It must have taken you ages!'

The kitchen table transforms into a still life with yellow teapot, salt and pepper and toast rack, fat with left over toast. All on a surface thick from layers of polish. The traitor, which is the bag of muesli, is placed next to my new unused sketchbook. A temptress, *Elle*, the magazine, whispers: *read me*, to Emma.

Footsteps pat the floor outside the door. A knocking sound, 'Can I come in?'

'Yes,' says Emma her hand thumbing the magazine. She sighs, turns around and her red satin slippers disappear away, out of the door, leaving a shrunken me.

In his Dad's musty, fusty, old, leather slippers, Nick slips in.

'I heard the shouting. You've been eating the nuts again, Alice. Come here, have a hug. Have some proper breakfast. I'm going up in a minute to see if Joe's ok, coming with me?'

As the warmth of Nick's hug drifts away and the clashing of Emma's shouts quieten the room becomes a vacuum.

Looking at my sketchbook, it looks back and begs me to pick it up. But tired, in a single movement with my arm, I push it aside. The magazine seems to fall into my hands. Fingers stroke the cool shiny cover as I look up expecting Emma to return.

Elle, is written in big pink letters across the top of the magazine. A beautiful woman, pale blonde, silky hair and eyes the colour of my turquoise dressing gown, in a pencil thin polka dot dress, has text falling over her head. It cascades down the cover following the shape of her hips and legs, saying in the bottom right hand corner: *Do you think you have normal eating habits? Read this article and find out! Page seventy-three.*

Scrambling up to my bedroom, the candlewick bedspread tickles my anticipation as, like a cobweb, I sprawl my body over it and open the magazine. Fanned by the flickered pages eager to find the article, I see it gobbles up half a page. Inserted into it is a picture of a man with a red bow tie and hair swept back in the same way Stuart's is. The man's teeth are beacons beaming a friendly smile and layers crease around his chin doubling it in size. Under the photo, in tiny print, is written: *Professor Lucas.*

My eyes skim the text unable to settle until they reach the last sentence, ending with a phone number for a helpline. Glancing at my easel tucked away in a dark corner of my bedroom, unused for months, looking again at the restless number. It stares back at me begging for a decision, and I know, the impulse to draw would sigh and die if I didn't say, yes.

Crinkly lines criss-cross the page. Smoothing it out with sweaty palms softens it. My heart beats loud and fast as the Professor and I lock our gaze. *Will you be able to help me?* I ask.

*

On the phone the sharp sound of a woman in control comes down the line and pins me to a date: Tuesday, 23rd October. A time: 3.00pm. And, a place: Outpatients, Heathstead Morley Hospital. I have an interview with Professor Lucas's Assistant.

*

The scraping of knives over plates breaks the silence. Nick and Emma eat their dinner. Emma, in one of her rare yellow days, dresses in a canary coloured, long woollen jumper with pink and orange striped tights. Sniffling, Nick begins reading a newspaper. No one's eyes are looking at me while I eat, thank goodness. Joe's arms, hands and face are tattooed with sores. He's sleeping. His only other comforts are Nick, a comfy place to sit and doing heroin.

It is the day of my interview with Dr Lucas's Assistant. I say goodbye to Nick and Emma and hop over the small fence of our neighbour's, tatty front garden with its Tescoe's trolley parked on the oil stained patio.

What a trip it is! On the bus, off the bus, steps and escalators, Black Heath Road off Tooting Broadway, all on a smelly, grey, dull day. But, as I walk along the last road, above the noise of angry, steel beasts working hard on a building site, separated from passers by with wrought iron railings, I hear the sweet trill of a blackbird and it lifts me.

Following a turning into a row of trees and up a leafy drive, I come to curved concrete steps and a large oak door. A standing man, tweaking cigarette in mouth, looks up as I walk over.

He does not acknowledge me, just looks. I am confronted by the door.

Doors are like people, there are many different types. Most lock me out. A strange unfamiliar one frightens me as I do not know what will be behind it. This one is a heavy, slow, hardworking door, its brass knocker a sinister hand. I look for a bell, but do not find one. The knocker thuds a dull, monotonous sound. No answer. I push the door. Wood bruises my shoulder before a gap appears and I hear scraping on the linoleum. The door swings back with a long whine.

Squinting along the never ending corridor, stomach muscles tight and hands moist with sweat. My steps are tentative. Rough stone walls catch my nails as I search for a light switch. A temporary light, a feeble yellow, glows on a spiral staircase. Worming its way up, me following its twists and turns, certain

15

I'm walking with spirits.

On the first level there is a great big cheese plant with so many holes like mouths. My fingers, restless, crave for a pencil to draw it, but I remember my sketchbook stays in my room, neglected.

A large fierce window faces the park. The man is still standing, smoking, looking at the ground then, up at me!

After three more flights of turning stone steps I come to a door "Outpatients waiting room."

It is like any other: rectangular tables for magazines, one or two plants, notice board, wastepaper bin, except this one has a nice man mopping the floor. His gold watch on his tanned hairy wrist and gold medallion around his neck pick up the sunlight. He has a forest of hair and a cheerful smile which lightens up even the long dark corridor.

3

Breakfast Time

I sit and wait. The mopping man leaves.

'Alice?' I look up.

'Come with me please.'

Into a room the woman goes, bending her towering, narrow as a lamppost body to fit under the doorway. I follow.

A string of light from a small square window breaks the darkness of the room and I smell polish.

The woman sits down on a long backed chair. I notice her slim hands are so bejewelled they shine like a Christmas tree. I sit on a small squat chair opposite her. The electric fire behind the desk sweeps its heat over her legs but doesn't quite reach my cold toes.

She tells me she is Mrs. Brew, Professor Lucas's Assistant

'Your name is, Alice Smith? How do you spell your surname?'

Not knowing if this is a test or not as no one has ever asked me to do this before I say each letter with precision: 'S. M. I. T. H.'

'What is your age?'

'Twenty four.'

She continues to take down personal details.

'Okay Alice. I'm going to ask you a few questions. What did you eat today?'

'72 French Fancies.'

Her forehead frowns forming a furrowed field. 'And were

you sick after?'

'Yes.'

'You realise what you're doing to your body, your liver and your potassium levels?'

It's difficult, too painful, too silly, the whole thing.

'Am I anorexic still, or bulimic?'

'That's for Professor Lucas to decide. You are obviously underweight. Over half of people suffering from Anorexia also have bulimic symptoms and frequently depression. You're probably a bit of a mix. That's normal.'

The questions drone on. I put my head on my arm. A sound like small cymbals shouts twice at me in my muffled sleep. I awake properly and count two more. It's four o'clock. The leather of the brown notebook competes with the smell of polish, as I draw in a deep breath. Mrs. Brew's pen is still scratching over the page.

I look around. There are no white-coated people with needles.

'What now?' I ask.

'We will write to you. Everything will be explained.'

Out of the dark room and down the stairs into the brightness of day. I climb up the steps of a number forty-two bus. I jump off at Dandsworth High Street. Walking very fast, footsteps tapping the pavement, my head down, I don't see the migration of children pass by. They snatch my bag. I turn to reach out to them, but it's too late. They run to a place where they can unpick the ten-pound note, letter from Stuart, keys to my front door, old short stubby pencil 6B and blackened rubber.

The theft has taken everything out of me. Too tired and weak to do much, but drag my feet home, hoping someone will be in. I don't even think to call the police.

A bright green Emma opens the door. Emma has colour days and by the end of the month she has gone round the rainbow several times. She is biting into a crisp apple. It is a Granny Smith. As her teeth sink into it, I imagine the sharp, sweet taste. Her eyes open wide as she waits to hear the news.

'A letter is going to come,' I say, trance-like, imagining what kind it will be: a short one, one side of A4 or a long one on several pages, and what will it say?

*

The postman comes twice a day and each time I hear his van crunch on the gravel, my heart misses a beat and I wait for the shuffle of letters through the box. Today two weeks after the interview, the letterbox snaps shut, startles me as usual. Turning off the tap gushing with water, I rush to the door.

Like all-important letters it is squashed between less important things like: Thompson's garden centre offers and the electricity bill.

The only other letters I get are from Diana. They come with things I don't need, like cushions and bathmats. Once, three bras all different sizes, arrived. I became afraid after that as she sometimes cannot stop. I imagined her filling the post office with her packets of underwear, which I would have to collect. But she went onto teabags.

'Alice, more T-bags, Love from, Diana.'

The very proper envelope crackles as I open it, clambering upstairs to my room. A breeze plays with my laced curtains, causing pools of light to dance on the ceiling as I lie facing it, holding the letter.

There are two signatures. One is the size of an ant, Mrs. Brews. I can tell that by looking at the other, which is like a harvest spider, all long, thin and legs going everywhere. It is easy to read and says: *Professor Lucas.*

Heathstead Morley Hospital offers me a place on the unit.

19

The team hopes I will get well during my stay and expect me to be with them for at least three months. I can't help thinking that is an awful long time and there will be nothing for me to do. Maybe I could paint.

*

'You're doing great Alice. You've made a brave decision and have our support but you can't make yourself homeless!'

Diana's voice shrill and anxious spirits down the phone to reach my numb ears.

'I'll be living in the hospital.'

'Not forever! Why do you have to be so extreme.'

'I have to do something. I can't go on like I am. Besides I have no money, nothing.'

'What have you spent it on? Drugs? Food?'

The conversations stretches on, my eyes are sleepy, I sit down on the stool and rest my head in my hand, saying,

'I have to go now. It's late, in fact it's late for you too. Speak in the morning.'

The landlord, a grim man with a fearful moustache takes my letter confirming I'm leaving.

'Don't worry about the phone bill,'' says Nick.

'We'll cover it. Just get better.'

My things find different homes in other people's attics. The green rucksack comes with me. It smells of college days as art materials, pencils, charcoal, sketchbooks, oil paints and pastels, bulge out of its sides.

Three more days and I will be there. At least somewhere to live for a while, but will Professor Lucas's magic wish away the hated habits, which pull me back from the world?

*

It is time. From my window I see the dipstick glint jet-black in the sun. It is wriggled back into the hole it came from and the water cap is twisted off. Drops spray from a shaking finger. Stuart, wearing his polo-necked jumper, carries out the same oil and water checks he did yesterday. Now I see him take on one of his favourite tasks. He dusts the seats and polishes the windows. Retired from his job, transporting chemicals and explosives, his once dark hair and moustache long since turned grey, he now carries Diana to the shops and me to my new homes. He is always there in his dusted, polished Golf Estate.

On the kitchen table, white powder trimmed to a line waits. Emma nods towards it. Waves of smoke from her, once a day cigarette, float in front of her eyes. She has cut down from thirty.

'You said you wanted to try some love. It's a good-bye presy from us.'

I sniff. Wait a few seconds. My nose twitches and I wait some more but nothing stirs. Perhaps there is something wrong with me.

Emma smiles, 'Doesn't always work first time. Here let me give you a big hug instead,'

Nick holds me in his fragile, limp arms, and looks at me. His eyes have never looked into mine before, 'Listen Alice, don't be a waster like me, make this work. Get well.'

*

It couldn't have been a prettier hospital, winding up a long road, all tucked away behind trees that are alive with the singing of birds. Smiling people greet me, except when I get to the top of the stairs there are lots of unhappy faces, too. Stuart puts down my bags, says goodbye with a wet, cigar kiss and hurries off down the brown stairs. His feet tap the tired patches, which hundreds of footsteps have worn down.

I wait on a bench in the middle of two large rooms with beds. One of which has a snooker table. Men shuffle around silently, unshaven faces, hands in pockets, tired eyes. I can almost touch the smell of the hospital ward, linoleum floors and the last of dinner still in the air. The other room is full of women; lank haired, chatting or sitting.

A jumper-red man asks me to follow him. We arrive at a tall, double, wooden door. When it opens we come out into a lovely, white airy room. At the other end there is a long desk and one, two, three, four, five people including Professor Lucas sit behind it. He has exactly the same smile as in the magazine. They all smile and nod hello. Professor Lucas gets out of his chair to greet me. His strong handshake devours my small, bony hand.

'No drug abuse, no physical relationships, no abuse of food, no alcohol abuse, no self-harm and no stealing. If you break any of these rules you will be asked to leave.'

Red hot I stare at the ten shoes, all different shades of brown and black, tan and green; all in a semi-circle. My chair seems to get bigger and bigger until I almost disappear, and in a very small voice I ask if it's okay to paint. I tell them I have my sketchbooks and oil paints with me.

'Sorry, Alice but we can't allow you to paint while you are with us. It will distract you from your therapy.'

'But I have to paint. I'll be ill if I don't. That's why I'm here. You don't understand!'

'You will be able to do art therapy, but of course that isn't the same thing.'

My feet fix to the floor, I lower my eyes, my hands begin to feel cold and clammy and when I swallow, I'm sure everybody can hear.

You'll find a way Alice, the words cling onto me.

All the art materials in my bag, and my clothes, which I couldn't fit in, left at home. And, what is art therapy?

My bed is halfway down the women's ward. The walls are white. A curtain draws around leaving enough space for dressing and visitors. A white locker is next to the high, metal bed. Everything is clean, part of my perfect new life. If you look at the ward from one end, you cannot see colour, except the red on the man's jumper. On the middle table are jigsaws, unfinished. The more I look the more I see people, in bed, on bed, sat up around tables, looking out of windows, walking, standing, two twins together on the floor near the double door and two very thin people.

But I don't belong here. I'm normal!

In bed by ten, lights out, happiness tingles up my spine and inspiration comes like a sparkling light.

I can save them and the nurses, too. I can save everybody.

But, in the morning lead-heavy and as if an iron flattened me, I lie there belonging to the bed. I move my hands and push the top part of my body up, leaning on my elbows. I look at my hospital nightie. I like it very much. It is pale orange with white stripes, and is made of cotton, has long arms and goes down to my feet. I think of the people in the beds either side of me, perhaps with the same nightie. I think of Dickens' *Great Expectations*, the scene in the dormitory. I catch the smell of bacon and toast. See people walk past my bed, ghosts behind blue curtains. Like a cock crowing, I hear: 'Breakfast, breakfast.'

It must be eight o'clock, time to get dressed.

4

Under the Storm

My first day on the ward and I can't wait to meet Elsie, my new neighbour, who has the bed next to mine. To my surprise Elsie is much older, in her sixties, very wrinkly, stick thin and pale as a cloud. Perhaps because she wears a white dress, she sits on a white bed cover and disappears into the white hospital walls. She seems to have a chill over her. It's as if she has stepped out of a freezer. She doesn't say hello, her eyes quiver and look all around, but not at me.

'Elsie has to have electric shock therapy every week. Now can you understand that's why she is this way? Her memory is poor too and she is often confused,' says the elderly man next to her.

I imagine the waves, like sizzling lightning zinging her brain and I shudder. I don't think the treatment is working and I see she has worn the skin on her forehead thin and red, from rubbing on and on. She doesn't look at her husband, but lets him hold her hand.

Am I going to end up with someone holding my hand like that? I wonder.

Like envelopes, days are opened. Everyday goes in my diary. Saturdays are the best days because family and friends visit. Emma comes. Her high voice rouses the quiet ward as if a strange noisy bird has flown in.

'Alice, my love, how are they treating you?'

'Am I fat? You have to eat three meals a day here. I look

huge in the mirror.' My eyes widen as they beg the response to be *No you're thin.*

'How heavy are you?'

'Weighed in at 45kg.'

'You know you're too thin. Now come on what's up?'

'They wont let me paint. Not that I've got the energy. Being in here makes me so tired . . . You look beautiful.'

Emma wears her long, red, velvet dress. A strange sight especially, in a hospital ward. It has pleats down to the ground and hides her little black laced boots. She just needs a wand to make her the good witch.

The blue curtains have become walls surrounding my throne-like white bed. They move if someone walks by or a draught from an open window catches them, rustling the pictures I have sellotaped, forming a thicket of early, charcoal drawings of fish—prawns and mackerel.

Art therapy days are full of matchstick people. The other patients paint seas, volcanoes, coffins and houses. One day I paint a black spiralling circle and add more and more black. This brings a wide smile on the face of therapist Mary, a big, flowing, gentle-voiced woman who wears skirts the colours of spring and necklaces down to her creamy, bulbous, enormous bosoms. A thin gold one with a tiny daisy falls down between them and only appears when she bends forwards.

Sundays are dreadful weighing in days. We go to a little room with a large sausage-shaped boiler hot as a green house, with no window and no pictures except a "No smoking" sign. The scales are so heavy they could squash our toes. Anxiously I wait for my turn, wishing the queue would never end, putting the cold metal scales further away from me. I feel like a fat African toad when I step onto the scales, and I'm a sumo wrestler when I get off them.

Mondays to Fridays are group days, even more dreadful than

Sundays. Sitting in a circle around a green carpet, like bats we hang, brooding. The therapist nods his head patiently and through a two way mirror we know we are being watched, but I can feel all of their eyes on me. They are saying, we are watching you, Alice, so I try to keep as still as possible.

Sam reminds me of my brother. I meet him on a Saturday. I have seen him once in the food queue and liked his dark eyebrows and admired his thin body which is unlike Stuart's, who has a bulging, beetle stomach on top of skinny crooked legs. Sam is a patient from the men's ward. He wears a black sweater and slacks. We find each other like two cats on the prowl ready to steal a walk in the world outside.

The front grounds are sublime. The green lawns spread to the edge of the road, held in by gracious, wide oak trees, pink and yellow flowering shrubs and a new, wooden fence. It's a rule never to cross over and out to the grey damp roads, but no one is ever there to stop you. The Iron Gate swings open. The only sound it makes is a soft scraping noise when it falls against the bushes.

It's a heavy day sweating with near thunder. A few drips of rain fall, wetting our foreheads. Twenty minutes later and we are on the verges of Wimbledon Common, following a dirt track pitted by horseshoes. I imagine people riding and wish I could be on a horse cantering with them. But, I'm with Sam who has his hand laced through mine.

The rain starts to fall with drops of certainty, never stopping in its pace. It falls on our eyelashes, our faces, drips from our noses and soaks our clothes. Our hands become wet white knuckles. We don't have any coats as they may give us away, clues to our adventure. It's not freezing, but cold enough to make us walk faster so we are soon in the small forests of Wimbledon Common. Edges of silver run through the sky and the enormous shout of thunder comes. We count the seconds.

The storm is almost above us, a curtain of darkness falls. Quickly we meet the night.

I'm with Sam now snug under an oak tree his arm around me. 'Kiss me,' I say under the storm, the leafy branches of the tree and beside the rain. As he does, his dark eyebrows meet. It's the most delicious kiss I have ever experienced. In a deep dark soft centre I taste the salty earth. A fleshy alien forces its way through and explores my mouth. His manly odour penetrates the air around, not like boyfriends before who smelt of aftershave or Stuart who smells of Old Spice.

When we return it's just past midnight. The nurse on night duty, like a kind of beaver moving busily, gives us two hot cocoas. But, suddenly as if seeing a fish, she stands up straight and says, 'I will have to report you tomorrow.' She has one eyebrow raised so much it falls into wrinkles and a crease of a smile fills the corners of her lips.

5

Natasha

The next day, sunbeams bursting through the windows, my body tingling all over, I feel so alive. I run across the velvet green lawns. Flapping my arms like a bird, cupping my hands over my mouth yelling YO OO! YO OO! YO OO! I scream—the whistle of a steam engine, until I feel myself disperse in the air.

Calmer, I sit down and watch gentle blades of grass tilt in the breeze and make crisscross patterns on my legs.

In the distance two white coated people the size of ants, become bigger and closer, until their large white forms surround me. I recognize the tall one, Luke and the other is a new nurse on the unit.

'Come on Alice, back inside.'

I feel a heavy hand on my shoulder and the other nurse take my arm but it was no good I could not stop laughing and falling over. My sides creaking with the sting of laughter stitches.

'Are you going to pull yourself together, Alice or do we have to sedate you?'

In the afternoon, burning up with a new desire, to eat and eat and eat, wishing I could be a cutter, or overdose instead of being an anorexic, bulimic muddle, I seek out the large Steinway tucked away, alone, in a small room. It is like a tired oversized shoe. The almost black wood is soft and smooth to touch. The keys are yellowing and the middle C is out of tune so it plays awkwardly, like someone walks with a wooden leg and its peddles creak and yawn. My fingertips touch the keys and each as if with a memory, begin to play, hard, fast, and determined until nurse Jake falls into the room,

'What's going on? Don't play like that or you will break the keys and disturb every one!'

After all the screaming, shouting and playing the piano, it's as if someone has pulled the plug and all my strength leaves me. I carry my limp-leaf body down the aisle of the women's ward. I pass the windowed room where they serve you medication morning, noon and night, past the office, the small kitchen, never stocked with much and into the aisle of the men's part.

As if by instinct, I glance to the left, and there, through a window I see, in the half empty hospital car park, a huddle of black by a blue car. Looking closer, pushing my nose flat up against the pane of glass, I see it is Sam with a lithe and tall George. They are kissing in a passionate strong embrace, the force almost hits the window pane. They are glued together. The way George holds tightly onto Sam's jacket, you would think he owns him. I reel backwards, for a second remembering Sam's kiss with me, my eyes begin to glint with tears.

Rushing out, I bump into David.

'Hey! What's up, Alice?'

Tears sprout like seeds and I bury myself in David's large wholesome arms, soothed by his, running like a river, talking— always about the latest pill system. David is a vitamin fanatic. His days are spent in his bedroom, his meals left by the door, once a week he visits the chemists in his black gear, black visor and on his black BMW motor bike. He goes to several and has long lists of which vitamins to take. He likes to take them beyond the limit and recover so he can take some more. His stories carry me away from Sam.

After seeing Sam with George, I stop going to the groups, except art therapy. I can spend all day with Mary. She makes pictures flow out of me. Instead of commenting on my furious outpouring of stick people and black holes she comments on the way I hold the pencil and the kind of marks I make on the paper. At one point she asks me who I'm hurting, me or my mother. I don't know. To pass away the evenings I make earrings in the art room. The enamel drips into whirling forms on metal, creating joys of colour. I think if I make enough I could start selling them at Camden Market.

My weight drops as I begin running everyday around the park. Dr Watchit, my psychotherepist appointed to me by Professor Lucas, at least notices. I wait by the men's ward hoping to see Sam. Sometimes I walk up and down the corridor, sure that I will bump into him. My stomach sickens with a different kind of hunger, a physical hunger, to touch, to hold Sam and feel his warm skin against mine.

One day in Dr Watchit's office, with the window open just a little so I can smell the fresh rain, I talk a lot about Sam. Dr Watchit's thin, delicate face and his fragile, sparrow-feet hands seem to catch my words midair.

'I think you are heading for a crash, Alice.'

At that moment Anne, the secretary, knocks and puts her head around the door. 'I've had a call from Vanessa. Can you come? It's an emergency,' she says. Dr Watchit vanishes.

With jagged thoughts I am left to wonder what a crash could be like.

His notebook is still open on his desk. Drawn to it like a magnet I tremble as I look around then, close the door. Scanning the page I read: Alice has difficulty forming relationships with her peers, is unable to participate in group therapy. If she continues to abuse food her place on the unit must be reconsidered. Footsteps disturb me. I grab my cardigan and leave, frightened by the cold clinical words.

But I have one friend, I think to myself. Natasha, the only patient who looks at me long enough to start a conversation.

'I wish I was dark and petite like you' she says to me. Surprised, because I would love to be as tall as her and slim and strawberry blonde with sky blue eyes. She is there for nymphomania. Spends most of her time on her bed reading women's magazines. Anorexics and bulimics aren't allowed the luxury of seeing thin, beautiful women, on satin pages.

'You already have a distorted body image. Concentrating your mind on your body, food, weight, being slim is a diversion from your real feelings. You are here to find yourself,' Professor Lucas's words run around my head, making me dizzy.

Natasha could have been a model, but she always has her fingers in a knot.

At suppertime the smell of roast beef fills the rooms. My senses can taste it. Reluctantly I join the queue. How can I get out of eating this time. Peering over the shoulders of the person in front, trying to see the size of the portions, in that moment, my head turns as if by instinct. At the same time a piercing scream enters my body, a voice in me cries out, *Natasha!*

Leaving the queue, I rush out of the canteen, following the scream and onto the ward where I see a nurse supporting Natasha as she sits on the edge of the bed breathing hoarsely, tears running down her reddened cheeks. The bottle of bleach stands by her bed, half empty.

'Take that bottle away Jennifer please,' calls out the nurse. The smell of bleach fills the air. The curtains are swished around Natasha's bed shutting me out. My hands tremble and I sit down on a nearby chair.

'Natasha has swallowed bleach . . .'

I hear the beginning of the conversation then the words become slurred in my mind.

Afterwards the nurse tells me they made Natasha drink an awful lot of milk. Her stomach must have been red sore.

The following day, I awake shrouded in shadows. I see the skies preparing once more for rain. Rushing black clouds allow the sun to peep through small holes and then, shut it out again. My stomach gnaws with hunger. I pick up a brown glass bottle of homeopathic pills and eat them, 500 tiny Rosa Damascena. Their sweet flavour bursts on my tongue. I have a headache all day. I tell the nurse and show her the bottle. She says, 'It's not food, you know! And' phones the laboratory.

The laboratory confirms 500 Rose Damascena are harmless. The next day I'm called into Professor Lucas's office.

'Alice, I'm very angry with you. What you've done must be taken seriously. We give you support with the groups, you must use those more when you need to ask for help.'

He didn't say it, but I realise I have opened another door. A door to taking pills.

One week later me, Natasha and four other patients sit around a circular table in the Elephant Pizza Restaurant, staring at our food. We prod our margherita with our forks. This is the food therapy day out. No talking about weight allowed, but I notice the tidy, *thin* waitress, with a big gorilla smile. Certain she knows we feel like hulks. Sue, one of the nurses sips a glass of chilled white wine. I remember my session with her, in her squashed office, full of paperwork and housing a nasty pair of scales.

'Eat slowly so you don't feel out of control,' she advises me.

Cutting into the middle, avoiding the thick step of dough, I begin to eat my first pizza in over ten years. It tastes delicious. I panic. Frightened I might want to eat it all. My eyes glance up ate the sign 'Toilets.'

No! I'm not going to do that!

My horrible thoughts are interrupted by a quiet, slow voice, 'I have to leave the unit.' Natasha puts her knife and fork down and tucks her hands under the table. She fixes her eyes, not looking at anyone just through the air.

'What!' We say in unison and look up.

'Professor Lucas says I need to be an outpatient. He doesn't feel they can support me here.' And in a rush she splutters, 'It is just because I drank bleach!'

'You'll be here in the daytime though, Natasha.' Says Sue.

Tears spill down Natasha's raw face. I take her cold clammy hand and hold it, squeezing gently. Remembering something Dr Watchit had told me.

You need to have a strong sense of self to survive here. It's easy to get lost amongst the other patients with their problems. If it doesn't work out you can become a day patient, but we'll see how you go.'

A short week passes by and I miss Natasha, even before her footsteps pace down the corridor towards the front door—I catch her before she leaves in her green Citroen.

'Wait! Natasha!'

'Bye Alice. I'm not coming back to the unit. Give me a call sometime, let's keep in touch.'

The old sheets are taken off her bed. New ones billow like snow in the wind then, flat hands brush and pat and tuck them into place, ready for another person.

I wonder whether I will be next to be told to leave.

6

The Mist is Rising

My pencils and sketchbooks stay under the bed unused. Sometimes I imagine picking up a pencil, but my hand feels clay heavy and clumsy. Perhaps I'll do some drawing when I go home for Christmas.

Rolling mists on a chilly day and already I'm dreading the twenty-fifth December, which is falling as fast as a shooting star in my direction.

Stuart fetches me. The shiny seats of the Golf will have been dusted. He'll look pleased to see me with a big smile on his face. He climbs into the car, coughs, sneezes into a large white handkerchief and switches on the engine. Off and away to Haystart, our home town, which is famous for its dreariness. Everyone's train stops there as it is the end of the line. A distorted voice echoes: 'All change—This platform for this destination and that platform for that one.' Confused passengers study the flashing boards, anxious to get on the right train.

Our house is in a walled garden and has a smelly fish and frog pond. I used to scoop up the tadpoles and see their wriggly tails. In Stuart's part hoards a large selection of well loved vegetables. In Diana's, a little, curved stone wall and steps, islands of flowers and secret paths.

*

I wake up on Christmas Day in my old bedroom. My age falls

to twelve as the pink and purple of that time still surround me and the mural of a jungle, with cockatoos, swallowtail butterflies and a giant tiger, which I painted one Easter Holiday, transports me back. A pillowcase full of daring things, like chocolate, socks and pants, slips off the side of the bed. I can smell squashed fresh clementines. Today I will stay in my dressing gown until lunch.

In the middle of the morning I am hit by a craving to eat. It is as strong as a gale force wind. The Christmas cake calls out to me. A giant block of earthy mince swallowed up in a fold of thick icing. Its smell is sealed into it. I open the squeaky, pantry door into the cavern stocked with towers of homemade jam, cornflakes, biscuits, bread, and the big cake. Stretching up and slithering the knife flat against the plate, I manage to slice off some of the dense, brown, sticky mixture. Catching the crumbs I eat it behind the sofa. Half an hour later, a thief, I creep along the dark shadow up the stairs to the small room.

'Come out of that toilet!' cries Diana,

'I know what you're doing. It's Christmas for God's sake. I thought you were better now?'

I wait in silence until her slippered footsteps disappear down the stairs. I can hear a sigh followed by arguing. Craftily I nip into my comforting bedroom.

But, at lunch my mouth as if stitched with cotton, controls my, animal like, hunger. I watch Diana cut the turkey and divide it up. I hope my portion will be the tiniest. My heart beats fast at the thought of the cement brick Christmas pudding. Will I still be able to control myself. I stare at my plate with suspicion.

The only part of Christmas lunch I enjoy is pulling the cracker and the smell it makes bringing the memories of Guy Fawkes night, the cracking and sizzling of burning bright fireworks. If I survive Christmas it's either because I haven't eaten anything or I am like a whale eating everything and have made myself sick after.

Diana's eyes are on me everywhere. Stuart eats, smokes his pipe, and listens to the Queen's speech and sleeps.

Under the tall, wide Christmas tree, heavy with gleaming balls, is a present. It's wrapped in silver and blue paper. I tear this off to reveal the smile of Mona Lisa on the front cover of a heavy, tomb-like book five inches or so deep. A woody smell hits my nostrils. I begin to turn the thick and shiny cream pages. Each one reveals drawings and paintings by Leonardo Da Vinci.

So they do know how much I want to paint and draw. My fingers play with the small card and its picture of a dancing fish. And they remember how much I love drawing fish.

'You draw fish beautifully Alice. You make them surreal and give them heavenly colours' Emily had once said.

On the card Diana has written in capital letters: *Love Mum and Dad.*

Three days after Christmas and it's time to go back to the hospital. Diana and Stuart sit like waiters in the car while I chase my clothes into a rucksack, squeezing in the last thing, the pink t-shirt from Diana. My book goes in a separate brown paper bag, protected in more paper. It would make my rucksack too heavy for me to carry.

'I'll take the book,' cries out a helpful Stuart.

'Yes, she has been good.' Diana's voice rises higher as she talks about Christmas. She has one hand clutching her handbag looking efficient. Stuart stands behind her, hand in pocket, he looks sad. I wonder perhaps if it because of me and being in the hospital. He asks: 'When can she go home? She has been here for three and a half months now?'

'Her weight has been fluctuating. She has to attend the groups more. They will give her the structure she needs. If we

36

don't feel we can support Alice in the unit, we can continue her treatment as an outpatient which means she will live outside the hospital but can come here for the daytime groups.'

Professor Lucas's stomach is round and from the way he leans back in his chair it seems to form a bridge between him, his desk and my parents. He quite rapidly leans forward and places his two elbows on the table, forming a triangle with his hands, and says: 'It's Alice's choice to be here, but if she continues to break the rules she will be asked to leave the unit.'

My parents are free to go. I can see their relief once we are outside and the fresh wind is on our cheeks. Stuart lights a cigarette, 'We must go, Alice,' he says, 'We have an hour's drive, as you know.' His face sags as he sighs, 'For goodness sake Alice, get well love, for us, for your mothers sake.'

I say 'Okay,' in a faint voice, but really I want to bury myself under a ton of sand.

*

I leave my rucksack open. The contents flow over like intestines, wrapping themselves around the legs of the chair as my feet push them out of the way. Gradually, I put them in drawers one by one.

It's the twelfth day back in hospital and with dull sloth like thoughts I sit waiting for my meeting with Dr Watchit. Wearing my thick, grey long jumper trying to disguise my weight—since Xmas I have lost another 4kg. He suggests group therapy might make me feel better. But the black veil over me tightens. I'm even excused from the once a week ward round.

Dr Watchit looks worried in our next meeting.

'You're behaviour is concerning us and also your recent depression. I suggest that for a while you remain in the hospital.'

'Can I go to the shop?'

'No. You'll be under supervision.' Easing over me comes a sense of relief, even though I know I will be watched when eating.

Every night for six weeks, to help me sleep a nurse called Rebecca gives me tablets, sometimes Tamazepan. I fall into waves crashing with terrible nightmares. Strands of rubbery mozzarella reach out from giant pizzas to strangle me and I suffocate under the lids of Mr. Kipling's apple pies. During the day there is a thick fog wall between the patients and me. The only person I talk to is Rebecca. She stays by my side all day. At night the night nurse watches over me. Even after I stop taking the Tamazepan I sleep for hours, only waking up at meal times. Food tastes flat and sticks around my mouth. Then, one morning when I wake up I am not afraid of the black cloud, which fills the sky or bothered it is going to pour down. My own mist is rising. My thoughts are beginning to take form and colour.

7

His Palette is like an Exotic Bird

Weeks are stacking up until another full three months fly by. My appetite begins to come back. I eat three meals a day and put on four pounds, but feel full of energy. I skip along the corridor to Professor Lucas's office.

His face guards a serious expression.

'You'll need to start thinking about your life after you have left here.'

'But I'm not ready!'

Professor Lucas shifts uncomfortably in his leather, wine red chair.

'You've been making excellent progress. I think it would be a good idea to set a discharge date for the end of the month, that gives you four weeks to prepare yourself.'

'But . . .'

Twitching his nose, Professor Lucas says, 'We need your bed Alice. There is a waiting list. You have gained all you are going to from being on the unit. It's time now to go outside and practice what you have learned here.'

I sit up on the edge of my seat, cheeks feeling cold and hot at the same time, sweaty palms, I forget to close my mouth which hangs there in an 'O'

Needing something to occupy my mind, which is now a nest of ants, I drag out the dust covered box of crayons from under my bed and from memory, in a frenzy, begin drawing. First Elsie's sad, lined, raw-red face. My memory recalls her vividly. I write a list of names of the people I want to draw. This will be my way to hold onto what I have here. My body relaxes, muscles unwind when putting the tip of a 4b pencil onto the smooth surface of paper from my thick A4 sketch pad. I feel a sigh followed by a smile coming on—the first in months.

*

Just before breakfast, off comes my orange striped nightie and I fling on my black and white thin-striped top and leggings, wriggle on a pair of extra large blue dangly earrings. Peacock proud, with crown raised I arrive at the group and flounce in late, to the annoyance of everyone. Nobody says anything about my new look, I must be invisible, but Sammy looks at me sternly,

'Why did you stop coming to the group before? Why come now? Aren't we good enough for you?'

'Sorry, I'm ill, but I'm getting better.'

'We're all ill,'

Only Ruth doesn't say anything. She has her long-lasting smile on.

Unpopular and free, I'm given the okay to be out for an evening. Away and loud we all go to Soho. Hopping on and off the tube, letting out sighs and laughter, we are glad to be released from the prison-like walls of the hospital. Soho is full of lights: red lights, yellow lights, green lights and Neon signs flashing as if singing to tunes.

We arrange to meet at the kebab stall in one hour. Suddenly I'm alone. The others all disappear into the night, a huddle of silhouettes. The street is dark and like a medina with its narrow passageways. I walk down the centre wanting to see everything, my very long neck turns left and right, my eyes are big. It is a colourful feast after the sombre hospital rooms. Dangling from his arms and strapped around boards, an array of glittering silver and gold watches is touted around by a dark coloured man with shining clear eyes. Next to him a woman shows her wares of large, heavy, sparkling earrings that would make your ears very long.

After passing all the people with something to sell, I come to a sign saying, *Enter*. Inside is a long corridor with walls covered in red velvet. All along it, men, their backs bent, peer through small windows. To see through one you have to have three pounds to put into a slot machine. Curious, I put my coins in and slide a metal bar back to reveal a hole. Out comes a naked, slim, pale-skinned woman. She doesn't look much older than me, but seems more grown up. I am surprised by the look on her face—fed up and bored. I wonder what it must be like to be watched. I'm embarrassed as if she could see me.

Before this my experience of naked women's bodies has been mixed. Diana tussling off a jumper, covering her head like a bandit, is white as a cloud and her skin is like porcelain. And then, in the Turkish baths, which are full of women, eleven or twelve of them. Pink, browns, dark browns, white, every colour, but most turning to blue when they come out of the cold bath. Everyone has a great, big, white towel to cover them. I have mine on all the time because I never go in the cold bath. In the steam room, it's so hot we lie like sea lions. There are women with breasts hanging around them like handbags, others have round apricots. Some have perfect skin like Diana's and some have veins like the roots of trees. They shout above the steam, their skin glistening and their eyes bright. Their bodies move to the sway of laughter, as they talk about their husbands.

Then there are the life models at college, they always look serene and perfect, even if they have lots of fat or are pimply or very big. There is something about their stillness, which makes them sculpture like. The thin women are the hardest to draw. I hold up my pencil against the model searching for the exact angle of the bone. For voluptuous women my pencil glides over the paper discovering rivers and valleys in the folds of their flesh.

Its 10.30pm, I'm forty minutes late. I hurl myself forward, run through the streets, hearing the sound of my footsteps clattering the pavement and imagine the voice of Sammy drumming my ears and him sneering at me like an ogre.

'You're late. We've been waiting ages. Now we're all late.'

I am full of apologies spoken breathlessly.

'Alice, where have you been, we were worried to death about you!' Ruth says.

We take the Northern line and fall into places on the tube. Sammy sits by Rose, Duncan and Harry sit together, and then, Dave and Natalie. I'm on my own. I catch my reflection in the window and think about the woman in the red room. In my pocket the fifty pence coin sweats my hand as I hold on to it. I let go and open my purse and count the pennies. I will need to find some kind of work after I am discharged from the hospital. I shiver and the cold wind grips me as I think of leaving.

It's midnight when we climb the long hill, open wide the large gates and enter the silent hospital. Sometime after two I fall into a deep sleep. Like shadows my eyelids cover my eyes, roll over and shut tight.

Shimmering through this veil of slumber a pair of vast, deep-red curtains glide apart like two graceful swans, leaving a clearing in the centre of a stage. Bejewelled bars form a dome shaped cage, which hangs from a faraway ceiling by a golden thread.

A naked body crouches inside the cage. The face lifts and I see it is a young blond haired woman with an ashen pale complexion, a forest of freckles, lips dipped in peach rose, mediterranean-blue eyes and eyelashes like feathers. I think of a butterfly. Startled as if she's hears something, she sits up.

I can hear it too. Raucous cries from behind the cage where a sea of men, whose shadows make gruesome silhouettes, creep, slide and crawl on their stomachs, dragging their bodies. Dressed in long coats and hats, torn and scratched, filthy and worn, they wear old, vile shoes. Some of them stalk, until they form a human robe around the cage, trying to pull it lower.

Plunging and reaching through the metal bars with their arms outstretched and their coarse hands spread like fans, they brush her skin roughly. Nails scratch her, fingers pinch. She strikes out to protect her face, but she is dragged forwards by her arms. Her cheeks slam against the bars as the men tear at each other trying to reach her. Their cries are one continuous sound of waves crashing against the rocks.

I get up from the seat, where I have seen all. Clamber over the rows of empty chairs around me, until I reach the stage. Walking to the cage is like walking through a spider's web, beads of sweat tumble down my back. For a moment I stand in front of it, my eyes are misty and I can smell vanilla perfume. I step closer and closer to the woman, with a feeling I am stepping closer to myself. In her eyes I see my eyes. I see fear.

Stepping back I feel something knock my shoulder, turning round I came to face a surge of trembling hands reaching forwards. Forcing my head back, before they smother my mouth, I scream long and piercing, until I begin to feel something solid. I wake up, eyes wide, gripping the metal bars of my bed.

'Hey, hey, you're having a nightmare'

I hear a familiar voice of a nurse, I smell the newly painted ward, and feel the cold metal frame of my bed.

The next morning I have my session with Dr Watchit. I can hardly keep my eyes open and I rub them red trying to keep awake.

'It's almost time for you to leave, Alice.'

'But it's still too soon,' my sleepy eyes meet his.

'It's not good to be in hospital for too long. You will become too dependant on us.'

'What if I fail.'

'You'll have the support of the Outpatient unit. Have you seen Mrs. Clements about somewhere to live?'

Mr. Watchit's session is full of: You have this and you have that. Instead of: Why this and what is that. I feel his thin little body tensing up. I can imagine them preparing my bed for another patient. He always shakes my hand after every session but after this one he forgets.

I hear the peal of a bell. Its lunchtime, I grab my Morley Times and walk quickly to the queue. The other patients are coming out from behind curtains, from the games room, out of the kitchen all forming a long worm of a line in front of Lottie, the lunch lady. Lottie has large friendly breasts and a round tummy. She is very plump with pale skin and light chestnut hair and is about thirty years old. She wears a diamond ring on her wedding finger which is plump, too. We are lucky to have Lottie. She makes lunch time a treat. She gives us anorexics little balls of potato and gives large balls for everyone else.

The sun makes patterns through the rain splashed windows to clothe the red vinyl topped table as if it is covered in lace. When I sit in the chair with my back to it, it throws my shadow forward so my plate is in semi-darkness. If I read while I eat I won't even get to the egg by the time I reach the job page. When I do, I see the position, which beams at me like Lottie's smile: *Painting Restorer Assistant Needed.*

I leave the plate of soggy spinach and egg leftovers, thrust the paper under my arm and walk quickly to the phone box, hidden by the booth, at the other end of the canteen. But inside is Nigel filling up the space—a large unshapely sack. Cross, I frown. His words, joined up by medication, make a thin trail of sounds. I look around at the cream walls of the corridor and to the notice board, read the fire notice and a poster for a film night, until at last, the phone is free.

'A man's voice comes down the line, mysterious and quiet. I have to squeeze my ear to the phone to catch every word—my first contact with a stranger. After answering his questions in a fast eager voice, excitement peals in me like a shining bell and a silken thread is sewn from my stomach to the world outside.

*

My first proper interview dressed in blue, smart as a pansy. Catching the tube to Islington, so many people on the move my head feels dizzy. Up the escalators and down they go, in and out of cars, queuing for taxis, callers calling. In the hospital everything seems to stay still, except the nurses, who glide around in quiet, steady movements, not in twists and dives like swallows as all the things around me are doing. I feel upside-down.

I don't like being in the room on my own with this strange man. He reminds me of the lonely men in Soho, scavenging for a naked woman's body. Slippery thin, a shadow, he moves in and out of his canvases, one very large one, upside down, which hides even his shoes. Paints and tables are everywhere and jars and jars of brushes and a strong smell of turps permeates the air. The man tells me how meticulous I need to be, but I know I can't work for somebody who spends all his time on his own, that is, until I see on the table, his palette, like an exotic bird dotted with every colour of the rainbow.

He tells me he will let me know if I have the job, soon.

8

The Protector

After the interview the next biggest adventure is going to be leaving hospital.

I unpeel my paintings and drawings from art therapy off my curtain walls. There are twenty-four, displayed as if in an exhibition. Push and squeeze my clothes into the rucksack, strip the bed ready for the linen basket.

With a face like a full moon the clock shines 4.30pm at me. Stuart is to pick me up at five thirty. Awkwardly I wait on the bench in the corridor opposite the exit, watching people pass by. I feel like a traveler on a platform waiting for my train. Through the swinging doors I can see my bed stripped naked, waiting for the next patient. I clutch my drawings and paintings from art therapy, rolled up tight and kept in place by a blue band. My sketch book now full of portraits of the people on the unit, also stays by my side.

My first night sleeping is on Simon and Jane's front room floor. It's a tiny room with a rug in different colours, mainly red, and Indian patterns, which lies between the electric fire and the settee. Under the settee there are lots of bumps and dust. I can see that because I'm in my sleeping bag right up to its base. A television stands at one end of the room and nothing else at the other.

Simon is a tall, thin, theatre director and Jane is his girlfriend. Jane is tiny. Her eyes level with my chin. She has short hair dyed at the back—green and yellow horizontal stripes—like a cushion cover. Jane is a costume designer. They both work in the East End of London. They hardly speak to me except in a very gentle way as if I'm a wounded bird.

In the morning, another drizzly, misty morning, my stomach feels flat, but my thighs gigantic. I'm a mix of fear and excitement. I look at the objects around me. They are welcome strangers, no more white hospital cupboards or blue curtains. I can hear low voices coming from the kitchen—Simon and Jane. Keeping still as an owl, ears leaning forward, I can hear what they are saying:

'How long is Alice here for?'

'Until she finds somewhere to live.'

'But we'll need the space for Ellen. I hope she finds somewhere soon. She's quiet and a bit sullen.'

'So might you be if you had just come out of hospital!'

In the attic lives Frank another person staying with Simon and Jane. Frank came here four months ago. He is long and skinny and wears green cotton, loose trousers, which sit on his hips and have lots of pockets. He wears a black t-shirt. It hangs off his shoulders and has a hole in it. His fingers twitch around a joint. One late evening we are in the sitting room. I'm snuggled up in my sleeping bag and the curtains are tied back, revealing the night—a horizon of rooftops rising up the hill and cloud-like forms of trees, all in an intense black against the blue-black of the sky. We whisper, but I can hear movement upstairs. Frank sits on the settee, bony knees apart, arms resting on thighs.

'Do you want some?'

He thrusts out a hand towards me, holding between his fingers the fat joint.

In this room now is only me and Frank. Noone is watching. Wanting to impress on Frank I am older than I look and at the same time not wanting him to think I am a bore I say, 'Okay.'

'It's grass,' He says, a little hesitant.

I know what hash is and hash cakes are, speed makes me walk very fast, but I have never had grass. I take the white, wrapped joint and put it to my lips. I inhale the strong odour and my head begins to feel weightless. In minutes I'm soaring above the clouds.

The images in my mind come clear as photographs. I see a mass of stumbling skeletons crossing a desert-like landscape, the sweating blue sky and a large, black, eagle-like bird poises to dive. I open my eyes fearful it will reach me.

It's darker in the room. The curtains have been closed. Frank has gone. I bury myself in the sleeping bag, damp with perspiration, no longer certain I will survive life outside of the hospital.

*

I'm waiting for a place with Aspect Housing. They are sometimes called halfway houses, so I must be a halfway person. I wonder what it must be like to be, an all the way person? These half-way houses are peopled with ex-patients from hospitals and ex-criminals from prison. You can even choose your own futon— from the hospital to a palace!

Three weeks later I receive a letter offering me a place in a house in Dandsworth. It comes like snow in July because it's the only letter I have had for months, that is, besides Diana's containing teabags.

On a Tuesday morning for the last time I roll up Jane's sleeping bag and leave it on the dusty carpet, water Simon's Yucca plant, and with a little prayer it will be forever, pack my rucksack. Stuart is there ready, waiting, hands stretched out to take my rucksack.

Suddenly I feel too big and embarrassed. I fold myself up

like a chicken and squash myself into the car. Even though there is space I nestle up tight against the window watching Stuart thank Simon and Jane, apologetically, for having me.

*

'This is your bedroom', says Sara with a beaming smile in contrast to her burning deep frown lines. Big bead bracelets run up and down her arms like tails. I peer in, *all this space for me. I wont' know what to do with it.*

'It's a lot bigger than I expected' I say, eyes open wide.

'Oh, Aspect Housing Trust is very generous. We're all lucky. My room's upstairs with my piano. You wont see too much of me. I spend all my time playing and teaching.'

'How did you get it up there,' I ask looking up at the twisting narrow staircase.

'With difficulty,'

A man in a white shirt, buttoned up to the top passes by me, with a tense, serious expression on his face, says hello and disappears through a white door.

'That's Stephen. Brendan should be here any minute. You know Brendan's the resident carer for us loony lot,' she says smiling.

Ah Brendan! Meet Alice, our new housemate.'

'Welcome,' Brendan steps towards me lit up by his glossy mop of blond hair, twinkly blue eyes. A hot spring of energy gushes from him, rushing through his fingers, and when he touches my arms I light up too. Overcome with hot red embarrassment hoping nobody notices my new flush-red colour, I look down at the carpet.

'I'm here to help. If you have any problems just come to me,' he says in a soft Irish accent.

'Hi, I'm Mike' a long lean man at that moment comes in

49

rescuing me and holds his hand out. He has a modest grip and a clean medium sized smile, speaking with a Scottish accent.

'I hope you don't mind my motorbike being in the kitchen, I'm giving it a good clean,' he says holding a rag in his other hand.

Stephen and I are the *not okay people*, Sara and Mike are okay and Brendan is double okay, because he is our protector.

9

Antique Typewriters are Heavy

An insignificant looking brown envelope peeps through the door. I scramble with my fingers to open it. My eyes pick out the word "sorry" and I know I haven't got the job with the beautiful palette and the shadowy man. My breath slows with relief.

Red, plastic chairs startle the dim, grim social security office. People slouch, others sleep, some sit up, rigid, waiting, it's their turn next. We all grip our tickets watching out for the number to come up on the screen. My ticket is thin from the wear and tear of my fingers pushing it around my palm. Some people argue, their noise battling the otherwise silence. There is a stale smell of dirty clothes and unwashed bodies mixing with the passing scent of cheap perfume. A plump child, with rolly polly pink arms in a grubby pushchair whimpers, its mother swears and shouts at it, 'Shut it Peter, or I'll thump you here and now!'

My turn is next. I've filled in my forms, white forms, pale blue forms. When did you last work? Why did you leave your last job? How much money is coming into your household? Typical Social Security probing, wanting to know everything about me.

The window separates me from the woman with grey, curly hair and a thin, pointy nose. I think she is about fifty. She wears square, dark blue glasses and holds her hands clasped. Her face is pale and oval like a spoon. Her painted, shiny rose lips narrow and as if with pleasure she tells me, 'It takes one month for your money to come through.'

'One month . . .' My panic makes me gasp in a deep breath. 'But, why so long? I need money now.'

'Sorry, but you will have to wait.'

'I can't, I have nothing. I have just come out of hospital!' A sob chokes my throat. 'I need money, please!'

The thumping of my fist on the counter silences the room, even the child stops moaning and sucks on a thick, soiled chunk of material, eyes wide and fearful. Waves of emptiness spread through me, distancing me from all the looks. I lower my head not wanting them to see my tears. A man's authoritarian whisper marches through the quiet. *'Okay, Jean, I'll sign for an emergency cheque.'*

Jean, I now know her name, leans forward. Her glasses reflect the fluorescent tube light as she nods. The cheque she passes through the letterbox-sized hole slips in my sweaty palm.

I come out into the cloudy, wind whistling day, reach home, and tackle the pulling in the breeze, chilli-pepper-red door.

Down the dark, long, like a tunnel, hallway, I pass the staircase and register something is missing. There is a line along the turquoise green carpet, which leads to the cream door of my bedroom. Someone has dragged my port-folio along and left it leaning on the wall. This has happened twice before. 'I'm fed up with this. There isn't even enough room here!' I shout.

In my portfolio are drawings of fish: mackerel, trout, pinhead fish, puffer fish, fish markets, and life models, large A1 drawings, and small A6 pastels. They are the most precious things I have recovered from Diana and Stuart's dark and forbidding, covered in cobwebs and full of oddly shaped objects, attic.

Frustration grows inside me, an army of red ants, biting through my clothes reaching my mind. In hospital I had very little money, enough for coffees and apples, with that and the groups and the rules, for a while it had felt as if I had an iron bar wrapped around my waist. I thought when released everything would go well, but almost not getting money from the social security office, and then, to come home and find somebody's moved my portfolio again, trembles my insides. Don't people understand? I don't want anyone touching it. Mike has his motorbike, Sara has her piano, Stephen has his antique typewriter, and I have my portfolio. I am not eating cakes, not stealing; it is my art work which keeps me going. When I draw something in front of me all my worries vanish. Hot flushes wash over me as I anticipate all the terrible things I might do if I found out who touched it, but I tell Brendan and he says he will find out who is responsible and tell them to leave my work alone.

Sara is playing the piano, her student sings in a high, lyrical voice. I wonder if they pay less for having to learn the piano in her bedroom. It isn't very big and it has all her things in plus there are family photos on the wall.

That evening after supper the sky is an orange rose. Brendan comes in later with his girlfriend. Chestnut hair—shiny as a conker and big, Jan has a smile like the sun and rocks slowly to and fro as Brendan sings and plays his guitar. He has a lilting, soft, Irish voice. He comes from Dublin. Mike taps his heels to the music, while Sara sways left and right. I stay as still as a rock, listening to every word. Stephen is up in his bedroom resting. I forget to ask Brendan about my portfolio.

In the middle of the night I lie awake thinking about the conversation with the woman in the social security office. I think it is a good thing to cry like that sometimes and to shout. A noise outside my room stops my thoughts. It is like someone is dragging something along the carpet. I want to go out and see, but am so afraid I can't move. I grip my duvet and hold it round me. In the morning I try to open the door, but it resists.

Finally, I manage to push it far out enough to squeeze by and there, leaning against it is my portfolio. I take a deep breath then, move it back to where it should be.

Under a bright blue sky I take a walk hoping to find a good café. At the top of the street, turning left, I can see the road is a long one. A lot of big, red buses are passing and I can see bus stops along the way. The grey pavement grows longer like a stretched piece of elastic. I begin to think it will never end, and don't know where it does end because I decide to turn back.

When I open the red-chilli-pepper door the same, night-time sound, is happening. I look up. Stephen is moving my portfolio back to my bedroom.

What are you doing? Leave my drawings alone. They go here—not there.'

'They are in the way.'

'No they are not, no more than your bike. I'm putting them back and don't you dare touch them again!'

Stephen swings himself around the banister and disappears like a blown out candle. His face is white and tired.

Everything in the house is still. We are all in our beds. I stare up at the luminous sheep decorating my ceiling. After a while I look at the glowing hands on my clock. Four a.m. My eyelids fall and dreams rumble and tumble inside my head until a warming light wakes me. The sun is streaming through my window, catching millions of speckles of dust dancing in the band of light, thrown across my lime green duvet. I need the bathroom. Standing, I brush the creases out of my orange and white striped, hospital nightie. I had asked to keep it and they said, yes.

With sleep fogging my brain I don't think there might be an obstruction so when I press the door handle and try to push it I feel surprise as it inches open as if it has to move something out of the way. I peer round and there it is again: my big black portfolio, with a puddle of drawings spreading on the carpet. I have stepped through and now have my toe on the edge of one. I stand like a statue, unable to believe what I see.

Heavy and tired and with fists clenched, I stomp into the sitting room. It is gloomy as the thick curtains are still drawn. I pull them apart and open one of the windows. I feel the sun's warmth on my hands. On shaky legs I walk up to the bureau, gathering momentum as my body awakens. Stephen's antique typewriter, black with round keys, which have tarnished silver rims, stands on the navy, leather inset of the drop-down desk top. It has an arrogant stance. I lift it. My back bends under its weight. It is too heavy to throw. I balance it for a moment on the window ledge, and then, let go. Pings and loud thumps make me think everyone will hear.

I had forgotten about the marigolds Sara had planted. When Stephen finds out his face drains of the little colour it had. His red eyes sink into the black, sock-like bags underneath them. He looks like a zombie. Sara is furious about her crushed marigolds.

10

Sara's Venom

Brendan has a happy face, a million miles away from the sad ones in the hospital. I look up to him in trepidation. His eyes take me on an adventure; I want to hold his gaze. His talking voice is like music. I like it more than when he sings as his songs are embarrassing. They tell of losing someone.

Jan is always here, on the doorstep to the patio, rolling up and laughing. She calls herself, Brendan's Jano. She squashes her curves into tops that mould her boobs into two mounds each side of a valley and trousers or jeans that leave a roll of squishy flesh on the outside. She gives her hair a lot of attention. Alice-band pushed in at a slant, then removed and swept back in at a different angle. She never lets it hang in its natural bob.

'Jano, do you want something from Dennis's?'

Brendan often buys stuff for Jan, something to do with textiles for her work. Brendan-Jano . . . Jano-Brendan, their names jumble up together. Jan asks lots of questions, which pull me out of my awful silences. She has kind ways and she bakes very nice cakes for us all.

I think of the few weeks they told me I would be in hospital and how it stretched into seven months. A time when the same sounds and sensations shifting and shuffling dimmed me like a sedative. I lived on a plateau, a low grey one, where nothing had shape. Now I pick everything out. The sky, when it's blue, is bluer than blue. I hear like a musician, singing notes of a violin, threads of water gushing over stones, drumming feet, a nightgale out of the dark blue night and voices like scales, high ones, and low ones, some a deep base. I want to touch things, rough sand, slide my cheek up the side of a mug of hot tea, soft sensations like bird grain and hard coal and things that change, like the rubber covered handles of my bike. They start off cold and solid and become warm and pliable and tell me they can take me anywhere. And, I love getting post. Especially stuff with my name on that is just for me, but even junk-mail has potential. Sometimes the letterbox springs back into place as if it is a hungry mouth chomping on food and it traps everything, creasing and ripping, spitting it out.

*

Nobody tells me wearing a short skirt is flirting. Fluttering my eyelashes is something women do. But, it's those two things, which get me sitting on Brendan's large, square knee and us both on to my bed. A kiss comes when I'm not even looking and he stops being my protector and turns into the blue eyed, soft like cotton wool, Brendan. He calls me his sexy kitten so that is what I must be like, a small ball of fluff with large brown eyes.

In my bedroom secret, short moments gather together like snowflakes, until a great big snowball is made and that's when we roll out into the spacious world of Dandsworth.

All the time we are running, running to catch a tube, running for the bus, running across a park or down a lane. I'm always out of breath and when not running we are in the pub. With Brendan, my laughter seems to come out of the depths of a deep cave and up like a bubbling stream. We always go to O'Rileys pub around three in the afternoon. Even if busy, it takes a lot of people to fill O'Rileys. All around the sides are comfy, leather-backed, wine-red chairs. They smell of polish and face each other with a wooden table between. The seats hidden behind screens are our favourites. Here I listen to Brendan's well of jokes. I don't understand the punch lines, but watching Brendan tell them makes me laugh.

I find out about America when I ask Brendan which is his favourite country, Ireland or England and he says America.

He tells me he and Jano and her brother stayed there for six months and says, 'I wanted to stay longer, but my visa ran out. I want to live there. The Americans are free spirited. There is so much space and I don't feel trapped.'

I have to imagine living in America with Brendan, as I can't imagine life without him, but otherwise all I can think of are the big spiders.

It's a merry, sunny Wednesday; I sit in our local, The Trout, for a pub lunch, with Jan, Mike, Sara, and Stephen. The pub's theme is a strange mixture of fishing and hunting. The walls enclose us in a cosy space. Stuffed fish in tanks on wide shelves and windowsills and prints of horsemen riding to hounds, some hung in clusters others in straight lines, military fashion. It's a proper pub, not one of those made in a day with African looking objects bought in from China and horrible, plastic menus with lurid coloured ice-cream pictures on them. Its real wooden beams have soaked up years of smoke from cigarettes, cigars, and wood fires. Good, home-cooking smells waver out of the kitchen and influence our choices.

Jan does more than look at me. She looks right through me and I think she can see our many precious moments. Her questions come fast and furious. Some she asked me before like, "Are you staying in London for a long time?" Like an interrogator she doesn't give me time to think before onto the next question. She has an intense look, with forehead creased. Brendan comes with a round of drinks. He sits next to Jan and me. He is the same distance from us both, about a foot. Stephen sits on my side, but with an extra large gap between us. He hasn't spoken to me since I threw his typewriter out of the window. I prefer it that way. Mike sits there next to his biker's jacket, helmet, and gloves. You need two seats when you have a bike, one for you and one for your gear. For a while Jan stops asking me questions and turns to Brendan to talk. I sit in one of my awkward silences and Stephen talks to Mike with Sara butting in.

The next time I see Jan it's in my bedroom. It's four in the afternoon. The sun radiates through the white, bright-with-light, net curtains.

'Where is Brendan?'

Her tone demands an answer. My nose, already quite long because of the times I have lied, grows longer. Now it is very long.

'He's not here.' she says in a sharp rushed voice, disappearing around the door.

On another pub day with just Brendan and me, we sit in silence. Brendan's gift of the gab deserts him and there are no jokes. He moves his knees a little away from mine and looks into my eyes. In barely three seconds he says, 'Alice I'm going to America with Jan.'

He is serious because he says Jan, not Jano and I've never heard him say that before. 'I maybe coming back, but I don't know.'

Maybe, is like one of those push-me-pull-me animals in Dr Doolittle, you never know which way it's going to go, but it's all I have to hang on to, except for my drawings of fish, now of the ones bought from the market just down the road, silver scales, mouths open and with beady eyes accusing me.

Brendan plans to leave in the autumn. He is going to be living in Dallas. He tells me not to be there on the day he catches his plane. He says it's too difficult.

Before Brendan leaves we go to O'Riley's. I wear Brendan's favourite skirt, grass green with a wide waistband, short and pleated, not good for a windy day. The familiarity of the pub, the place we sit in, hidden behind the backs of wooden screens, loses the sadness of the day.

'I will write, I promise and I will see you again. I'm not leaving you behind.'

Holes don't stay holes for very long. I refill them as often as I refill my wardrobe. I pack the big hole Brendan leaves with lots of things—his black, racing bike. It's too big. I don't care. It's his.

Sara takes a dislike to me. She makes me feel I'm dirty because she likes Jan, and part of the hole fills up with Sara's venom. Cleaning fills up the rest of the hole as does a man called Peter Macdonald.

11
Windows and Bathrooms

I meet Peter at a conference for the arts, in a great big hall that echoes. You can tell an artist by their clothes. I see a lot in colourful clothing, so I suppose the monochrome people are not artists. I'm relieved I'm wearing a bright yellow shirt, and my skirt with large pink flowers, which buttons from bottom to top.

Peeping over people's shoulders, carrying a white, plastic cup of grey tea, time comes and goes. When enraptured by a speaker, minutes fly, but sometimes, bored, I fall asleep, and it's as if days have passed.

At the end of the conference I start to help put away the chairs and that's when Peter approaches with his soft voice and mouse brown hair. He is wearing corduroys, not very colourful, and his clothes are a bit outdated, like a farmer on his day off.

'Excuse me, excuse me, my name is Peter Macdonald.'

He has a confident voice but the words seem to turn up at the end and it makes me think of a boyfriend I had at school, who made me a wooden hedgehog. I used to hide behind the curtains when he came round looking for me.

I recognise Peter; he is one of the speakers. He gave his *Learn how to photograph your art* workshop.

'I wonder if you would be interested in being my studio assistant. I hear you would like to learn how to paint. I can help you.'

Peter lives near the Elephant and Castle tube. He fills large canvases with what he calls *City Landscapes*. Flyovers, he especially likes flyovers.

My first lesson with Peter begins with a large piece of board coated with button polish oil to stop it from absorbing paint. I squeeze out chunks of oil colour luxuriating in their intensity until Peter tells me to use less.

'Paint's expensive, you don't need all that!'

My board gobbles up the paint. Sometimes I have so much on, my brush is muddy brown from mixing, and my board becomes a slushy grey.

For the first few weeks I'm nervous of meeting the students. I hide in the horrible, porta-cabin, outside toilet, when they come. It's always raining on student days so it's smelly and humid. One day Peter reddens in his bulldog face, his taut neck stretching out from his shirt collar.

'Why are you never here to help the students? It's your job. Please be here ten minutes before the students arrive.'

But then his face softens,

'Come on inside. Into the dry studio.'

They are all diplomats' wives, rich, with perfumed accents. There's Naomi, Dominic, Donna and Lily, they all come every week. Lily is very elderly. I help her with her easel and sometimes help to put her arthritic fingers around a brush.

Still Life days are my favourite. The students huddle around a group of colourful objects, arranged on a decorative cover: teapots, wine glasses, cups, and pepper pots. They take measurements with their brushes in the air and bits of paint blob on to the floor from the bristles. Lily squints up her eyes and they disappear into the smoothed out wrinkles and her makeup cracks and flakes.

I paint my first proper *Still Life* painting. Peter says I achieve a perfect finish. 'Not a brushstroke wasted.'

Then, he walks up to Naomi, and is surprised to see her

confident painting.

'Naomi has done a terrific little number here. See the way she uses the paint to create a variety of brushstrokes. See that?'

Peter points to a brushstroke of cadmium red crossing the path of cobalt blue.

'That's a good example of wet over wet.'

At the end of the day the room is full of content smiles, occasional puzzled faces and the smell of turpentine. People start putting their things away; paintbrushes into canvas holders and lids on jars. I help Lily untangle her fingers and fold up her easel. Donna is taking her work home for her. Donna is a very handsome woman with a square jaw. She paints City Landscapes like Peter, but they are dark and brooding. Peter's are blasting out loud with colour and contrast. I hope I don't start painting them, too.

Off to Brixton next where I clean for Lily. Lily's house is a dust house, everywhere there is a layer of grey. The bathroom is my first task. Lots of little things, pots and jars and shells from the seaside have gathered here. The bath is white and yellowing in the centre with a horrible stain near the plughole. It stands on four fine legs with paws. I clean under everything, lift it all up, and put it back down in just the right spot. Lily feeds me bread and cheese and since it's hot and I am hotter from cleaning, her homemade lemonade is very welcome. Lily is thrilled with her new clean bathroom.

Naomi lives next to Lily and Donna is just down the road. They gossip about how good I am, which makes Naomi and Donna ask me to do for them, too. So now I clean windows and bathrooms for all three of them. The windows are lattice with glass like hundreds of little diamonds so small I have to clean each one with a cotton wrapped finger. I make them sparkle and they splinter colours in the sunlight, just as though they are fireworks of reds and greens and blues with hints of yellows.

To me it is like giving them a new life.

Sometimes, when at Peter's, I'm so tired I crawl into the backroom and sleep with his paintings and canvases. Protected from the bare floor by a blanket, all curled up tight to keep the world out, I dream jumbled up dreams. Peter knows I have been in hospital and puts it down to that.

12

Almost Unoticeable

Soon my favourite place becomes Peter's studio. I like tearing up clothes for the rag box and cleaning brushes in the way he shows me, with soap so they keep their shape. And, I find things for him, his keys under newspapers, the tin of turpentine, Peter's colour chart book. I know where everything is and if Peter loses something I know where to find it. Peter doesn't know what to do without me, though if there is a single thing out of place he bursts into a flurry of muttering and cursing.

'Alice I have lost my car keys again!'

'They're under your diary.'

During the lessons there is the pale swish of wet brushes stroking the board or the faint scraping sounds of pencils, sometimes hurried, scratching shade into a space. Peaceful sounds, often interrupted by the jingle of the turpentine jar as someone cleans their brush. Some afternoons we go to art galleries. I bob from painting to painting dodging the hushed tones, not speaking in case someone quells my spirit with a cross look. I know I can put my nose close to a picture to study it, but if my feet cross over the line I'll have to leave. I curl my toes and turn up my soles to help me to be near enough to see everything. My body is stiff and poker-like as I tread the boarded floor. I check the notices in large red letters, dotted here and there on walls and doors and some hanging on the ropes. Do not touch, No Photos, No smoking, No eating, or drinking. Sometimes the white walls hypnotise me and make me feel sleepy, but today I'm more awake. Peter gives us a task. 'Everyone choose a painting.'

I choose one of many bright colours by Marc Chagall.

'Now count how many times each colour occurs in the painting.'

Well, I did that and then I had an image of the painting in my mind, like a person does who has a photographic memory, but not quite that good. I think this is a good trick. If I want to remember a painting I now know what to do.

Visiting Peter's apartment feels strange. We are in an almost empty living room. There are no books on his shelves and a musty, damp smell hangs in the air. He points things out like the fridge. 'That has to go to, Nancy.' Nancy is his ex-wife. Peter has been divorced three times. This is a different Peter. Not the man whose voice fills the studio with authority, here it's as if seeing him naked, a vulnerable man with a fragile, thin body.

One day when in the studio Peter picks up two big potatoes and starts to juggle with them. His laugh's like sandpaper on my skin. Nervously I look away. The space around us expands, but in the distance we seem to get closer.

It's Tuesday when I see a women he calls, Debbie. Debbie is tall and glamorous with nutmeg coloured hair and red rimmed, sexy glasses. Debbie looks the same age as Peter and she is a sculptress. Peter starts to lose even more objects and stops doing odd things like throwing potatoes up in the air.

Now, I have a routine. I get up at six in the morning, cleaning first then, cycling back across London on Brendan's black racer, across the big roundabout to Camden to study life drawing. Back again for cleaning and on to another night class, there isn't a minute to get too upset about Brendan or to think about food. French Fancies don't exist in my life and if they did they would be Arab Desserts now, because these are so tasty.

My life is pressed and vacuum-sealed, not a minute left to spare. It's like treading on that thin bit of wire. I keep busy until eleven at night. I eat supper in bed. It feels safer eating there than on the table downstairs where temptation claws at me to take Sara's healthy biscuits. It is strange to admit it, but I feel comfortable in my new life and a part of me is glad Brendan is not here.

Letters come through the post. They are always short, some having only three words. Some are in gold and others made of torn bits from newspapers stuck together to make sentences. The sentences often say something sweet, they all come from Brendan. I write long letters back, imagining writing them in my mind between sleeping and not sleeping and while on the tube, but I always know when my stop is up.

One Wednesday early morning I take the bike out of the hallway. It's pelting down with rain and drips hang from my eyelashes blurring my vision as if I am wearing a thick veil. I have my yellow, red, blue, and green, Mary Quant cape, bought from a second hand shop, to protect me and bright yellow waterproof trousers. Cycling away I start to prepare a letter in my mind for Brendan. I'm getting used to cycling on the roads. Love the feel of turning a corner; carry my head up proud, owner of the big black racer.

It happens when I'm freewheeling down a long sloping road. The roundabout is an oasis of green, seen through the wall of grey rain. I look back over my shoulder; my view is half inside of my hood, half road. I signal right, turn right. Bang! Hit the front of the van and slide to the wet, hard concrete. I stay still, hear the faint sound of an ambulance, in the distance, and then its siren is taking more and more of the space around me. A voice asks, 'Why did you do it?'

All I can remember is the rain, the pouring grey rain.

Back in the hospital, snared again, the smell of linen and

medication, but this one is full of machines and drips and nurses in uniform, a different kind of hospital.

White ceiling and glaring lights are like a silent train above me. The tall man in a cotton, green uniform and a nurse in blue joke together as if on the telly with the sound turned down, as they pull me along a corridor on a narrow bed. I juggle what is in my brain, only an hour ago and I rode the black racer and thought of Brendan. I try to move my arms and neck, pain stabs, the bed stops; a man comes up in a white coat.

'In a rush were we?'

His hands are cold. He checks me all over.

His touch sends a tingling feeling to my spine, alien but welcome.

'You've bruised your back and have some whiplash. Keep moving so you don't seize up. Nothing we can do for you here, go home, and take some painkillers.'

A thin grumpy looking nurse comes. She could be Italian; her face is brown, like a crumpled leaf and her hands are big. She wears flat black shoes. She asks me to leave the bed, points to the phone signs; they are there to telephone someone to collect me if I need. I don't think people should work in a hospital unless they have a smile to cheer you up.

Sara is likely to be the only person at home and that is—if I'm lucky.

'It's, Alice, I have had an accident. Can someone come and collect me?'

'Suppose I will have to.'

For all Sara's bluntness she is a kind person and wouldn't have let me stay in hospital waiting and did not suggest I take a taxi, which is good, as I have no money.

The accident pulls my busy activities away, like a loose thread until my day lies bare. Not a single one of my muscles move without aching so I make a cup of tea and sit down. Thoughts tip-toe in at first: Brendan, cleaning, Peter's exhibition, Donna on Friday, Naomi on Thursday.

Head like tumbleweed, don't know which way to go. Then, I see Brendan's bike on the patio, its frame twisted, its wheels buckled and all my thoughts blow backwards to a place where I'm holding Brendan's hand, running for the tube, running across the park, laughing. What would he say now if he saw his bike? I don't know if he would be horrible or nice.

There is an eerie feel about the house in the middle of the day. The sun catches the dust and clings to the cobwebs. I feel like I'm in a tense movie. The silence has a sound, the hum of the fridge, the ticking of the clock. I want to pace to make my feet shuffle along the carpet, but the pain in my back stops me. I lie on the sofa, but no matter how I arrange the cushions, one under my head makes my head ache, one under my back makes my neck hurt and my back hurts whatever I do.

I manage to get to the library. Down the long grey road, stopping to sit at bus stops. Red buses screech to a halt, air hisses out of their brakes, doors concertina open. Angry scowls from the drivers when I just sit there and do not get on. They shroud me in fumes as they move off. Passengers glare at me. But, now I am safe. The boy with a pimply face and teeth encased in a giant pair of braces with bug-like dark glasses squints at his hardback book. Perhaps he will grow up to be handsome. I notice he is not yet a shaver. Fluffy hairs protrude from his chin. Out of the door, clinging to the rail with one hand and, *Goodbye to Back Pain* in the other, I hobble down the steps.

In tiny movements, every day, my back improves so I'm able to walk without a stoop. Two weeks later and Stuart comes up in his dusted, red Golf to take me home for the weekend for a rest. That is all I can bear in this house.

A long time has passed since my last visit and I have to get used to it and Diana's ways all over again. I look around, William

Morris design, velvet wallpaper and proper sofas with beautiful patterned material on them are overshadowed by a tall, like a bird table, ashtray. It smells of stale smoke and sometimes if Diana hasn't stubbed the but-end until it is out, a curl of smoke winds itself up to the ceiling. Stuart in charge of polishing and dusting, sprays with the can, in the air, pretending to be at work. It's the sitting room I'm going to stay in to rest my back. All I do is sleep and daydream. I think of nothing else, but Brendan.

The swishing of the wiper blades lulls me as Stuart takes me back to Dandsworth. He's pleased he doesn't have to dust his car because of the rain, but not pleased to be driving in it. On the way he sighs a lot and shouts at other drivers. I sit in the back, even though Diana isn't with us, the front seat is her place. We all have our places in the family wherever we are, in the car or in the kitchen. I'm always in a corner or behind something.

'Okay, wake up.'

We are there parked on the roadside next to 140 Tearlsford Road. Stuart turns round to look at me.

'Well, that's another journey over.'

Stuart never stays very long anywhere. Once he has done his duty he is off, but it's wonderful to have seen him. Stuart doesn't need to say much; he comes with nice memories like the two palomino ponies with their flaxen manes, we used to give apples to and the walks through Bluebell wood.

The radio is on in the kitchen, but no one is around. I call upstairs. Stephen could be in his room, but he wouldn't answer. Maybe, there is no one in. I don't mind, I look around; the house feels like a distant friend holding out a hand to me.

There are some letters on the kitchen table. I have three, keep the one with Brendan's handwriting 'til last, the other is a get-well card from Peter, and there is an invitation to Donnas' exhibition. I open Brendan's and sit in my favourite chair, which has arms you can hug and a seat, which hugs you. Brendan's handwriting is large and open with lovely tails that sweep around and lots of space between each line

'Alice how's things? Where are you? I tried to phone. I miss you."

The other paragraphs are all about Dallas, but there's something wrong as if a dark cloud hangs over him. None of his sentences end with a happy thought. I look to the end of the letter to see if it's going to tell me if anything is bad. It says 'Bye Alice, Love Brendan.'

He has been in Dallas for five months. He's telling me about the rain there saying it's like London. But my eyes start rushing through the lines looking for something missing and there it is.

'I'm coming back.'

Four words, they aren't in gold or cut outs, they are handwritten. They are almost unnoticeable, but as soon as I read them they become gigantic.

13

Source of Craziness

My routine is shattered. Brendan is back. Crashing waves around
me as he comes in like the tide, over my life. But inside a part
of me tingles, remembering firefly moments, in my bedroom,
O'Riley's—behind the screens, running across the park, holding
tight cupped hands, kissing melting kisses. I need to watch
him talk, throw myself into his world, ears touching his lilting
voice, but he tells me someone is coming to visit.

'I have a favour to ask.' Brendan's skin is tanned so now his
laughing eyes have a new lighter blue and today they have a
twinkle which says 'I want something from you.' His eyes are
puppy-dog wide as he says, 'A friend has come over from Ireland
and he wants to see me before he goes back. His name is Joseph
and he's a bit crazy. He once climbed up a church steeple with
no clothes on. I love him for that, but he ended up in a hospital
a bit like yours. He'll just be staying the one night, if that is
okay?'

A crow's shadow passes by my face and my smile disappears,
but I don't say, no.

He tells me he hated America, the blistering heat, the accents
and I think he lost his confidence. Here, people know and respect
him, he has a good job, he is a protector, there, they laughed at
him when he didn't even mean to be funny.

'You'll think I'm mad, Alice, but I spent hours in shops
trying to keep cool, staring at clothes, taking my mind off
America. I shouldn't have gone back, I'd remembered only the

good things, but in reality they were not many. I'm so glad to be back here with you.'

'Where's, Jan?' My nails dig into my sweaty palms.

'Jan stayed in America. We split up. We couldn't stand each other any more. Don't worry, I'm here now. '

Mike is cleaning his bike. He spits and rubs the dazzling silver metal. It looks perfect as if it has never been outside on the dusty roads. Sara is upstairs playing Chopin, her favourite music. It's Diana's favourite too. Stephen is out at work, cross-eyed over numbers, calculating totals. Four o'clock and in comes Joseph, flaming red, curly hair, freckles and a strong body, taller than Brendan and with a big smile and steel grey eyes. Not at all like my mental picture of someone small, dark haired and with an unhappy face. He throws his brown rucksack down and opens his arms. 'Hi, you must be, Alice, heard all about you.'

We go for a walk down Tearlsford Road and around to the park. Joseph and Brendan step out in front laughing, like two dancing hyenas. I walk behind trying to keep up, my legs stretched and straightened like an ironed shirt and I know I have aches building up for tomorrow. In the pub I sit on a chair all on my own. They sit on the bench opposite. Their Irish laughter peals away. I can feel a lump arrive somewhere in my chest and my breath is getting slower and quieter until I can't feel it and my body is still. I can sense a sulk coming on. I stop looking at them; stop trying to keep up with their chatter. They become like one animal, gyrating and bubbling. I look down at my lap in silence.

'What's up, Alice?'

'Nothing.'

'Joseph and I are best mates, Alice.'

On the long walk back the sulk on my face doesn't go away. I try, but it's more comfortable having it there. The smell of

73

vegetables sizzling in oil greets us when we get home. Sara is cooking up a stir-fry. I think of how Diana, when she was in one of her frequent hurries used to serve us with peas and carrots from the freezer, though Stuart did grow delicious corn on the cob and fluffy potatoes, which made great *smash*. The thoughts lighten my sulk.

Sara is cooking for us all. Dressed in her long turquoise skirt with tiny pieces of glass stitched in, making a spray of mirrors, reflecting the light and a silk red scarf flung around her neck, she plunges a spoon into the pan. Mike is still cleaning his bike. Stephen is somewhere else.

Pondering over the activities in the house and where everyone is dilutes the laughter of Joseph and Brendan and I am glad to see them sitting on chairs at a distance from each other. Joseph likes roll ups and I like watching people roll up. He winks at me watching him. Now I have his attention, I ask, 'When are you going back to Ireland?'

'Oh, tomorrow, I'm only over to see my brother and to catch Brendan.'

I search for something that would place him in a hospital like mine and can't see anything. He has energy bursting out of him like a racehorse pushing at the bit and he looks and acts, 'normal', even though he climbed the church steeple with no clothes on. I try to picture him, his body is covered in the red, curly hairs, cat-like he is climbing the steeple, stretching out his arms on arrival, reaching to the skies, I can hear him shout in exultation. What it would be like to be there with him. If only I wasn't nervous of heights.

Some dinners at the table are in silence, some with the noise of chatterers, and others ghost-like with hushed voices spoken so as not to upset somebody. In our family that somebody was Stuart. Stuart used to have a loud army-voice, which shouted at you in short cross words if you broke one of the rules and, you had to put your hand up if you wanted to leave the table. This dinnertime is a noisy chatty one, mainly Sara, Brendan and Joseph. Comforted by the presence of Mike and Stephen, I begin to enjoy eating vegetables cooked with spices, which I have never tasted before.

I come to bed early. I can still hear them laughing. It's after twelve when Brendan comes in and slips beside me under the cool, white, cotton sheets. I feel his large soft hand on my breast. At first I shrink away—my breasts are small like pinheads and they always embarrass me, but he persists. Seconds leap into minutes. Sleepily I move to fit around his searching hands. They visit every part of me in a rough urgent way. Aroused by his excitement, I let him cover me like a hairy cloak, folding out the light until I can only see his heaving, sweating chest.

In the morning Brendan signs on early to avoid the queue. Everyone has gone out. The bed feels empty. My space is beside the window where I can hear the birds sing and the sound of the number seventy-seven bus from Wandsworth to Oxford Circus. The sunbeams catch my eyes and warm my face. It's time to get dressed and go. Joseph is downstairs sitting on the settee, his dark blue sleeping bag in a bundle on the floor, next to his feet.

'Morning, Joseph . . .'

He doesn't answer. He starts to make a roll up. His fingers space the tobacco out in an even row and push it down as if sowing small seeds, then delicately, spreads it over the white paper. With little movements he rolls it and licks along the edge. His fingers work in light, but firm movements from side to side to seal it. Intense with concentration, he strikes a match and lights it. He still hasn't spoken. There is something different about him today. He keeps his head held down quite low and with his wild hair you can't see his face, not a freckle. I make some porridge. A lovely smell after it's been cooked in the microwave.

'Want some tea?'

I wait for an answer but his continued silence fills the space, 'Can I get you anything?'

The silence is several seconds longer. *Has he heard me?*

I sit down in the large, leathery armchair and its soft, fleshy arms engulf me. It's the one farthest away from Joseph, but I feel uncomfortable being so deeply embedded so I move to a chair with a paisley cushion. That's better. I sit there, arms folded, legs crossed.

'Mind if I put the television on?' I ask.

The silence has loaded the air and the space around Joseph is physical as if you could put your hand into it. I stay there eating my porridge, my hands shake, a heat creeps over me, reddens my neck and now my face, it is like I am being watched, and yet, Joseph isn't looking at me. He leans back in his chair; his movement lightens the heaviness of his silence. His big body fills up the well of the seat. It touches the arms and the sides, not leaving any room in-between. He turns his head to the right and tilts it back to look outside. His neck muscles show the strain of this position, but he holds it for some time. His eyes are still and emotionless. There is nothing to see outside just the black dustbins and a bike. The sun, weak as it came through the window in my room, has gone and it's now a grey day. For a moment I feel sorry for Joseph. I start to talk about the weather, get into a conversation all by myself.

Joseph moves. He clasps his hands and rests them on his knee. He lifts his face and looks at me as if I'm his prey. I look away and get up. I walk with caution into the kitchen, which runs into the sitting room.

I wonder if he is punishing me for something, then indignation at the very thought, makes me brave. I call out questions in a careful, but direct way, 'Why are you doing this?

76

Why aren't you speaking? You can talk can't you?'

Joseph taps the ash off his cigarette into an ashtray.

'What have I done? Have I been rude to you? I don't know what you are upset about but you've got to start talking. Say something, say hello, just that, but don't be so silent.'

I'm standing a little away from him, calling over an invisible fence, frightened of his size and his silence.

I go upstairs to my bedroom, relieved to get away from the possessed space. I wish Brendan would come back. Minutes tick away, some move fast, some slow, but altogether they group to make one whole hour. It's 12 midday, four hours have passed. Joseph doesn't say hello to Brendan at first, he keeps his head bowed down and his hands clasped. Brendan makes himself a cup of tea, the noise of the kettle and the chinking of the china break the silence.

'Are you alright, Joseph?' Brendan has a light tone as if nothing is wrong.

'Fine, Brendan, fine.' Joseph's voice is quiet. I only just hear it from my position upstairs leaning over the banister, but I think I can go down again. I take each step in a deliberate way, holding on to the banister, listening for clues that everything has returned to normal. The cup rattles in its saucer. Brendan is carrying it through to the sitting room. I step through the door. 'Hello, Joseph.' I say again.

'Hello, Alice, where have you been?'

Relief at hearing him speak releases the breath I didn't know I had been holding.

I show Joseph my portfolio. He loves the charcoal drawings intense, supple, black lines together with the contrast of white chalk.

'Their eyes are so real.' He turns the paper over revealing more fish.

'Can I pose for you?'

'Yes of course, I'd like that.'

Joseph is a statue for two hours, with two, five minute, cigarette breaks. He keeps his eyes on my movements and rarely speaks. His madness is contained. I draw him in his colourful clothing. Blue shirt covered in red and yellow star-like flowers, black rubber tie, studded with orange and yellow shapes and dark trousers with swirls of light blue. He looks like a tropical fish. I draw his face, smooth and pale, against his ginger hair. His eyes pose a challenge. In them I see a deep anxiety, penetrating all that's around him. They reveal the source of his craziness and I know he is manic and inaccessible.

14

The Fog

Hurricane Joseph disappears as quickly as he appeared, leaving us alone together.

We walk across Hyde Park. It's so hot you could fry an egg on the pavement. The smell of just cut grass, scents the air. There are still patches of green from spring, but most has dried out and become dusty. My eyes open unblinking for a while. I'm talking in my head. Brendan is wearing his white shorts. I'm wearing a knee length, yellow, gingham summer dress and plimsolls.

It's eleven in the morning, most people are at work, but there are the wanderers, a few wide-awake tourists and a woman jogging by in blue silk shorts, she has globulous thighs and a slim waist. I notice other women's bodies. I note if they are too fat—Michelin tyre fat, but they can never be too thin. I imagine which one I would like to be like. I am not happy with my body and still hate parts of it, something no amount of months in hospital could change. I listen to Brendan as he chants songs about falling in love. His songs feel stronger than his fragile feelings for me.

We come in from the hot day and lie like drunken lizards on the sofa. The blazing heat has followed us in. I close the curtains to block out the sun and flop down beside Brendan. My fingers search for the palm of his hand. A memory, small as a daisy, slips in and I see myself as a child, running across the fields, palms slippery from sweat, clutching a bunch of wild flowers. I get to the front door of our, very proper, detached, square house. A few crumpled dandelion heads and violets fall to the ground. The fun had been in picking them. The next treat was pressing a cold glass of lemonade against my face.

*

We rest, asleep on the sofa until Sara comes in with plastic bags bulging and weighing her arms down. When Sara comes in with bags like that it means she's preparing to cook something. She suggests another house meal. We have a house meal about once a month and usually take turns, except when it comes to Stephen. Stephen only knows how to cook packet meals in the microwave.

With everyone around the table, the glow from the candles, the curtains closed to keep out the disappearing sunlight, the pan-fried fish glisten like tinsel.

Questions follow Brendan: Did he see any big scorpions? What is the social scene like? How is Jan, is she coming back?

'No, no, not in Dallas, plenty of dogs and cats, but no scorpions, yes, the music scene is good. Yes, Jano is well. No, she is staying out there. She sends her love.'

On hearing Jan's name I can't concentrate on the conversation. A low headache moans as it tries to become full blown. My stomach bulges and I remember pumpkin days. Have I eaten too much? I stare at the fish-skeletons. Brendan's is still in a perfect fish shape. 'Keep your fish bones,' I interrupt. 'I'm going to draw them.'

*

Philip, the community nurse, visits the house once a month to see if everything is alright and there are no unhappy people

80

and no problems with the rent. He is the kind of man you wish would hug you, there is something fatherly about his roundness. He practices aromatherapy massage when he can. He rubs sweet smelling oil into his palms and then, covers me in it as he massages my shoulders and other smaller areas. Sara loves his massages and always has a big smile and some carrot cake for him.

Soothed by his calming hands I ask, 'Phillip can I talk to you about something?'

'Sure, fire away'

'I'm worried, Brendan might go away again. I don't think I could face it.'

'He's very independent and free spirited. I wouldn't set your heart on things. Take each day as it comes.'

A black, bottomless cloud drifts over me and hangs there brooding. When I move, it follows me, even out into the sun. That's where it hurts most of all. I can't enjoy the sun with it over my head. It's Philip's fault for giving me the bad thoughts. I'm confused. Jan, Brendan, Ireland, and America—all go like a merry-go-round in my head.

When Brendan comes home from signing on, I immediately say I have to talk to him, to lift the heaviness off my shoulders and to see if I can look right into his eyes and know the truth.

'Are you going away again?'

I can only look at the tip of his nose. 'Well, I might be going back to Ireland.'

'Can I come with you?'

'No, that's too complicated, Alice. I'm best on my own.'

My eyes don't meet his. They fix onto the edge of the table.

The cloud is now a shroud. All over I feel grey. For the next few days, unable to eat, even porridge, I can't laugh at Brendan's jokes, though he tries to lift me out of my misery.

I'm just too good at being miserable. We even play the game—whoever is first to smile loses. Normally I lose, but this time I win.

After asking questions Sara gives up. Mike watches. Stephen, with his head in a magazine, seems to be eating all the time, sandwiches or something. The whole house becomes silent and the damp, grey fog spreads from me into every room. It seeps under the floorboards and stretches up to the ceiling.

'Oh come on, Alice, this has gone on for long enough, it's affecting everybody's morale, what is the matter?' Sara says, with a big sigh.

'Brendan is going back to Ireland without me.'

Like a balloon shrinking so does the atmosphere, till it shrivels into a tiny piece of grey cement in my head.

15

Like a Parcel of Fish

Often I sit in silence holding Brendan's hand, too upset to speak about 'it'.

Tonight, face turned towards the cool breeze, I'm startled by the sound of an orchestra of cats. I sit closer to Brendan wishing he would say he's not going, but instead out shoots, like a poison arrow, 'I might not be coming back.'

'Why can't I come with you?'

'You have got your painting and Peter's studio.'

'I'll give them up.' I wipe away racing tears, rushing down my cheeks. My shoulders and elbows are jumping and jerking. I can't stop them. Brendan puts his arm around me to contain my sobs, but that makes more come even faster and thicker.

The next day, warmer, with running-away clouds, is the last day of the term at Peter's. Donna and Naomi attend and Lily, with her suffering hands. Peter tells me to keep painting. Lily says I will meet a nice man soon who will sweep me of my feet. Donna buys two paintings, one of a leaping trout, another of some minnows swimming in a purple sea, made from torn up paper and ink.

The day finishes at four o'clock instead of five. I am sad as I walk back and make each step slower and shorter. I don't really want to reach home. I take in all there is to see: the large man with the two, clipped like topiary trees, white poodles, rotting vegetables left over from the market hanging out of a cardboard box and a man—twentyish—with a long thin face like a stalactite, hair tied back, gold earrings catching the light as he sweeps the pavement.

On the way I discover a shiny new shop, it has replaced 'Pritchard's Antiques'. The large windows, for a long time dirty, with pieces of cardboard shutting the room inside out of sight, now displays brochures, insurance company adverts and a poster of a woman with long chestnut hair in a little, light blue bikini. She walks along a flat as a table, cream coloured beach. If only I could look like that. I never wear bikinis, since I can't bear my stomach to be seen.

The lady in the shop has straight long hair, of gingery blond with light streaks, which make me think of tigers. I ask how much it is to go to the Algarve. She shows me a hotel with a picture of a swimming pool and trees all for £99 pounds including breakfast and evening meal. I say I will come back.

*

'When are you going? What's the date?' I ask Brendan,

'Why do you want to know, now?'

'You know when you are going! Why don't you tell me?'

'Probably, the last week in July.'

July is the month for Brendan to go. I find his ferry ticket sitting on the table with the cream lampshade we bought together from a car boot sale. It's on a stand in the shape of a large paw. I only agreed to have it as Brendan likes it so much, but it gives me the creeps.

'Why didn't you tell me?'

'I didn't want to upset you.'

'It's okay, I'm not upset. I'm going for a holiday in the Algarve and won't be here when you leave.'

I say standing tall, pride in my eyes.

I have never seen Brendan look putout. It is as if he has

been slapped.

Pubs and tickets, telephone calls and tearful goodbyes are all mixed up, Brendan off to Ireland and me to the Algarve.

*

The still, warm air clings to my face. I cross the runway, through the customs, wait to collect my rucksack. I watch it travelling towards me, bumping and turning on the rumbling conveyor belt. I try to catch it, but miss and have to wait for it to do another round. I spot it with ease because I have tied a yellow ribbon to the handle.

Two hours later on a searing hot bus I arrive at Hotel Maraket. As I'm walking along the sticky-tar pavement I inhale the stale smell of dog excrement. I dodge a row of Prickly Pear Cactus, almost as big as me and step inside the hotel doors and put my bag down by the rectangular, wooden reception desk. I'm about to ring, when a bronzed man with blonde, frizzy hair, dazzling grey eyes, tight muscles and aged about thirty, approaches me.

'Hi, I'm, Derek. Are you, Alice? Excellent, I'm your rep for the week.'

I can see a dark corridor with shiny floors leading off to my right that must go to the bedrooms, but there is also a lift in the corner of the entrance. I wait for the receptionist.

'Come for a drink in the lounge, Susie won't be long,' the blond man says. I can imagine him on a surfboard, at home in the sea.

I sit on a high stool one elbow leaning on the bar. More and more I begin to feel pain across my stomach. I try to move a little to relieve it.

Derek orders me a Martini, 'That will relax you. Now, why are you looking so sad?'

Tears creep up. I gulp my drink, swallow hard and blink, but nothing stops them, they rush forth like a spring. 'Sorry.'

'Love life?'

'Yes.'

I screw up my fingers, holding back tears, pushing the floor down with the tip of my toe, which could just reach.

'You're here now. Try to forget about it.'

'I think I ought to go back'

'Stay a night and think in the morning.'

My bed squeaks and the mattress is thin, there are tea-coloured stains on the eggshell painted walls. There's a sink in the room and a towel on my bed. Rachael has got here first and chosen the bed nearest to the window with the light falling on its beige cover. Rachael has lush brown hair, a mole on her cheek and a Birmingham accent. Rachael, who is my roommate, is either out on the beach in her frilly tops or bikini or in the apartment sleeping.

It's Monday morning and I feel blue, not sky blue, but a deep blue-black, like ink. I'm missing Brendan. The pain has come back. I take two white paracetamals with a glass of tepid water. My tooth aches, too. I hope it's nothing serious. I gargle with large amounts of hot salted water.

Hands trembling, heart thudding, I open the door to the corridor and see a woman carrying a fat, round bulk of white towels. Disorientated, I have forgotten the way out,

'Where are the stairs please?'

'No speak English.'

Six doors closed, the seventh door opens out onto a stairwell. The passage down the stairs is dark and cool, no windows or pictures, just blank white walls. Steadying myself by a rail I enter the lounge, Derek looks up.

'Morning. Sleep well? Any better? Can I get you a drink?'

The heat suffocates and the Martini makes me lazy and

sleepy.

Rachael is out. A confetti of pants and tops litter the floor and the bed. I change into my swimming costume, navy blue with a spread of white daisies and yellow centres. The cool of the bedroom brings goose bumps up all over me. I'm like a plucked turkey.

The longer I stay in the sun, the more Martinis I drink and the more Derek comforts me with his reassuring chat— relationships are never meant to last, there is always someone else. He gives me a squeeze around my waist.

In the hot sun my sleazy, martini eyes linger over a lithe, tall man called Paul. He has a profile like a Greek God. From conversations I have heard, he is a bodyguard. Perhaps I could have a wild romance.

The pain in my side hasn't gone away, only dulled and in the morning my hands tremble. I've forgotten to bring Brendan's passport photo with me. I reach out for a memory of his face but can't focus on it. The room is hot, airless. Brendan's face fades. I clutch at it but it disappears. I give up trying to remember Brendan.

It's Tuesday, the fourth day of the holiday, only three more days to go. I lie like a contented cat on the warm, pale sand listening to the ruffle of waves climbing the shore. I hear children laughing and people talking, but above these I hear a scuffling sound and right near me a pair of feet and a bottom land in the sand. The feet belong to Rachael, I can tell by her anklet.

'Going to come to the party tonight? Go on, we're meeting at Rays.'

'Who?'

'Everyone, Foxy, Dave, Trevor and Tracey will be there. You know some of the people. It'll do you good.'

The evening stays light till ten, eleven is my usual bedtime, but this evening I begin looking through my rucksack for a pair of earrings, they are in the form of fish, made up of tiny parts, their bodies undulate like real ones. Brendan gave them to me. He never got me a birthday present, but gave me these fish earrings. I had only bought two going out dresses, one pink, long, cotton dress with thin shoulder straps and a green, light suede dress with a swinging skirt. I slip the pink dress on and my multicolored sandals, with thin wedge heels, brush my hair, which sits shoulder length on my bare shoulders and put on the fish earrings.

Dancing everywhere, on the streets, on the tiny nightclub floors, we visit them all and it's still only two in the morning. We are a herd of wild beasts tearing through the night, waking up the sleeping people, startling wide-awake cats, bumping into hungry stray dogs, sometimes falling across other night clubbers staggering their way home. Restaurants have closed. There is only the hum of the night, the warm air, the laughter in the silence.

I dance with the man called Paul, the lithe, tall bodyguard. Dancing with him makes me miss Brendan. Paul has a vacant stare as if to look through me, apologises and goes to steal a bar stool for the night where he stays sipping beer.

The bar at the Hotel is still open, but closing. Andrew, the bartender, clears up a few tables, but we all, like a herd of thirsty elephants, trample in begging him for one last drink and sink into the leather, black seats. In the quiet, under a lamp, is Derek, hunched over a newspaper.

'Had a good time all?'

We sit around Derek with gin and tonics, beers and whisky. Derek is drinking Orangina. I have a Martini. My legs are spinning from dancing, my feet want to continue, I can feel them tap tapping, but the top half of my body is ready to sleep.

Whilst Foxy is talking, holding the conversation like a king,

88

everyone all ears to him listening to his stories, I feel, from under the table, a hand reach for my bare thigh. It is warm and pressing. I'm sitting so close to Derek, no one notices. Foxy, named Foxy, because of his pointy nose and red hair, slight build and cleverness, decides it's time for bed, at least to try to find the bedroom, in a drunken haze.

As if held together by a rope they all stand up at once, grabbing handbags and finishing off drinks, saying goodnight. I can't move. I still have a hand on my thigh. Even Andrew has gone. He switched out the main lights not noticing ours, not knowing we are still here. In the dark I feel salt-tasting, fleshy lips pressing against mine. Derek eases me down across the seat. Damp with sweat, his and mine, it's like having a huge heavy snail on top of me. A glass crashes onto the hard, stone floor. I lie still, hardly breathing. My hand reaches out for the cold top of the black marble table. Thoughts of Ireland come. What is it like? I have heard it's a very green country, full of myths and legends, Leprechauns and fairies. Another glass smashes, my mind comes back to me. I push Derek to the side and roll off the seat to the floor, not sure how, but I miss the glass.

'Sorry, but I'm too tired.'

Derek is surprised. With his help I stand up and straighten out my pink dress. Derek pulls on his blue shorts.

'Oh, I'm sorry I didn't mean to . . .'

'Don't worry, it's okay, I'm okay.'

I'm so glad to get back to my squeaky bed. Rachael is asleep with two pieces of cucumber over her eyes.

*

The walk down the ramps and through customs takes ages. It's like a busy motorway not a passageway. My rucksack bumps along the floor, straps fly everywhere, my feet walking on them, tumbling into people, and knocking elbows. Carrying bags like camels, step by step, we are all determined to get home.

At ten o'clock I arrive in Gatwick. I catch the tube, the familiar blue-white, metal bullet, shooting through London, but very calm inside on the blue vinyl seats where I can think and sleep. My rucksack seems heavier and messier on the return home.

Night in the house is still as still as a stone. I switch on the light and tiptoe into the sitting room with my luggage. Have a drink of water and sit on the sofa until my head sinks and my eyelids begin to close. It's time to go to bed. With fairy-like steps I go down the hallway, past the bikes, up to my bedroom door and open it. The moon is a thin slice of lemon and affords no light. I find the switch, flick it and from the doorway I see the lump, like a human form, in my bed. I think it might be a friend of Sara's staying the night. On the floor next to the bed Brendan's white trainers say, 'hello' to my heart, making it bump. Next to them is the familiar crumpled heap of his honey coloured trousers.

I switch out the light. Brendan hasn't gone, but I am not ready to see him. I make my way back to the sitting room and on the sofa with a blanket I wrap myself up like a parcel of fish.

16

Summoned by a Bell

The closed, laced net curtains glow lemon in the sunlight, while the sun's fingers run through their pattern, tickling the kitchen table. I lift the black-bottomed kettle off the stove and take it to the tap. It used to have an efficient whistle, until that died as if a cat got it. I'd forget the kettle, be in the other room, not hearing the impatient whistle. It seized up. It's a good make too. I hold it high under a slow running tap. I don't want to wake anyone, but a noise like thunder reverberates around the silent house. I hold my breath. The stairs creak, I hear Brendan's familiar voice, 'Well, aren't you going to say hello?' He says as he comes through the kitchen door. It has only been a week, but he looks like a stranger. I touch him, his arm, his faded-tanned skin.

'Saw your shoes last night, didn't want to wake you.'

'I had no idea what time you would be here. I have been waiting for you.'

'But, you're supposed to be in Ireland.'

'I've been thinking a lot about you. I've missed you.'

My legs are weakening and my toes scrunch up as if to grip the floor to stop me falling. I move back, away from Brendan.

'I'm tired from travelling.'

'Shall we go for a little walk?' His voice is tentative. 'To the cafe?'

'Why not.'

We turn in the opposite direction to the charcoal grey road and walk, single file along the narrow pavement of the fast paced, direct-route road, between the industrial estates, and retail parks. Lorries and sales rep's cars whiz by. I feel like I am in a tunnel. My eyes blink away the dust wafted into the air around me, but it is all worth it as ten minutes down this road is a transport cafe, the best. I ask for two mugs of tea. Another customer orders coffee. Ours slurps, thick and dark, out of an ageing and battered, steel teapot, theirs sets the steam machine into motion and a noise like a jet engine revving up drowns the chat of the working men with their tattooed arms, rough, tough shorts and enormous breakfasts. The flowing smells of bacon, sausages, eggs, tomatoes, topped with a handful of mushrooms, makes our hungry stomachs growl in protest.

The wooden legged chairs scrape on the red, sand-ingrained, meant to make it non slippery, linoleum. We sit opposite one another. Brendan's words float far away—small ships in the sea. I snatch only a few haphazardly—Ireland, together . . ..My mind is like crazy paving. I clutch my corn-coloured mug with both hands. The tea is still hot. Its steam dampens my nose. Putting the mug down, I begin to scratch the varnish on the wooden table.

'Are you okay?' Brendan looks pale, grey lines etch under his eyes.

'I'm sorry to mess you about. I want you to come back to Ireland with me. I need you. I realise I can't face Ireland on my own . . . and, my parents . . .'

The objects in the room stir with his words. I put my hands behind me and hold onto the back of the chair to steady myself.

My thoughts are limp. I'm tired of him throwing my hopes up in the air with his laughter and then, crashing them down, leaving me all alone. I remember Derek. He's kind. He doesn't tell jokes, but he is easier to be with. Being with Brendan again is like falling down a deep well, with only a tiny parachute.

*

Now, at night, with everything unresolved, we take up a space either side of the bed, which seems to open up like the parting of waves in the sea, as we climb in at different times, me with a book at ten and Brendan after the pub, bringing the smell of beer into our bed. I rise earlier than usual, for a walk to the newsagent to buy a paper and to avoid Brendan.

Sara has a lot of people for singing lessons and Mike is away. With the silence between us, the house seems bigger. We are polite to each other, especially in the kitchen, where the cooker is next to the sink and the sink next to the microwave. It doesn't matter what you are doing in the kitchen, you are only inches away from each other. My eyes roam across the tiled floor, afraid to look up. Frowning and puzzled we try to finish what we have to do. I must be as silent as a blue, June sky. Brendan is a man behind a mask. I can't tell what he is feeling.

One day we walk down Tearlsford Road together, Brendan has to sign on. I want to go shopping. We walk with two feet of space between us, commenting on how the weather has changed. Fine drops of drizzly rain land on our shoulders and heads. A harsh smell of fumes penetrates the damp air and coats my throat. I step aside to avoid a puddle and the dirty, black smoke belching from the number seventy-seven bus and bump into Brendan. The bump holds a tingle of electricity. Brendan puts his arm around my shoulders and releases his breath on a sigh. 'Let's make up.' he whispers. I squeeze his hand.

It's a dewy, next morning, with a rainbow yawning over the sky. The sun lights up the pearl-like clouds. I leap out of bed saying, 'Yes, I'm going to Ireland!' But then, I realise I'm in a dream. Later, the dream and the reality mix up, like the eclipse of the moon, as the wide-awake me says yes.

I make long lists, which I write out into smaller lists, on bits of coloured paper. Red for very important, this is the longest: passport, bank details, letter to Diana—that is, before a phone call telling her not to worry and not to have nightmares, and despite its size, the most precious of my things, the painting easel. The yellow list is for everything else.

Every morning brings a sharp breath of excitement. It's as if I have decided to jump into the ocean. The kitchen becomes a meeting place for me and Brendan. We shuffle through the small space, touching hands from time to time, jostled by people and brushed and bumped by elbows and knees to a background of noise—Sara humming, Mike on the guitar in the corner, only Stephen flits here and there, bat-like, soundless.

There are two post deliveries, one at 11.00am and one at 3.00pm. Nothing comes for me in the morning. I didn't expect anything. There are two for Stephen. Sara always gets the most because she likes making friends. She writes lots of letters and sends off for freebies, belongs to clubs and emails lots of people. Her email list of addresses is as long as my arm. But, in the afternoon I get a letter, the envelope states, 'Miss Alice Smith', very formal. I think it must be something to do with me leaving. I open it and read it out loud.

Dear Miss Smith,

I'm writing with regard to the post of, Paint Restoration Assistant. The position is now open again.

The previous assistant has left due to unforeseen circumstances. I would like to offer you the post. It would be preferable if you could start immediately, due to the amount of new work.

Please let me know as soon as possible if you would like to accept the position.

Yours Sincerely,
Roger Wright

For a moment I see Diana's happy face and myself, holding a paintbrush, instead of a ticket to Ireland. After this there is a hole in my stomach getting bigger with all the things I will have to leave behind: Tearlsford, the parks, Sara, Mike, Stephen, Emma, even the cat next door, Ginger, who I give milk in spite of being told not to. If I leave I will never see them all again. What about Professor Lucas, how will I manage without him? Will I be able to paint in Ireland?

I don't tear the letter up, that would be too final. I fold it in four and look at the expectant faces around me. Brendan's expression holds concern, he asks me, which Alice I am today. I hesitate, but all at once I drop the letter in the bin and say, 'The Irish Alice. I want to go to Ireland.' And, as I say it, all the rogue thoughts and worries leave me as if summoned by a bell.

17

Stuart's Plum Jam

The following Thursday I leave for Haystart to say goodbye to Diana and Stuart.

It's a hot day. Both Diana and Stuart are out shopping for a new wheelbarrow. I decide to visit the local church. I find churches peaceful. I let my fingers rap against the railings, which are not very tall and have spikes to stop people from climbing up them. Duncan White's image shudders through my body. From a tree, after school, he fell onto some railings like these. I didn't see it, but a picture formed of him impaled and stayed with me. I break out in a sweat. Jeans, black polo sweater, socks and black pumps, while the sun is sizzling, has more to do with it than my thoughts, but I'm having an all covered up, day.

I walk along running my fingers along the rails until they touch the cool, grainy stone gate posts. The iron gate smells of fresh paint. Black and majestic its hinges swing in a silent movement and I think the absence of a, metal grinding against metal, groan means the oil can has had an outing as well as the paint brush. I step through onto a path, bordered by velvety grass, like a tail of stone-stitches threaded into an emerald coat. Once, the lawns housed grave stones, but now these ancient, grey-slate relics, telling of people who roamed here in years gone by and died of consumption, or measles, but never old age, stand like soldiers worn down by battle, against the dry stone walls.

I look up to see the great, big oak tree, the oldest in Europe. Its trunk hollowed by age is like a gaping mouth and I remember I buried a note, containing my inner thoughts, inside the trunk, under a piece of loose bark, when I was twelve. But still, I was afraid someone could read the secrets in my mind. The note soon disappeared, probably with the damp.

The pointy triangle roof of the porch holds the church door in a tight grip. It makes me look up, because it's so tall and I think they built it like that to make you feel closer to God. The smell of grass passes as soon as I'm under the porch, with its thick oak beams. To me all wooden things are oak. It's the only tree I know apart from the willow tree, which is full of caterpillars.

The church smells musty, like an old wardrobe and reminds me of a tardis—it seems to expand once you are inside. The pews in their, close together, rows trip you up as you try to get out of them. The alter sits under the only stained glass window. The iridescent light pours through, its clearly defined beam divides the church in two. I follow it with my eyes and see the magic of the beautiful, blue, red, yellow and green myriad of colour. It reminds me of Marc Chagall's paintings.

I stand behind a seat. After a few minutes, I begin to feel the presence of a person, but when I turn around no one is there. The church feels full of people coming to pray. But there are no people. I lean with my back against the wall to stop the uncomfortable feeling of ghosts behind me.

Ten minutes later and a hundred feet away from the church, I look back. I see a person wearing a long black coat, changing direction away from me and disappearing around a white, stonewalled cottage with a thatched roof. For a moment I think they are trying to hide from me. I'm beginning to feel very alone, though it's only a twenty-minute walk home. The experience of the church hasn't been so peaceful and I'm glad when I pass through our gate and walk past the cherry tree, up to our front door.

Home feels quieter than in the church, even with the sound of Diana sewing. Her needle pierces the satin and the silk thread flows through carrying streams of colours, silvery greys and blues, making pictures of rivers and mountains. The gentle rhythm soothes me.

I can smell something strong and sweet coming from the kitchen. Stuart is leaning over a large pan with a brown wooden spoon stirring.

'Is this more jam you are making, Stuart?'

'Yes, plum, with plums from the garden.'

'But the pantry is already filled up from last year's.'

'Good, we will have lots then.'

Stuart blows on the hot jam with such force he makes tidal waves.

I have only four mornings to go before taking the ferry to Ireland with Brendan, four more days with Diana and Stuart and four more days with Bobby. Bobby is a mongrel with a wet black nose and white paws; he lies near Stuart while Stuart towers above the jam.

'How is Diana about Ireland now?'

'You will have to speak to Diana about that.'

You will have to speak to Diana about that—is one of the longest things Stuart ever says to me. There are others: 'Alright love' and 'Get off', or 'Do as your told'. Diana talks more, but only before mealtimes. She's quite chatty then.

'It's not that I don't want you to go to Ireland.' She says. 'But, I want you to be happy . . . I don't know this man, Brendan. You say he's nice, but you can't trust people. Besides there have been a lot of bombings in London. Your brother's in the army. If you got married he would never be able to come to your wedding. Alice, you are going to Southern Ireland and you're a foreigner and you're English. Don't blame me if you get into trouble . . .'

'*It's not my fault if you get yourself into trouble.*' These are Diana's favourite words to me.

After the walk and the church, I can hardly keep awake, but it's dinnertime. Somehow the stalwart silences always bring me to attention. Must eat properly, sit up straight, Stuart is at the head of the table, Diana fidgets in the chair, dog's nose points out from under the heavy, velvet cloth. The silence starts with hot steaming plates put on the table, lasting through to pudding, with just the clinking of forks and knives and the scraping of dessertspoons finishing off the apple pie and custard. Not a word is mentioned about Ireland.

Deep means quality in our house, regarding mattresses. I sink into my bed, whereas only a heavy man can crease my futon in London, which came new and firm and never gives up being so. It's a treat to sink into something as soft as the bed in Haystart. It's only nine o'clock, still in my black polo-neck, jeans and socks I fall asleep into a collage of dreams: Ireland and planes, Brendan and horses, explosions, blue skies, red buses and Stuart's plum jam.

18

Waiting for Brendan

I've never been on a ferry, it's like a large flat foot with a dirty, chips and cigarette covered floor. I've been on a hovercraft and on a plane, enmeshed between rows, blocked the aisle with my hand luggage. But, on the ferry there's room; room for your feet to walk, your arms to swing and even to skip and leap across the squeaking, maroon carpet, to weave around the empty chairs. Telephone signs disappear and appear like the white rabbit and Alice and smells waft through the air of the salty sea.

Brendan, confident of his way, takes me to the cinema, a tiny room, squashed with people. We watch Superman 3. It's twelve noon, two hours to go. I'm in the middle of the sea. The waves roll, the ship lurches from side to side and my stomach leap frogs.

Standing upright and still, feet at last on concrete, arm linked with Brendan's, my stomach, nervous from the journey over the waves is now a jellyfish wobbling inside me from worry at the thought of meeting Brendan's family, the O'Sullivans.

Thomas, his large flipper hands rubbing together as if they were cold, anxious, waiting to see his son after five years, opens the door of his rusty-white Renault. His cartoon stomach bulges, braces slide down his shoulders, his chin is like bread dough, squeezing out of his blue jumper. 'Brendan, Brendan! Come here, you haven't changed. Everyone is waiting to see you.'

'Da, great to see you!'

I step closer to Brendan. Thomas's eyes, cold and detached, yoyo from my mini skirt to my legs. I try to shrink into my clothes. The way he looks at me you would think I'm an unpalatable fish.

Bags stuffed in boot, me in the back seat hunched over my knees, already forgotten, we leave the dock with its ferries and freight ships and huge bird like cranes, their long necks swinging parcels and crates, and we travel the streets of Dublin. Grey buildings, smart shops running alongside the river, Brendan says is the Liffey, and on to Welnooth. The roads narrow and the buildings become scattered over the countryside. We turn on to an estate of red brick houses with small gardens in front, one of these, like a domino, has nothing to distinguish it from the others except the number, this house is number forty-four, Brendan's home.

Ma's there waiting for Brendan, sitting on the small kitchen stool, her large hands wringing and her small body tense. Out comes a delicate, little, loving twitter, 'Lovely to see you, Son. Come and have some tea. Sit yerself down.' But, Brendan has warned me she isn't like this all the time and little insects grab and tug at her: Stupid Shaun, stupid Thomas, why, why why can't they do things right? Why can't Thomas zip up his trousers, it's indecent. Why does Shaun sleep till twelve? Criticise, criticise, criticise . . .

It's my first night in the dank, blue, dark room. Barrie's old room, Barrie is Brendan's older brother. Over the bed a gold painted plastic angel looks down and on the windowsill a porcelain Virgin Mary, white and clean. The room is cold, a brown paisley carpet on the floor, old, with edges turned up. In the morning the sheets of soft cotton loosen as Brendan unfolds out of bed and into his jeans and shirt and leaps into his old life, breakfast in the kitchen chatting with Ma.

'How's, Jan, Brendan? Is she bad?'

'No, Ma, she's in America with her brother.'

Jan's name thrown into the air, casual, but loaded, jolts me. Why can't Brendan forget her? I'm here now. I enter the kitchen, wearing my little green dress, with a wide belt, which holds in my, invisible to others, falling out stomach. My stilettos make me tower above Ma. I hope my stocking tops don't show.

Ma whispers to Brendan, 'Has she no proper clothes?'

'Leave her be, Ma, not now.'

I sink into a comfortable old armchair by the fire, a white terrier at my feet, some tea and a slice of bread.

Eye catching the phone, Ma says, 'I think I'll give Moira a ring, she seemed a bit pale on Monday.'

Brendan comes and sits on the arm of my chair and holds my hand. Moira, I know, is Brendan's sister and the wife of his brother Barrie. Her words come over the phone.

'I'm sitting on the floor, let me just get up . . .' She tells Ma.

'What's happened, why are you on the floor?'

'Barrie knocked me down. I come home with the shopping and he asked did I see, Flora and Andy? I told him they were fine and he asks can he go to O'Hara's. I didn't say no, Ma, but when he asks for money I tell him I didn't have enough money for shopping this week and say he'll only waste it on the horses.'

I looked at Brendan. Brendan shook his head and lifted his shoulders to his chin. The knocking down of Moira hadn't shocked him. Ma carried on her conversation, agreeing with Moira, 'Aye, he would, too. What did he say to that?'

'Nothing, I thought he'd taken it well. He switched on the television, the one in the kitchen . . .'

'Oh, aye, the one as you don't like? I know . . .'

'Well, Ma, he has one in the living room and one in the bedroom, I've not the room for the one in the kitchen, but it's not so bad hidden in the corner like it is.'

'Oh, well, if it keeps him happy.'

102

'I wished it did so. But, he watches the end of the Manchester United game and when they win he jumps up and down singing, Olay! Olay! And then, taps me up again, 'Moira, please give us a tenner.' he says 'I haven't got it to give.' I say.

'So, that's when he hits you?'

'Not just once, Ma. He slaps me over and over and down I went, me legs like clothes pegs, laid out on the floor and me body all folded up. And all he says as he picks up me purse is, 'Now, for sure I needs a pint . . .'

A loud sob came down the phone. My body went numb. Ma talked as if this is the way to go on, men hitting their wives, spending the money in the pubs, on the horses and having televisions where they hadn't room for them, she condemned none of it.

'Will you be going to see them at the health centre?'

'There's no point, Ma, nothing will change. His mates praise him for sorting me out and when the doctor sent us to a councillor, she said, "What have you been doing to upset your husband?" Sometimes, I don't know if I can stick it until the kids grow up.'

Ma reminds her she has no choice and to try not to get under Barrie's skin. A man needs his pint and his mates and a flutter on the horses. Without them, he's looked on as a complete nobody and a sponger, and Barrie won't be standing for that. She'd just have to sort her budget out a bit better.

The shock of this conversation settles around me like contaminated rain. I want to shake it off, shake off what I heard. Brendan says nothing, looks at Ma knowingly and Ma looks at him. He doesn't even look at me. For a moment I don't exist. The O'Sullivans take up the space in the small sitting room. Ma replaces the receiver, looking pleased with herself. Moira would have to toe the line.

'What do you think, Brendan? Hasn't Moira a good catch in our Barrie? At the end of the day he's no womaniser. Oh, I know Moira's the best looking woman in Welnooth, with that lovely red hair, and she's a figure as would pull any man, so that keeps him on the straight an narrow. And, you can't better her loving nature, but she has her committees, the bingo, the village fete and the dance clubs, sure that should be enough for her.'

Brendan nods again. My insides scream at the injustice, but I stay quiet.

'So, Ma, where is our Shaun, then?'

'Sure, he's waiting in his bedroom for you.'

'Shaun's a bit different' explains Brendan. 'He wont come downstairs, oh no, he'll wait until I knock on his bedroom door and call out Shaun, only then will he open up and I get to see my little brother.'

'How old is Shaun?'

'Oh he's 16, but we treat him like a kid. He's the youngest.'

We find Shaun. His bedroom is dark. Elvis Presley posters overlap and hide the walls. He and Brendan talk music, have a jam on their guitars and play some pool. I sit on his bed and wait, bored I flick through some magazines full of photos of Elvis.

Owen is the second oldest brother. We find him in O'Hara's, finishing his third whiskey. He sits sloped in a worn and tired looking wooden chair in the corner of the pub. Brendan tells me, for Owen, days and hours, people and names jumble up in his head and the only place clear as a bell is O'Hara's. Though, he would have known Brendan was coming, it wouldn't make a difference. Everybody is the same to him and he draws crosses on everybody's forehead with Holy water, from his little plastic bottle.

Bridget is in the pub, too. She's Brendan's only sister and is as drunk as Owen. Plump and freckly with a very thin, sensible husband, Brendan says, they are the only two people in the family with a house big enough to give 'a welcome home' do.

*

Most days I return to the armchair. It's a refuge. It holds me down with a big hand so I can't move, not even to the little gate out at the front. Ma and Da feed me on chicken, cabbage and potato. The moment I move they spring into action,

Da asks, 'Do you want a lift somewhere?' And Ma asks, 'More tea?'

I have all I need here, most important, sketchbook and pencils with which I draw in expressive, dark strokes: a tin of sardines, the budgie and Thomas eating. I have books, paper for writing letters, but no stamps. Outside I can hear a few children playing and people passing. If Brendan comes with me, I will go out, but not on my own. In London, people don't look at my legs, here I think they will but, like Thomas, not in a nice way. I'm lonely and miss London where every pavement fills with moving feet, shop lights flashing: *open all night*, and shouting magazine men. I wonder where the people here are. Tucked away in their cosy homes, like Ma and Da's, by the fire with babies, tea, and whiskey, slices of bread, chatting? The chimneys of all the houses puff black smoke into the sky. Welnooth is too quiet. A City could crush you, but here you might disappear.

Every day I watch the room fill with people and every night empty by eleven pm. At twelve pm, in trickles Owen with his bottle of Holy water. 'God bless yer,' he says as he makes a cross on my forehead and on anything that moves. He whispers to the dog and the budgie.

Then, there is the oddity of Ma and Da. They haven't spoken to each other for fifteen years. They send messages via Shaun or Owen,

'Shaun, tell yer Da to buy a chicken for tomorrow, oh and soap.'

'Owen, give this to yer Ma, will you, it's for stamps.'

Brendan puts his hand on his head and to himself says, 'You have got to try and help them, Brendan.'

He has a go at fixing things. Thomas can't go through the narrow kitchen door, so he perches his stomach on the edge of the doorway. Brendan puts himself between him and Ma. 'Come on now, you can't go on like this forever. It's not doing you any good to be this way.'

'Brendan, it's his imagination. You know me.'

'Brendan, I don't forget things, and yer Ma's done something I will never forgive.'

And so the two stay stubborn and stuck and Brendan gives up.

It's around the neighbourhood that Brendan and I share a bed and whispers condemn us, *'It's disgusting.' 'They're not married.' 'It's because Martha's glad to have Brendan home that she allows it.'* With this and Shaun's shyness, drunken Owen and Bridget and the unspeakable violence in the house of Barrie and Moira, it is amazing Ma and Da's silence stays intact, but nothing shakes it. Fifteen Christmases of: 'Shaun, buy a little something for Da with this and don't say it's from me.' And, 'Shaun, buy something for Ma, I'll give you the money.'

It's not a wonder they all spent the last five years, waiting for Brendan.

19

Alone in Ireland

Outside Ma's house on the Riley Estate and with my new-found confidence cheering me on, I find my way around Welnooth. Welnooth Castle, Carol's Cafe, O'Hara's, the church, the newsagents and the Bridge over the river which reminds me of Peter's city landscapes. It's stone, grey, thick arch. Peter used to have a thing about arches. I can smell the oils and the canvasses, and hear the sound of ripping up rags. Naomi, Donna and Lily and bathrooms and windows all crowd in on me. Homesickness tightens around my neck like a noose. I take a deep breath and shake off the feeling.

Along the path comes a woman. She clucks her tongue as she passes and turns her head away. I watch her walk on: a paisley headscarf tied over her greasy, no-point-in-washing, hair. Bent shoulders, skirt a respectable length and flat shoes. How does she know I'm the girlfriend of Brendan O'Sullivan? *Does everyone know who I am?* How can I stay in Welnooth if people treat me like a hussy, clucking their tongues and gossiping?

From Ma's to the newsagents is a five-minute walk, with no elbows and thighs to jostle and only a few nods to the turned-away, tut-tut heads, just in case they look at me. Past the neighbour's garden with the ball that bumps on Ma's kitchen wall, left, unwanted on the grass. Past the next house with the old, rusty car, bike leaning on its stand and dog barking, all kept in with chicken-wire, and on to the corner house with the neat garden and sunshine dahlias bursting forth. Cross over the silent, car-less street, it's three o'clock, everyone is at work, round the corner and push the door with the loud bell.

'What do you want? It's over there. Quick now, I've a customer waiting.' I pay for the paper and stamps then, afraid of the woman's harsh face, her accusing, sharp blue eyes, I rush outside, lean against the shop wall and think, *she must hate me because I'm English*.

I carry on walking, over the bridge to Carol's Café, next to the car park. The smell of fresh baked bread teases me. With hunched shoulders, I walk, determined not to let the hunger in. The devil has his claws out, I grit my teeth and say: No. Inside on the left the counter holds cream cakes, jam donuts, iced fancies and fruit cakes, all homemade and all encased in fly and hand proof, glass domes. My fingers itch and my palms feel sweaty as I look behind them to the wooden shelves lined with greaseproof paper where I see the loaves. Cottage loaves, soda breads, twists and plaits, some golden brown, some dusted white with flour and others with almost-burned bottoms, tempt me. The young girl behind the counter has her white apron pulled tight round her small waist in such a way you could tell she was proud of her figure and knew she was the prettiest girl in Welnooth. She gives me my first friendly smile. I buy bread for Ma and cakes for Thomas and Shaun.

Cradling them in my arms all in their white paper bags I take them back home, over the bridge and along the street to Ma's house. I slip in not making a sound. Thomas is on the settee having his nap. His enormous belly and bottom like a giant dung beetle wedged between dung and more dung, sinking below the nylon, floral-coloured covers on the huge arms. Joey, the budgie chirping, excited to see someone, flaps his wings and almost falls off his perch. Like a sleeping alligator Thomas opens one of his eyes wide.

'Who's there?'

'Alice.'

'Oh, you . . . You've woken me up!'

'I've bought some cakes for you, your favourite—Lardy cake.'

'Come here a little closer, sit down beside me for a minute.'
He pats the cushion next to him.

I lower myself in a steady movement onto the arm nearest
me, not wanting to fall in, but before I feel the settee, something
firm grasps me from underneath. Not able to defy gravity I sit
on Thomas's clutching, squeezing hand, gasp, and using all the
strength in my lower legs jerk to a standing position.

'Got any knickers on?' His voice, a low growl owns up to
his lust. Indignation shouts, 'Oh, shut up!' from my lips, before
I can think.

'Shut up! No one tells me to shut up in my own house!
Get out . . . Go on . . . Get out now!'

The door opens, Owen, bleary-eyes widened by the surprise
of the noise, looks in.

'Hey do you hear that, Owen? That Alice tells me to shut
up to my face. I tell you, she's got to go.'

'Now Da, don't get into a huff, calm down.'

'Well, she's a slut, coming here in her short skirts and those
things on her feet she can hardly walk in. Get her out of the
room!'

I stumble out, catch my thigh on the corner of the dresser,
breath in a sharp breath with the pain of it and knock into the
bird cage. Joey screeches like he's an air-raid warning.

'Get that damn bird out of here as well. Sure, a man needs
his peace come the afternoon.'

Into my bedroom I tumble. The Virgin Mary is lying on
the floor. Feeling comforted at having her there I pick her up,
hold her in my hand, careful not to break her. *'Oh, please don't
let this happen.'* I say aloud, my voice quivering. Climbing on to
the bed, with the duvet round me, I weep into my arms. I'm

not ready for leaving I've only just arrived.

*

The next morning Ma tells Brendan and Brendan tells me I have to leave.

'Ma says it's because we're not married and it's upsetting the neighbours. We'll find you a good place.' Brendan says in a reassuring voice.

'*You* . . . What do you mean by, *you*? You're not going to leave me alone in Ireland!'

'I can't come with you Ma needs me, she hasn't seen me for five years.'

I wanted to say, *You Bastard!* But, like tar, the words stick in my throat.

Sitting back down on the bed, spaghetti thoughts run around my mind. I'm unable to catch just one of them. Instead my eyes seize the objects in the room and hold them in a dazed glaze.

20

Somewhere More Private

Today is Wednesday, Wednesday morning. I have a 2.00pm appointment for a room in a house-share. It's always raining in Ireland and it rains until I step off the bus. Then, under a sunny rainbow, glistening on the pavement, I walk all the way up to number 44, Kilkarney crescent. A mint-green door opens like a snapdragon, quick and quiet. A woman, who I think is around thirty-ish, smiles from out of the shadowy hallway.

'You must be Alice?'

She folds her arms and stares at me with beautiful, green, oval eyes through a pair of tinted, black, thin-rimmed glasses. Her nose is long and elegant. Her chin juts out like a beak. I can't concentrate on what to say because of the loud, dull thuds coming from the side of the house.

'Oh, that's Aiden chopping the wood.'

'What, now?

'Yes, preparing it for winter.'

'I'm wondering if the room is still vacant.'

'Yes, of course come in. My name's Claire.'

Claire starts to show me around pointing to the rooms. Their are six, squeezed into the shoebox-sized house. My bedroom would be a room for the bed and not much more, nestled up to Claire's room, the biggest. Claire's ornaments are everywhere, glass hedgehogs, china foals, wooden mice, all animals; it's like being in a jungle. She has animal prints on the walls, too. A leopard glares at me, bright pink flamingos pose like ballet dancers and a smiling giraffe eyes me from a great height. Unlike Ma's house there are no piles of unwashed and washed linen or not yet ironed or ironed clothes placed around the house like a lot of cairns. Here, I smell polish and my feet squeak on the red-brown wooden floor. The stairs and banisters match the floor. Dust does not have a place in this home. Claire likes cleanliness and order. The kitchen is the size of two bathrooms; Ma's is the size of one. This one doesn't look much used, not like Ma's, with rambling carrots and weeping onions, spoons and knives in piles, like jackstraws.

I become aware of a man, tall, thin as a blade of grass, standing in the doorway to the back garden, which leads out from the kitchen.

'Aiden, Alice, Alice, Aiden.'

Aiden doesn't say hello or smile, but scrutinizes me from under his thick brown eyebrows.

We sit around the round kitchen table with its red gingham tablecloth. The white squares are very white and the red flash like traffic lights. There's a pot of tea brewing and slices of bread on a plate. Without me prompting my mouth rushes out words. The house, the place, the rent, and on it goes, into Ireland, Irish, English, and awful Margaret Thatcher. Dates and facts come out like badly cut suits; my history lessons didn't cover Ireland enough. My nerves have got on his, he stands, whips out a knife and bending over the table, he points it at me, 'If you talk about Ireland again I'll fucking kill you!'

'Sorry! Sorry.' My plimsolls stick to the parquet floor.

'Put it down, Aiden!'

His hand moves to take a slice of bread, mine stay in my lap, wet with sweat. The knife goes back in his coat pocket and he gulps his tea.

'I hate you because you're English!'

'It's not her fault!'

112

He gives a deep sigh, pushes himself up with his hands on the table and leaves clicking the door shut behind him.

'Honest to God he wouldn't hurt a fly, but please don't talk about England, and Margaret Thatcher or just anything, okay? Do you want the room?'

'Where does Aiden live?'

'He lives at number 88 Kilkarney crescent.' *A bit too close,* I think to myself but Claire likes me I can see that and I need somewhere to live, now. Mind all jumbled, but moved by her gentle warm smile and soft whispering voice, I say yes and take the key, it's lovely, three metal circles welded together, like a Celtic symbol.

*

My first night at the new house, I have two hours to unpack before Brendan is due. He arrives at eleven, late back from the pub, with beery breath and smoke tainted jacket. Up the squeaking, wooden staircase we go.

'It's a bit small isn't it?'

'Its big enough, but I'm worried that Claire will hear us.'

'She probably will, but then, she looks like a woman who wouldn't be saying no to a bit of fun, herself. Don't worry, she has her radio on.'

At first, fingers on lips shushing and strained we manage not to make too much noise, but soon my bed starts to move as if on a ship, it slides, squeaks and grunts. Brendan's arm flies out and swipes the alarm clock. My left foot drags the tablecloth off and everything falls hitting the floor, like tell-tales. On to the floor clatter, watches, pens and books. His head bangs on the wall, the sheets are in knots, I'm trussed up like a mummy. We hear Claire go to bed, by the tick of a light switch.

'Did she hear us?'

The passion pricked, we lie still like two nervous rabbits,
Unable to move again in case all the objects rattle and roll! I try
to whisper something but Brendan can't hear.

'Couldn't you have got somewhere a bit more private?' He
mumbles.

21

Words Belong to Another Person

It's Tuesday. I can hear Claire getting ready to go to the shops. Claire likes to shop. She's a mature student with a part time job. She struggled with the rent and the bills when she first took this house, but now she has me to share the cost. I think she manages well.

I hear the front door open. It lets in the sound of the church clock striking the hour. Then, the door bangs shut and the last of the ten bongs fade into the distance. A silence descends on the house. Emptiness a presence, ghost-like it haunts the rooms, leaving us clues, a sudden creak or a cold draught. The 'Bring! Bring!' splits the quiet. All the parts of my body jump in unison. Telephones shout the same thing in lots of different ways, *answer me now!* This one is a heavy, old type phone with a big handle. It's red like the colour of a London bus, and when it rings it's to tell you something important.

'Hello . . .' I can hear steps padding the stairs followed by breathing, a frail voice, frail as eggshell says, 'Hello, love.' The red telephone continues to deliver Stuart's message, his breathing uncertain until a tired Diana takes over, 'Still raining in Dublin? We are fine; yes Stuart's fine and Bobby.'

The next day and the big red phone shakes again, Claire is out with her plump cousin Kelvin. Diana speaks in slow deliberate tones, not like normal, very fast, like a runaway train.

'Alice, I couldn't face telling you yesterday. It's . . . well, your father has only got three weeks more to live. Can you come home, dear? I'm so sorry to have to tell you on the phone.'

When I look up the room seems to be bigger. My legs have no bones in them. I hold onto the square telephone table as if gripping a rock in the sea. It stands quiet and still. I don't know how I'm going to reach the kitchen without falling over.

*

Grey clouds fill the sky and the wind blows a few specks of rain into our faces, we take the train and bus to the hospital, it's a big hospital, blocks of pale grey squares put together, the reception is nice and warm with a semicircle desk, its curves friendlier than the square ones. We follow the directions—purposeful signs and white arrows, up several levels, to level eight, down the cold floored corridors into a white room.

Stuart is a little person now; his skin is sallow and hangs limp over his bony body. A head popping out of an envelope of starched white cotton. His world and his life reduced to blood drips and blood bubbles and horrible, yellow, transparent tubes. He lies on his side. Big metallic bars stop him from falling off the bed, but without the sheets holding him he would slip underneath one. He doesn't recognize me. I don't recognize him. Diana tries to comfort—'Your Father's been waiting for you.' I think the morphine stops him from feeling and stops his will, his will to live.

Because Diana's a nurse they let us take him home. Tender, loving care is all he needs. Diana lays him on his side with his legs a little up like a fetus, his arms like a praying mantis. Her movements are gentle. She says he won't die until my brother, Lee comes home. Diana sleeps and I watch and then, she watches and I sleep.

One evening I take a piece of paper and a pencil and start sketching, I draw his big brown eyes, large forehead, furrows, thin lips, and his big wide nose. My eyes and nose I took from him, so I know them well, see them every time I look into the mirror. The more I draw, the more the Stuart I know comes back, even though my sketches are of the little person wrapped up in sheets slipping away from life.

Lee comes home and Stuart dies.

They leave Stuart in the dining room an extra day because of the holiday, we have more time to say goodbye, except Diana, who can't open her eyes from tears and exhaustion. The black car arrives and in we all filter, Uncle Brown, my brother, Diana and me. Diana asks the driver to drive faster, Stuart is on his way now, and she wants him in another place out of her world.

*

The Crematorium, a simple building, smells of new wood and flowers, carnations and roses for Stuart. Diana asks for there to be no candles. The vicar speaks in a tomb like voice: 'Generous and devoted father to his children. Loving and loyal to Diana, his wife; A man with a great sense of humor, an adventurer and a great golf player, everyone loved him and we will all miss him; Stuart Peter Smith.'

But, I have a foot in the door for other memories to tip toe through: *He wopped us with his slippers, kicked the dog, Brave Diana handled the neighbours while Stuart hid in the kitchen. He hated black people, hated fat people; said I had an arse like an elephant's and cried when he swallowed a fly.*

Another memory begs me to let it stay. Me, twelve years old out for a walk with Stuart around the old sewage works. In the long grass, I saw a big, round ball the size of a football, beige with dust coming off it. It felt velvety to touch. Suddenly I heard Stuart shout, "Don't touch it, it's a bomb!" Frightened I ran towards him. His head went back and his laughter bellowed out, 'It's a puffball,' he said, 'A giant fungus.'

The long elegant box he lies in disappears into the black hole like a magicians trick, the red curtains close—goodbye to us. In recognition of his years as a soldier the guns go off outside, the insect type, red and black military men, stomp their left legs and unhinge their right arms. Diana, buried under sadness, stares at a vacant space, her cheeks hollowed from days of not eating. Lee looks at his watch. We are in this world. Stuart's in the other.

Like a big black cloud we drift into the church hall, which is similar to a school classroom, with white painted walls, a high ceiling and with echoes spinning around like afterthoughts. Thin tables on thin legs are set up with blue paper tablecloths, pink salmon, cucumber, cheese, tuna and ham sandwiches, and later, Victoria sponge and chocolate cake. When we have saturated our grief, coffee and an assortment of biscuits to tidy up the afternoon, reminding us it's the end of this day.

I lose myself amongst the black coats, swirling black skirts, black shoes and black hats. Guilt pricks my conscience for wearing a dark green jacket and I try to hide my dry eyes.

'Are you alright?' ask Diana and Uncle Brown.

'I'm fine.'

The words float out as if belonging to another person.

22

Tiny Pieces of Pain

Diana, Lee and I sit around the too small, pullout kitchen table, set for a full breakfast: Diana's pale-green, china tea set, toast marching up and down the toast-rack, yellow as a butterfly, teapot, white plates and knives with forks sitting, obedient, waiting by the, nagging to be eaten, fried breakfast. I sip orange juice and allow my spirits to awaken.

'I'm going to get ready and do my face,' Diana gets up, her movements slow, her breath coming in sighs. The silence expands until crashed by Lee. He scrapes his chair backwards; in clumsy movements he stands up, his size eight feet struggling to balance him. He holds onto the table, 'Got some things to sort out.' He says.

So, that leaves me. Rude sausages and gaping bits of bacon gawp at me. Their smell lingers.

'Right, that's it, in the bin you go.' I tell them. The table is cleared and cleaned.

The kitchen darkens by a brooding cloud. I walk up the stairs, each step slower than the last. No one tells me funerals can be so exhausting. Tidying my bedroom, objects like nuisances resist me putting them where they should go. I wait for Brendan to call. He's coming today,

Daydreaming to pass the time away I imagine Brendan waking up, his sleek body slipping into a bath of milk-soap water, squeezing the sponge over himself, all done in Ma and Da's tiny bathroom, made all the more tiny by the mounds of washed and unwashed clothing. I can see him leaping down the stairs three by three, in a hurry, a hurry to come and collect me and bring me back to Ireland.

Brendan always travels light. I can picture his economic sized, blue bag, with clothes rolled not folded as they take less room that way. You could send Brendan to the moon and he would come back, shirts and trousers packed in the same order. He loves traveling and telling me stories of his adventures. His favourite is the story of the tick.

'It was stuck to my head, Alice, a fat, black vampire drinking my blood. I itched, but I was too frightened to touch it. I didn't know what it was. A friend took a look, "Hey mate you've got a big, ugly tick stuck in there!"

I had to go to the doctors to have it taken off. I came out, smiling as wide as Liffey River, glad the disgusting thing had gone.'

*

But Brendan does have another tick. When he's apprehensive, in one movement he shifts his neck, tilts his head, first to the left and then to the right, before swinging it forwards and backwards, his shoulders tense up. The doctor says if he carries on like this he will get arthritis in his joints. For all his smiles and blue-eyed twinkles Brendan does get anxious, then is when I see his bones twitching with worry. It's the Brendan I don't understand, yet.

It's half five. Brendan will be collecting his bag from a hungry conveyer belt. Lee prepares his weary body for the climb upstairs to take his coat, say good-bye and make his way to the station to pick up Brendan.

Soon, Brendan's hand slips into my hand, his thigh touches mine, real and warm. We sit thrown together by the springy

120

sea of my old, comfortable bed. Thoughts of Ireland begin to cheer me up, the greener than green grass, smell of wood-fires and briquette, the pubs and the fiddlers who play in them. But somehow this small bedroom holds me tight, womb-like,

'You alright to come back to Ireland with me?' he asks. I can feel the tension in him and know he is wondering if it's too soon,

'I'm not sure, I was thinking of staying here with Diana.'

'What if I ask you to marry me?'

A warm glow showers me and eagerly I reply, 'If you asked me to marry you then I would come back.'

*

In Ma and Da's I get a hearty welcome. Even Thomas gives me a hug and a kiss, his whiskey breath fanning my face. I sit down in my favourite armchair and a plate full of potatoes, cabbage and chicken lands on my lap. Owen makes a cross on my forehead with his Holy water.

'God bless yer.'

Brendan takes me next door to phone Diana, 'she will be anxious.'

Later, sleep begins to cast a shadow over me robbing me of the light from the cream lampshade. Everyone has gone to bed.

I climb into the same unchanged sheets. It's a bit musty in the bedroom, where the heat of the fire doesn't reach. I don't think Ma cleans except for in and out the pans and around the bottles and tins and under the mugs. There's always a smell of wood in the living room, stacked up left over from winter and of vegetables and chicken cooking.

I wait for Brendan to climb under the sheets. Staring at the white Virgin Mary hoping she will send me her blessing. The same question lingers on my mind. It's done the round, from one side of my head to the other, all the way from England.

'Brendan.' I say his name with determination, and then ask, 'when will we get married?'

Brendan looks uncomfortable. I can see he thought I'd forgotten. Used to smoothing over every little inconvenience he puts on his low, soft Irish accent,

'Ah no, Alice, I said that 'cos, for sure, I was afraid you weren't coming back and I wanted to help you a little.'

I stop breathing. My face burns. I move my body away from Brendan, but the bed is so narrow it is hard to keep millimeters between us. Gripping the duvet my mind screams at me, *what am I going to do now?*

The shimmering, satin, cream wedding dress—bouquet of lilies of the valley entwined with fern—bridesmaids in pale blue—the proud faces of Diana and Lee—Brendan's family holding up shining glasses of champagne—All dreams, which now lie before me, shattered into tiny pieces of pain.

23

A Thief in the Afternoon

I don't know where I am, where I was yesterday or what I'm supposed to be doing now, so I stay still in my bedroom waiting for something to makes sense. After some time I take out the drawing of Stuart using it to start a painting, A4 size, brushstroke by brushstroke, in the small space between my bed and the window. After every 20 to 30 strokes, I lie down on the bed, tired. I sleep, paint, sleep, and paint. A week passes by. Stuart's face begins to appear.

Cups of tea with Claire's brother, Duncan, pass the painful moments and keep me going. He is a thin thing with pale delicate arms and long clinging fingers. He could have been a pianist with fingers like that, but he is a mature math's student, just like Claire, his ambitions came late. We meet in an L shaped cafe, which sells very buttery croissants and lies on the High Street between the bank and the Co-op. I walk there with small, feeble steps, staring at the cracks between the pavements. Duncan is grumpy about his sister. Today I challenge him.

'Why don't you tell her not to spend so much time on her make-up, clothes and going out? Shouldn't she be studying for her exams?'

'Yes of course.'

We both hold our mugs on the bare, wooden table in a sleepy silence neither of us knowing what to say when, Duncan suddenly speaks about Brendan.

'Why do you stay with Brendan? You don't live together.

He hardly phones you. It's not good for you Alice.'

Our chats chew around and around like a dog on a bone and there is always another Saturday. Until one day I walk into the house after one of our cup of tea meetings. On the telephone table two letters and two torn envelopes draw my eye. The text in red, capital letters, gives a wasp-like sting. The telephone and electric final warning notices—both cut off if not paid within seven days.

It takes minutes, as I'm slow with numbers, to work out my rent and Claire and bills. And where did my rent go? On Claire, yes, up in Dublin, swinging through the pubs, nice dresses and the good make up, Clinique, seen in the bathroom.

'Claire I'm not paying rent, any, until you pay the bills.'

'Jesus Christ, what!'

The following day I turn the three-circle key and open the door. The hallway is like a wardrobe, with all the doors closed. It feels like something's missing, but as I go upstairs the feeling disappears, I lie on the unmade bed, hands over face, trying to escape from the day. The missing thing comes to mind. The red telephone has gone.

I wake up an hour later, but it feels like a week has passed. For a second I forget where I am. I stand up dizzy and hungry and make for the kitchen, but the door resists me pushing on it. The handle won't turn. I try other doors, all locked. I only have access to my bedroom and the bathroom.

I hear a noise, must be Duncan, Claire would be at work. Duncan comes through the front door, a friend. Coming downstairs I call out his name.

Glancing up at me he says, 'you're not welcome here, Alice, You must find somewhere else to live.'

'But, Duncan, you're my friend.'

'You have a week to get out.'

Duncan disappears into the kitchen, closes the door. I hear

the key turn.

An old, rusty key sits on the windowsill of my bedroom. For one moment, when I first moved back in, I wanted to pick it up, try it out, but then, my thoughts went to the drawing of Stuart and I forgot about it until now. Now, I have good reason to find out which door it opens, if any. I try Claire's room first. It doesn't even make a noise when it opens, I slip in. And on the bedside table gleaming brightly, big heavy handle, is the red telephone, my access to the world and to Brendan.

Brendan has been busy with his band and writing lyrics. He has a new job in Laybridge, the village with the longest queue—all the people from villages around sign on there. I think the band and his new job are why he hasn't phoned me, I hope so. In a rush words spill, 'Brendan, help, I'm in a mess. I need somewhere else to live. I've no time to explain, now.'

'Okay, I'll be over tomorrow night.'

I hear Ma and know her nose will be twitching with curiosity. No phone calls pass by Ma. 'What's up with Alice, Brendan?'

When tomorrow night comes and Brendan is here he tells me Ma could do with the room, what with Owen on the sofa since Brendan came home. She'd told him to get himself a place. 'Alice needs you now and besides you have a good job.'

Brendan is fast and impatient when out on the search it doesn't matter what for. He gets an appointment to see a place the next night, a place looking over Belsize Park. The little park with shady trees and two park benches is his most favourite spot in Dublin. He could sit in it for hours with a Guinness in hand, singing his lyrics out loud.

Brendan is happy and I'm glad now that, like a thief in the afternoon, Claire took away my place to live.

24

Like being in a Museum

Today like every Tuesday I leave the house before 8.00. It's raining very hard. If I'm quick the queue will be shorter, but the rain pushes us all, on the way to somewhere, back under shop fronts or into doorways.

I like queues, bus queues, queues in church, ceremonious, especially supermarket queues—what's in other people's trolleys, if they have a cat or dog, which ones are on a diet, which one's having a party. Dole queues are miserable, like long, grey, ration queues, not like the bright butterfly ones winding up to the theatre doors, or the lining up for the catwalk where beautiful colours, shapes, hats and handbags are for me to see. The queue today is damp and smelly, dirty floor from wet shuffling shoes, people removing their hoods, folding their umbrellas and pushing wet hair from sticking in eyes. In the short distance from the bus, the rain soaked my hair. Cold droplets drip on my face as I wait.

I'm twenty-second in line and there are five behind me. I count them down as I move forward, 21, 20, 19, 18, 17, 16 and it's at number 15 a man approaches me. He's large with a very round stomach, a blue bobble hat stretched over his head. His teeth big, square, crooked, like Stonehenge, hold a cigarette that waggles up and down when he talks, the smoke squints his kind, blue eyes. He's wearing a long coat. There is something not frightening about him so when he speaks to me, I speak back. He asks me if I want a job. I have no money; just enough to cover my bus fare and a sandwich. Bored and tired of being in a dole queue I say, yes. He has dirty shoes and I read somewhere that shoes tell you something about a person. I look down at my own scruffy, sodden, plimsolls. He asks me to follow him, which I think is a bit optimistic but, follow him, I do.

A green door opens and in we go up a narrow and long staircase. It's like something out of Venice. Three women stand there with arms folded, two with dry cigarettes hanging over lips. Are they supposed to be explaining to me what goes on here? They all look at each other. I wonder who is going to tell me. One says, 'We'll let the boss explain.'

The time is now 11.00. I have missed my chance to sign on. Rain throws itself at the window like a wild animal. I can feel the wind around the building strapping us in. My bus back is at 12.30 and I want to catch a sandwich at my favourite cafe.

'I have to be quick. I have got things to do.' No one speaks.

On the way up yet more stairs, past vast walls, white, blank, unwelcoming. I find myself at the top in a tiny yellow room. The room is warm and has only what it needs: A shower, a massage table, a small table with a towel and some tissues. A tiny window of sky with the branches of a tree blowing across breaks up the plain walls.

I can't remember how I got here from the dole queue, but life is already looking up as my perhaps-future employer is a desirable, tanned Italian. The even more amazing thing is he wants me to take all my clothes off and to give me a massage. Nobody hits me on the head: I do it and, like yawning, it seems a normal thing to do. His firm, large hands, smelling of vanilla scented oil, flick over me like slippery eels.

The rain beats a comforting tapping on the window, glad to stay inside and happy he wants me to do something for him, I give him a quick, shaky massage. His skin is smooth, not a spot and not a wobble of fat. He doesn't ask for anything, but suggests a few things. By the time he is standing up again shoes and socks on, he asks me if I want to continue here and at exactly the same time my mouth opens and something comes into my mind, and I say, 'Yes, I would like to give it a go.'

He tells me, no oral sex, no intercourse, just hands, no obligation to take clothes off, extra money if you do and its twenty pounds for fifteen minutes. There is a bell by the table if there is trouble.

The rules snap at me like terriers. Afraid of being afraid, I breath in the silence and nod. Besides as I am now, I can never buy Brendan and me anything and since Stuart died, I feel swallowed up with loneliness.

I start my new job next day at ten. I sit in the coffee room with the other women. Two of them are knitting. They chat away have cigarettes flopping from their lips or sending up spirals of smoke. They ask me questions and talk to me, which, after a while makes me think they must like me. It isn't how I thought a massage parlour would be. I imagined slender, pouting women in mini skirts and stilettos, and a pimp, tall, mean and dangerous. This is more like a meeting for the Women's Institute. One woman catches my attention. Her name is Helen and she must be over forty. Her waist ripples and her big breasts are two comfortable, deluxe pillows tempting me from under an angora, pink jumper. I long to bury my face in her bosom.

Someone calls out my name. I go to the yellow room upstairs. I have a little, fat man in a grey suit. He is on his lunch hour and his breath fills the air with the smell of beer. He undoes his trousers, takes off his blue pants and out flips a little grey-pink, wrinkly willy. How on earth am I going to make that tall and big? I try to imagine I'm very grown up, but my hands are like flapping fish and won't move in the direction I'm telling them to. I'm glad when his time is up.

'But, it isn't finished!'

'It's fifteen minutes only.'

I say 'Sorry,' giving the sad faced and confused man a hug. While he dresses, I busy myself folding the towels. On the way down the steep stairs I see the closet full of clothes: nurse's uniforms, waitress aprons, whips, hats, gloves and a leotard with a large fluffy bunny tail. It's like being in a museum.

25

The Forgotten Bad Dream

Something has changed for me. Jan came back from America, Brendan's Jano, as she used to like calling herself, still rounded in all the right places, uncomfortable for me to look at, I like skinny, but Brendan had liked her that way. Perhaps he still does. She has a perfect nutbrown tan, plays tennis, bakes cakes, especially Brendan's favourite—brownies and lives just down the road, but more often in my head giving me thoughts I don't want.

It's my shift and my second client arrives, nerves drown my worries about Jan for the moment. 'He's all yours, love.' Pamela calls out, 'If he wants more than fifteen minutes, make him pay—now don't forget.'

Pamela and Isabelle settle down to their knitting, not on shift until lunchtime, they click-click away. Growing from their needles like exotic furry butterflies, socks and scarves, pastel shades for babies, tops. Between stitches they huff puffs of smoke from cigarettes and stub ends out in the bronze bird-shaped ashtray

'Go on then. What are you waiting for?'

I stand up and try to look enthusiastic.

'Look at her, she's terrified. You won't last long in this business unless you're strong. That's right isn't it, Isabelle? She'll turn into an alcoholic like Jennifer did. Do you have a boyfriend, Alice?'

'Yes, but he doesn't know.'

'For God's sake never tell him.'

I try to imagine telling Brendan. I imagine him very surprised, or would he be very angry? Not bothered? Pleased I'm earning money?

'You haven't told yours?'

'My husband doesn't know a thing about what I do all day. Anyway as long as there's a meal on the table and his shirts are ironed he doesn't care.'

Isabelle and Pamela have their day clothes on, not their massage-parlour ones. Pamela's black leggings and a loose floral blue top, chestnut hair wavy and long, web-like with too much hairspray, in a large bead necklace to reduce her Ostrich neck, gives her the look of an ordinary housewife dressed for afternoon tea.

Isabelle wouldn't look out of place in Macdonald's, with a cup of diet coke and a hamburger, in her Levi's and sweatshirt. They change in a dressing room when they have a client, whatever takes their fancy, or suits the customer's fantasy. Black leather, delicate slips, red lace, there's a kaleidoscope of possibilities to choose from.

Helen doesn't knit. She sits reading or writing letters. She looks up and smiles. It's a smile I want to go into. I like Helen. I imagine her wearing her angora jumpers when she is massaging a client, and wonder if they secretly like her in them. I still want to snuggle up into her arms. Once she did put her arm around me. It was like she'd wrapped me in a baby blanket. The tears queued up, but I ground them back. Not wanting to be embarrassed.

I wear my black polyester dress, which fits my body like a long sleeve, with a wide belt hiding my tummy that only I can see. Pamela says to me that I shouldn't worry. I have a pretty figure and youth on my side. All I need to do is take my top off. The boss says that comes later. His comment pokes me with a moment of truth—*Is this really my new job?*

Mr. Briggs doesn't fit on the table, his feet stick off the end. He is better looking than the first man, but his awful, limp, black, coarse hair circling a shiny, bald patch lets him down. He smiles a lot, like a bus conductor. He hasn't much time and his thing rises up like the Lochness monster.

'Come on, be quick! You're nervous aren't you? Your first time? Don't be afraid, it's not going to bite!'

I massage his powder-white, practically hairless chest. My hands move down to his legs and knead his springy, dough-like thighs. My eyes concentrate on the texture of his uneven skin. His voice bites into the silence. 'We've only got 15 minutes and that's passed already, haven't even time to get a sandwich, forget it, I'll pay you, love, but next time get on with it! Now, I usually pay you girls with a pair of shoes . . .'

My meeting at Briggs and Sons shoe shop isn't till tomorrow. The others tell me the shop is in Clergy Street, not far. I walk along the cobbled streets all the way to a café called Hewley's. It's my favourite place to be. I order my usual cheese sandwich: grated cheese fills up the white, crusty bread, without falling off, a delicious tomato and sweet with Branston pickle. Cheese is one of my safe to eat foods, even though it has a lot of calories.

Someone told me Hewley's is a place where artists meet, but I think the whole of Dublin does, too. It bustles: well dressed women with their well dressed children, women with hair out of control and too tight jeans; someone with a very long beard, trousers and braces. There are noses buried in books, hands grabbing sandwiches and holding cups of tea. The teapots are metal. The cups are plain white china. We all fit into the shop, entangle in table legs and chairs, while we try to find spare seats.

I feel tired after the parlour. Finding a seat I pour my tea. The pot drips in the saucer and onto the table. I try to drink and forget the morning's work, but pictures of Mr. Briggs's pink, hungry penis rising up from between his blotchy, pale, hairy thighs and his teeth, in tatters from too much smoking, smiling at me, keep popping into my head. I want to be the size of a pea, hidden in a corner and never found again. Feeling nausea I put my cup of milky tea down and think, perhaps I'll feel better when I have my new pair of shoes. I haven't had any for ages and most of mine have scuffs on the heels. Diana likes to buy me shoes, the last pair she bought three years ago. They're sensible, fit for everything the kind Diana always buys. She looks cross now when she sees me in my short skirts. *"It's not what a young lady should be wearing"*. I used to look as if brought up in a convent or some such place where they wear very plain clothes, and would still, if Diana had her way. I remember my red kilt and Aran, home-knitted jumper—they were my uniform as a child. I loved them and don't know what inspiration made her get them for me.

The man sharing the same table as me has a very square jaw and a grey ponytail. He doesn't look up from the 'Art' magazine clutched in his hands. I try to imagine him in the parlour. The woman in black, sitting opposite looks as if she has just stepped out of a funeral. She would look good wearing a teacher's uniform and brandishing a long whip.

'Do you want to read my magazine?' asks the ponytail man, catching me looking at it.

'No thanks, but I'm new here and I want to be a painter. I need to meet other artists.'

'Well, what you need will come to you. I have to go now. Here, take the magazine. It's probably of more use to you than me.'

His voice holds a very strong Dublin accent, but the tone is quiet and even. When he stands I see he is the same height as me. His beige waistcoat and light grey trousers fit his slim body and the buttons on his white shirt are done up to his thick neck.

Without warning he bends over. With his head near to mine, taking some of my space, he says, 'Go to Hemple Bar studios, Hemple Street. Turn left after the High Street. I'll see you there. By the way, my name is Michael.'

Hemple Bar Studios sounds more sophisticated than the parlour.

One cup of tea after another, my tummy is swimming. I'm waiting for Brendan as we planned to meet at three. He bounces into Hewleys on his new trainers with their extra padding, wearing all white. White shorts and white T. Shirt.

'You've been playing tennis again with Jan!'

I know this because he has Jan's smile all over his face, it's all over the table, the walls and the door—everywhere. Something I haven't been able to do with Brendan is play tennis and cook cakes like Jan's.

'She's my friend now. You're worrying for nothing.'

I squash the last bit of sandwich with my fingers then put it down feeling fat and disgusting. My hands are sweaty. I hide them under the table.

'Well, how was your day?'

'Okay. I went for a walk and met a man here called Michael, he gave me this magazine. I think he's an artist. He told me to go to a place called Hemple Bar Studios.'

'That's right, that's where all the artists go. There and the pub opposite called The Moon.'

'I thought they met here.'

'I think some do, but it gets too crowded.'

Brendan's in one of his twitchy moods. His body moves the opposite of mine, in short quick movements. One pot of tea later we gather up bags, ready to go home. My thoughts slow down as if to keep with my heavy-as-a-dinosaur body. Brendan is in the distance somewhere, daydreaming, but with a frown on his forehead.

*

We catch the five o'clock bus and arrive back at our new flat come bedsit. There is a small kitchenette at one end and the bed and sitting room area at the other. It's all we can afford, but it does for us, it's light and bright. We have large cream curtains, good for winter, pulled to keep out the streaming, late sun. Autumn creeps nearer. A time of scrunchy walks through fallen leaves, a hint of winter mingled with the last of summer and colours that dazzle, oranges and golds and yellows against a brilliant blue sky.

My last earnings have already gone on food and now we are still short of things: milk, flour, butter, and cereal. We have bread and plenty of jam. We have custard powder, spices, teabags, coffee, but the only things we have to eat for tonight's dinner are potatoes and onions. My last few pennies went on the tea in Hewleys.

Out of nothing Brendan cooks a warm, savoury dish with the fried onions and potatoes. But, still fretting and not at all seduced by the smell of food cooking, I challenge Brendan, 'It's not fair, you seeing Jan. Please stop!'

Brendan spoons out the potatoes and onion stew, trying not to drip gravy on the floor. I'm smoldering.

'I can't eat. I'm too upset.'

'Well, don't be upset, there's nothing to worry about.' Tension clenches his teeth and holds his body stiff.

'Don't lie to me! Why don't you marry her and have kids. What's the point in being with me?'

'For Christ sake I'm not lying. Stop trying to trap me all the time.'

Before I can understand in the few seconds how I have trapped Brendan, a surge of heat rushes through me—like a red-hot poker. Reaching out for his glass of whiskey I dash it on to the cream-coloured kitchen floor. It shatters into splinters, its golden contents splash onto the pale-green carpet. Like the kick of an electric fence, a smack lands on my left cheek. The force of the blow sends me reeling backwards. Brendan doesn't give me time to recover. He leans over me firing one slap after the other.

A few seconds later and he is no longer in front of me, the room is more silent than a freezing winter night. I can feel his presence, but can't see him. I shiver. Tears wet my face. Shock holds me. Then, I notice his still form near the curtains.

'You mustn't provoke me like that.' His anger has gone. 'And, you should know I've lost my job.'

When I wake up the next morning I find fear in bed with me, but then, the hum of the traffic penetrates my hazy world, the sun glints through the net curtains and Brendan's voice sounds so familiar. Confused, I search around for what happened. I feel tingling in my cheeks which are sore and I can sense a bruise coming, on my bottom where I landed. Rooted very deep in my heart I know there is no return.

*

I approach Briggs and Sons shop with its large front windows displaying men's shoes on the left and women's shoes on the right. I'm ten minutes early. The colourful sandals with striped delicate straps, high heeled and low heeled, sit on glass shelves, not straight and neat, but with one on its side and the other facing away from it, like someone just kicked them off their feet. Next to them, slippers with fluffy pink straps, against a large wall of card decorated with pastel shades of flowers and then I see little boots like Emma's. They bring her to me in my mind and I wonder what day she is having. If it is a green one, then she may choose the sandals on the right, but if blue, she'd grab the boots.

I keep my eyes searching on the street for a sign of Mr. Briggs. What if people passing know who I am and what I do? My head drops with the shame of it.

'Nicola . . .' Mr. Briggs appears from his brightly lit, shoe-smelling shop calling the name I have given him. I didn't want him to know my real one.

'I thought that you would come down the road, not from out of the shop!'

He makes a gesture for me to come inside. It's after closing time so it's just Mr. Briggs, me and the shoes. I can't see any that I like. They're boring or squash my feet, or my toes fold up at the tips. I'm embarrassed to be taking up so much of his time, but I see I have only been here twenty minutes. I begin to think I will have to choose a pair of sensible shoes, but then there they are, a pair of black suede ankle boots, with silver studs. Looking at them makes me think of stars and heaven. I'm beginning to think the parlour may be a blessing in disguise. With payments like these and the company of the knitting women and Helen to look forward to, Brendan slapping me is like a forgotten bad dream.

26

My Guilt Rubs like an Abrasive Stone

A week later and I'm due to go to England, it's the first of October, time for my appointment with Professor Lucas. I haven't let Brendan see my new shoes. I've hidden them in my rucksack. When I come back I will say Diana bought them for me. I'm looking forward to seeing Professor Lucas so I can talk to him about the parlour. I keep all my problems, waiting for his voice of authority to provide walls to my life. Diana is pleased to have me home for a few days.

Professor Lucas leans back in his enormous leather padded chair. It's far too grand for his office, which is about the size of a stable for an average horse, that's if you are a lucky horse. His desk is made of dark shiny wood. On it is a pad of yellow memo paper, his note book and a spare pen, his favourite one—the gold one—he holds clamped between his teeth. It glitters as it catches the light. He flicks the end of it before removing it to speak, 'There is a strong link between oral sex and anorexia. I take it you didn't know?'

'I didn't say I did that!'

'Working in a massage parlour is forbidden. For you it will lead to a relapse into the old destructive habits you have had. Now what else have you been up to?'

Some things I say he writes down. Sometimes I say things, which I think are important, but he doesn't write them down. His notebook is a mystery.

'You must avoid situations where the attention focuses on

your body. Working in a massage parlour, life modeling, modeling, all of these things are not good for you. As for your relationship with Brendan, do you love him?'

'Yes.'

'Does he show affection towards you?'

'Yes.'

'Are you sure?'

'Yes.' I scratch the back of my hand and rub my forehead roughly.

There is a pause when Professor Lucas lowers his head, then he lifts it up quickly and says,

'Right, Miss Smith, that is all for today. Arrange for an appointment in six months time.'

I phone Diana from the hospital to say I'll be back in time for dinner, the journey from London to Haystart only takes one and half-hours on the bus. Her voice sounds in the distance and she picks her words carefully, afraid of saying too much. What has upset her I wonder. It's Bobby, Diana's Cocker Spaniel.

'He's ill. I hope it's not a bit of plastic. He chewed some bubble wrap this morning. They are x-raying him on Friday.'

After Stuart died Bobby became Diana's best friend. Every part of him from ear to tail she loves, every bark he makes, the different ones, she knows them all and his funny little ways, like when he curls up, tight as a knot on the settee after dinner.

We both watch, waiting for him to eat a little, Diana kneels on the carpet to offer yogurt on the tips of her finger, she makes rice and fish, cools it down and gives it to a reluctant Bobby on a spoon. When she has to go to the shops she says, 'Watch him for me. Don't let him go upstairs.' By the time I'm ready to leave England Bobby has brightened up. His soft brown eyes look at me and Diana. If he could speak he might say, *thanks*.

Except for drawing Bobby curled up in his chocolate-coloured dog basket, shading his black shiny fur into different tones, and the flat, white, doleful sole on a blue plate, I struggle to do anything. The night before the ferry, we celebrate Bobby's recovery with a glass of sherry, the only drink Diana takes.

It's a slippery voyage back, nausea floods me as the sea rolls and the ferry slides. I go to the bar and ask for a coke thinking it will help. It does. I'm sitting up straight and I feel tall, like I do when I am excited, but in my stomach the small morsel of fear still lurks. Brendan's slaps have put a mark on us both, an unseen, blue-black mark, like an omen.

Off the ferry, a heavy bag of goodies from Diana weighting me down, I clamber onto the bus to Dublin. It takes me as far as my side of the bridge. Now on foot, up the hills and down and round the streets, getting tired, and teasing pins and needles flooding my hands from carrying my bags, at last home is in sight. It's a luminous, windy day. From the corner of the park I can hear music, a dull crashing sound of drums. The nearer I get to our big white door with its brass knocker, the louder the noise, and now, I can hear Brendan's voice singing, 'Merry-go-round'. The guitar and the drums loud and fast, they're having a jam.

I come into the sitting room. Brendan turns his head, but no hello, not even a nod and I know he is still upset and hasn't forgotten in my absence. I go into the kitchen area and that's where I see Jan in her white tennis skirt and blue T-shirt. Panic wells up, in her eyes and mine. We don't speak. My shaky legs take me into the corridor. There I see the prints of Vangogh 'The Sunflowers' and 'The Chair' hanging up on the deep red walls. I like looking at them. I check the post. All for Brendan, except one from Diana. From its shape I can tell it's teabags. I hold it and savour her handwriting. Homesickness joins my pain to nestle deep inside me. And there are things about Diana I've never liked, but today I love them and everything I can think of that's Diana, her company, her routines, even the switching on of the very loud radio at 6.00 in the morning as if it is her prayer to the world. Inspite of my stomach being in knots I have a feeling I belong somewhere.

What am I going to do? Go for a walk? Go to the cafe? Sit in the park? I decide to walk around the block. I like meeting the different cats on the way: loved fat cats with velvet collars, rib thin cats, wide eyed and hungry ginger toms and blue-cream beauties with black-green eyes. My favourite is the one with dark brown stripes, like a tiger and an 'M' on his forehead. The dog from the blue house shakes his waggy tail. He always barks at me passing by. Then there is the garden with a peacock topiary tree, only it has a big hole in it where the tree hasn't grown properly.

*

Half an hour later and I'm back at the house. What if Jan is still there? But I see her green racer, of course she would have a racer, being so sporty, has gone. Jan rode her bicycle all the time as natural as people breath.

The silence in the room sealed like air in a balloon bursts out with the rush of wind as the door opens and the noise of the street filters in. The band, instruments packed up, music abandoned, leave without speaking.

'You didn't say hello, didn't even look at me, you could have nodded your head. I do exist.'

'Sorry, but you know what I'm like when playing with the band.'

'Why was Jan here?'

'She wanted to listen, Alice, that's all.'

I walk to the settee and sit down, hands holding my face, my jealousy arriving like a crack in the earth.

In a quiet voice, I say, 'You know how I feel about Jan.'

'Let's not start again.'

'Listen to me!'

'Shut up!'

The way Brendan says this makes me stop breathing, because it comes with a wind of motion, of Brendan coming towards me like a bird diving onto its prey, his slap shakes me like I'm a piece of cloth.

'Stop it, stop it!' He shouts. Minutes later, shock holding us both, Brendan sits down beside me. His head buried in his hands.

'I told you not to provoke me like that.'

After a long angry pause, almost choking over my words, 'I'm working as a prostitute, to pay for food.' I say, *prostitute* as if it's a normal job. Brendan looks at me his mouth like a goldfish opening and closing then, in slow motion and as if he can't believe anything anymore, 'Oh my God. What did you say?' He raised his head and the words, 'That's disgusting!' Spat out of him.

I remember all the porcelain Virgin Mary's in Ma and Da's house and picture Ma with her Catholic soul, a halo of shiny yellow, hugging her head. Now I have done it.

I feel space appearing as Brendan moves away from me, leaving me enclosed in a circle of cold and loneliness. His voice steel-like, says, 'I'm going.'

'No. Please no!'

'I can't live with a woman who does that.'

All that I'm worth drains from my eyes as tears burn the sting of the slap. I cannot imagine life without Brendan. A small but stabbing thought crosses my mind, *It's your fault too!*

'I have to get money from somewhere. How do you think I paid for the food last week?'

'You can do other things. You don't need to do that. You can work in a bar, or a shop. I've seen notices about. Shop assistants wanted. Why the hell are you doing this?'

'You said how much you liked the way a prostitute dresses. I thought it would make you love me more.' The truth rushes out large and tough.

'That's in magazines and films. It's not reality. I don't want you like that!'

'Please don't leave me.'

I begin shaking inside and outside. After another long swollen pause he speaks. And, as if he is my jailor says, 'I'll have to keep an eye on you.'

*

Three long days away and with Brendan's disgust and disappointment ringing in my ears like an incessant alarm clock, I click clack in my heels down the street, striking out my legs, staring back at people who stare at me. Knowing Brendan's on a course and can't follow me, I feel safe. Its 10.00'clock, I'm due at the parlour at half past. I need the money. This time I've got to go through with it. I turn the door handle brusquely and run up the stairs, but there are so many, my legs tire and I slow down. If I keep doing this I'll lose weight. I hope.

'Great, you're here early, Pamela's ill, she's at home, I'm busy and Helen's shift is later, can you take care of a client, he's new, but he looks okay for you.

So soon the little yellow room has become familiar. As I put my bag down by the wooden chair there is a 'rap, rap, rap.' With apprehension tingling through my blood I open the door, to a short man with an enormous belly thinning down to his smart black shiny shoes. Grey hair flicked back with grease, a puffy hand reaches out to shake mine, and surprised, I take it. He wears a chunky gold ring, and a Gucci watch, steps inside, his breath heaves and rasps, tainted with the smell of cigarettes. He holds the palm of his hand against mine, unwilling to let me go. Frozen, fish-eyed, I stand there staring at him. This is Mr. Chip my next client. After a silence the size of a whale, he studies me from my legs upwards to my breasts, his eyes leaning forwards, his fat lips parted, 'Yes you'll do.'

Seconds tap, tap, moving time on. My eyes, trying to blink my nervousness away, wander briefly to the discrete clock on the wall.

'Take your clothes off.'

His steely grey eyes hook onto mine. Possessed, I undo the button to my skirt and let it fall to my ankles. I step over it and push it aside with my foot. The room fills with the noise of my heart beating. My hands feel clammy and cold. With trembling fingers I undo the buttons of my silk blouse, I hate the way the material falls so easily. My bra comes undone at the front, revealing my defenseless breasts, seemingly lost in what has become a vast unwelcome space. Mr. Chips undoes his belt in a relaxed confident manner. He only glances now and then at me, while he struggles to remove his black trousers from his penguin shaped body. Wriggling out of his white pants he climbs onto the bed nimble as a cat and lies on his back. His stalk is red and angry, vertical with a faint banana like curve to it.

'Come closer, bend down over me, no further down, touch me with your breasts.'

I could feel his member rubbing against my breasts and smell the faint odour of urine. Guessing what he wanted me to do next and desperately trying to focus my eyes on something, I find the edge of the bed and as I stare the sheet becomes clear in its whiteness. I notice the box of tissues, the tree swaying behind the window, which gives me a throw away thought: there must be a slight wind. The room zooms in as I take in all the objects around me, before coming back to the truth of what

Mr. Chip is about. I step back and say, 'No! It's against the rules.'

'Suck my cock and get on with it.' He cries rasping, his head bent at an awkward angle

'I said it's against the rules.'

'Listen I'm paying for this. You do what I say!'

He grabs me by my arm, but twisting it away from him I step back.

'Touch me again, I'll scream.'

'Okay, okay, calm down. Bloody bitch.'

Pulling my willing clothes on and without waiting another minute while Mr. Chip puts on his trousers I open the door, but before I leave I look at Mr. Chip, a half naked man with a sunken penis. He grabs his trousers, an angry scowl on his face. Relieved I had made an escape I close the door.

My thoughts wriggle to get away. I just can't make a decision. Mr. Chip disgusts me with his glaring, staring eyes, but the money is good. But then, I think of Brendan and the guilt rubs against me like an abrasive stone.

27

Confession

If only I had someone I could talk to. Then, I remember the sign I had seen at the doctor's, 'Community counsellor visiting Friday morning.' Hand flipping over the pages I search for the number—as if circled in red it begs me to dial it.

'What is it for?' asks the secretary,

'Sorry, but I can't say.'

'Okay, well come. It's Mei you'll be seeing.'

Mei frightens me a little because she is from China. I'm not used to speaking to people from another country as far away as that. She wears a dark green tunic, embroidered with pink flowers and a long flowing, green scarf. You can't see her legs because of her black, loose, silk trousers. On her feet are green-strapped sandals. She looks like a bird—an illustrated bird out of a book on ancient bird paintings.

She sits on a plain wooden chair with metal legs, in a simple room, a little larger than a bathroom. Children's drawings adorn the walls making them a rich tapestry: mothers with mouths open like coins, men with big feet and long arms, girls floating in the sky with angel wings, skies painted, hanging mid-air and large angular faces with tiny noses and eyes and wide smiling lips, like crescent moons.

Stuart had called people from other countries nuisances, and said they should go back to where they came from. But Diana is a nurse and has come across all different kinds of people. She says, "Everyone is the same—people are people."

This person looks at me through thin sleek eyes that scan the whole of my body. They do not appear to blink. I sit down.

'Hello Alice my name is Mei. How can I help?'

'I'm not sure if you can. I work in a parlour, a bad parlour, a massage parlour and I do things I shouldn't do with men.'

Mei doesn't speak for a while then, she says, 'There's nothing to be ashamed of, lots of women do that, they have to.' Her eyes fix on mine so I look away. I see her plumpish arms, supporting an army of green and gold bracelets.

'Perhaps you need to do this.' Her voice remains calm.

'Yes I suppose,' shrugging my shoulders. 'But it's illegal.'

'You'll need to have some tests. Just to check you haven't caught something. It is wise to take care of yourself. The nurse can offer some advice.'

'But, I haven't done anything wrong.' Tears beginning to surge forward.

'I know you haven't.'

My face feels as though it is on fire. What have I done to get myself in this situation?

I want to hear something different, but I'm not sure what, and somehow, one person isn't enough. I need to tell someone else. There aren't many places in Welnooth, there is the café, the doctor's and the church. Maybe the answer is the church.

The next bright day I pass the large stone cross on my left as I go up to the notice board of St Peter's Church. I see, pinned with golden tacks, on the dark wooden walls of the church porch, a piece of paper with the hours of confession, written in small letters. Someone told me about this church, they said in the sixteenth century paintings covered its walls. I hurry by three tombs. For some reason I think looking at them will bring me bad luck.

The arches are beautiful; their curving forms make me feel serene. There is a table near by full of bibles.

147

The confessional box is made of dark wood. Inside is a wooden stool and to my right, the little square window out of which speaks a quiet voice—serious, with words drawn out as if on elastic.

'How can I help you?'

'I've got something to confess.'

'You can say whatever you want. Don't worry. It's confidential here. Only God is with us.'

'I work in a massage parlour and I know it's wrong.'

He doesn't say anything. I carry on talking. I tell him about Mr. Briggs and Mr. Chip, about how I like being with the women there because of the loneliness in my life in Ireland. How incompetent I am and guilty for not having told Brendan straightaway and the disgust I feel, but I need money because we have none. As I speak, thoughts come to me and I wonder if the priest has ever been to a massage parlour.

After the longest pause he starts to talk, in hushed tones just above a whisper. I only just catch his words.

'In Jesus's name I absolve you from your sins in the name . . .'

I can imagine him making the sign of the cross, in the air, near to his chest.

A sudden pang of guilt runs through me for everything I have said or imagined or done, even for taking up the space in the confessional box, when someone needier could be sitting there. Upset and confused I open the door and step into the light of the church, which, though dim, is a lot lighter than inside the confessional box.

On the way back from the church I take a different route as I think I will drop in on Bernadette. She and her fresh baked bread are my one true refuge. Bernadette is a friend of Brendan's sister, Bridget, but now she is mine, too. We met when Bridget brought her round to Ma's. Being the only ones not family, we have something in common and we both find the O'Sullivans a

148

bit strange. She'd look at me and raise her eyebrows if something funny happened. It always made me giggle, and then, Ma and Da were suspicious of me, but then I came from England and that couldn't be helped so they resigned themselves to my ways.

I turn into the quiet road which leads up to a small, new estate, full of families, where Bernadette lives, with her three children, all snotty nosed, hands over faces, covered in the pudding of the day, ice cream and jelly, and her husband who sells double-glazing and is never there. Her bungalow, like all new buildings, has a sparkly clean feeling to it. Recent scuffmarks on the doors seem out of place. Toys—splashes of colour—paint the unmarked blue-grey carpets which cover all the floors except the kitchen. The kitchen floor is beige linoleum. All the walls in the bungalow are white.

Bernadette has shapeless floury hair, as if she washes it too much. It isn't very long, which is a good thing. She isn't slim and she isn't fat, somewhere in the middle. You can just about make out her waist from under the apron and out of all the tea cloths tucked in. She spends most of her life attached to an oven baking fantastic bread full of nibble grains and nutty seeds and the best thing about it—it's a bright cheery yellow. What I like about being in her house, apart from the bread, is that you can have long silences with her without feeling awkward. Often she is doing things, drying up, ironing or folding clothes. I help her with the large sheets. Tiger, known as Tim, Ben and Rosalind frequently interrupt Bernadette. She never gets angry at them just cross and that happens often because they are always fighting and falling over.

When Bernadette speaks, it's all about Adrien, where he is and his terrible long hours, that, and the bread. She talks about her buns and loaves as if they are new born babies. I would love to draw them one day, their buxom bottoms, stolid rectangular loaves and curvaceous swirls. I talk about England,

149

my family, the horses in nearby stables and how I used to enjoy riding them and about painting and Brendan. I don't mention the bad bits or want to talk about the parlour with her. Our conversations today are light and airy like Bernadette's bungalow.

*

After the cosiness of Bernadette's and all that confessing before it, I feel lighter and stronger. There is one thing on my mind— money. I'm going to knock on shops doors till I find some work. There must be another way of earning a living. My face screws up into a ball at the thought of Mr. Chip, Mr. Lipper and Mr. Briggs, but especially Mr. Chip.

My feet become flatter as I walk until I feel as if I'm walking with hardboard soles. I stop at shop after shop after shop, like links in a chain.

'Sorry love, no vacancies.'

'Try December, might need someone for Christmas.'

'Post taken, you're a day too late.'

'Can you type?'

My feet stride across the pavements, closing time is coming in like the tide. I still haven't a job.

Deflated by so many rejections I enter the Globe restaurant. The seat in the corner by the window calls me over. I slump in it, order a pot of coffee and stare out at the passers by and the endless sky. Around me the busy, to-ing and fro-ing of staff and the noise of cutlery clattering on plates and shouting chefs whose voices come in and out through the swing doors behind the counter, pushed open by the waiter's bottoms. In and out they go with a sculpture of dishes stacked high, some balancing on arms, wine glasses precarious, teaspoons and forks jutting out. But, despite their efforts vacated tables remain cluttered. Perhaps they need someone to wash their dishes or clean?

My visit to the Ladies is a discovery of pink. Pink doors and pink pearl walls and inside, pink toilet paper and washbasins, a box of tissues, hand towels, hand-soaps and moisturizing cream, a pleasant, pink place to have a pee. The Globe has thought of everything. In front of a large mirror I stand still and stare. Am I tidy enough? Will I do? I shake my hair then swing it back and flip it up into a ponytail with a band from my bag. I examine my face and stroke some lipstick over my lips and un-ruffle my skirt. I'm ready.

I ask one of the waitresses if there is any work going and she tells me to take a seat and she will find someone.

A man in a black waistcoat and black trousers comes up to me and introduces himself as Neil and what can he do for me. At the mention of becoming a cleaner for the restaurant he pinches the skin above his top lips and holds it taught for a moment, his eyes lower. He is having a good think.

'Have you done waitressing before?'

'No, but I'd like to try.'

'Can you start work next week, on Tuesday?'

'Tuesday. Yes.'

'Well, be here for nine on the dot. You can wear clothes similar to what you are wearing now, except for the shoes. They must be flat, black.'

I have just the pair, still in their box, folded in tissue with Diana's receipt tucked inside.

'Now excuse me, must go.' Neil says. His busyness makes him forget to ask my name, but I know, it wouldn't be an important detail to him, not until Tuesday. He flits between tables, a word here a cloth flipped of crumbs there, like a tap dancer tapping out a rhythm, confident and precise. I wonder what it must be like to be there where he is. Not having to worry what people think of you or have done dreadful things which make you go to confession.

28
Just like Katy

Nervous as deer; I put liner on my lipstick, next the lipstick trying to stop the slight tremble in my hand. The mascara is almost impossible to put on. I smear some below my eyes, *damn*. Start again. After the tinted face cream I top up with a dusting from Diana's antique powder box. It takes me one hour to get ready for the new job. I stand in front of the mirror, pulling my skin this way and that, my reflection stares back not happy with the results. My mind fills with wasp-like thoughts: will I make mistakes, forget my orders or drop something.

'Do you need to do that? I like to see you look natural,' Brendan sounds aggravated. 'I like make up on women, but not necessarily on you. You don't look right.'

'Well, I have to wear it for my job.'

'You don't need to wear that much.'

A shade of sadness creeps over my face as I close the door behind me. There are wonderful light playful days when Brendan's spirits lift me through the air. Then, there are those grey trodden-on days where Brendan's spirits throw me down to the ground. And those black days, which I bury in a corner of my mind. This, the first day at The Globe is a grey trodden-on day.

At the start of the morning I have to fold the red napkins, two hundred. I like folding them, there is something soothing in the repetition, which dissolves the morning's bitter start. Then, I lay the tables after a quick wipe down with a cloth, put out the sauce and seasonings, shine and fill the salt and pepper pots. I have two hours before customers come. Soon it feels that Mr. Lipper, Mr. Briggs, Mr. Chip and the parlour have never existed, until, that is, I remember it's only just around the corner.

The Globe has been open for five years. It wears colours of autumn: Dark brown shop front, with a hint of red, polished wooden tables, rustic comfy chairs with pine-tree green, padded-cotton cushions, basket-woven trays of bread and red napkins. A coat stand of chestnut wood. Waitresses and waiters dressed in dazzling black and white. The waitresses wear skirts just above the knee not below. And none have an inch of spare fat.

Exactly two o'clock and the doors open, the warm air from the restaurant drifts out into the cold street air, a passer by looks up as if he has caught the delicious smells coming from the kitchen.

My instructions are to follow Liz. Watch how she serves people and what she says. I notice that Liz has a natural smile, a generous one for people. In return they smile cheerfully; I wonder how I'm going to manage that on my bad days. Then, there are the lists of sauces to go with the meats and fish. These I have to learn off by heart.

In the hot, steamy kitchen the chefs rush about like schools of chub, darting in different directions, colourful in their blue and white checked trousers and majestic in their tall hats, only the head chef doesn't wear a hat. He has a little bald patch and greasy hair like Mr. Briggs and appears shorter than he is as the others tower over him especially with their hats on. There's one female chef with auburn hair trussed up like a parson's nose. With all the shouting and the steam I know it isn't a safe place to be in for too long, but I love the smells, of meat grilling and fish frying, of potatoes sizzling and vegetables hissing.

Today I have three tables to look after. I'm doing well, until the steak. A large man, about fifty, with a wig of grey hair, in the company of two women, complains in a strong American accent, 'Excuse me! My steak is cold!'

'I'm very sorry. I'll bring you another one immediately.'

I have to return the meal to the kitchen of struggling chefs. Someone snatches it out of my hands and in a few a minutes replaces it with another plate topped with a freshly grilled steak.

I have no time to panic, my body is set for emergency mode, my shoulders become rigid and my hips take to a quick jerky rhythm. I'm doing the waitress walk, like all the others. It feels good like the best moment I have had for a long time.

The large man pushes the plate with his large red hands, 'Here, take it back! It's tepid!'

I take it to Timothy the headwaiter, who signals to a chef, whose face turns a shade and walks away with the plate in his hand.

On the third time running the man explodes, 'This is ridiculous! It's rare. I asked for it to be well done!'

As if my fault, the head waiter takes over from me and I move on to take care of table number six instead. I can see out of the corner of my eye the headwaiter carrying up yet another steak, and for a while the restaurant seems normal—like the parts of a clock with everybody set in motion, eating, serving, cooking, and shouting.

After work, on the way home, I stop by a grocer. At the restaurant I have eaten guacamole which I had never tasted before, it's the creamiest most delicious food I have ever had, and tapas. But, my stomach gnaws a desperate hunger at me begging me to seek out some chocolate.

The man behind the cash desk has a thin face and a thin body. He looks as though he has come from another country, perhaps Pakistan. I think of the story my mother once told about a family from Pakistan. They came here all squashed in a lorry and then, until they saved enough money to buy a house, they lived all squashed in an attic. The shelves in this mans shop are all squashed up with boxes, bottles, tins and packets and sometimes odd mixtures—a packet of razor blades next to a carton of milk, next to spices, like cumin, in large packets. I think he likes the all squashed up feeling.

The only bad thing about this shop is its mouldy carrots, seeping lettuces, bruised apples and brown leafed leeks, leaking a smell that overpowers that of the spices. I buy my bar of chocolate and like a bear to honey gobble it up, even though it has 220 calories.

Outside the shop I linger to read the notices. Next to the lists of what is on sale in the shop and the bright orange stars announcing this week's special offers a notice board blocks the view of the horrid vegetables. On it is a dolly mixture of treats. Baby cots, Belgian rabbits, settees, bikes, all manner of things on different coloured post-cards stating for sale and with a price and telephone number. Then, there are the ones for the missing animals, missing people and everything in a space the size of a large bathroom mirror.

It starts to spit with rain, little drops reach my hand. I take it out of my pocket and stand with my nose not far from the window. I sway forward and let my nose touch the glass for a second. I want to feel something firm, something to lean on, but it's cold and wet.

A picture of a large caravan appears in the corner of my left eye and I stand back to read its advert, in squiggly writing. Next to that a close up photo of an Alsatian called Pip, his big black eyes say, please give me a home. Like a map I read the board, my eyes searching, hoping there is something I need, because I don't really want to go home yet.

Eyes tired I come away. Taking small steps, my felt legs, just about keeping me upright, a thought wakes me up. Why not see the price of an apartment? Perhaps we are paying too much. I walk back to get this over and done as I'm now itching for a cup of tea and somewhere to put my feet up. With more efficiency I scan through the ads again. My eyes strain for the word, apartment or studio or even, house. They are all expensive except one, a studio for rent £60 a month, gas, water and electricity included. On the small bit of lined paper are the words in black, block capitals 'Artist's studio'—Telephone before 8,00am or after 9,00pm 01457 0352684.

*

For the next couple of days I try to be as polite as possible and I call customers Sir or Madam. My accent is very popular especially with Americans. This is why Neil doesn't ask me to leave even though I'm very slow. My hands pick things up as if they are made of heavy brick. My thoughts can't string themselves together and I keep forgetting which sauce goes with what. Tom is great as if he has wings on his feet. He speeds around the tables with romantic gestures treating his customers like ladies and lords. Karen keeps a stern face; smiles for herself only, but people give her big tips. My tips are modest.

'We'll keep you on Alice because people have commented on how polite you are and your lovely English accent, but really you're too slow.'

Perhaps it's because of the late nights staying up with Brendan, reading Brendan's songs, that I'm so tired.

'Read this one, Alice.'

'Okay.'

'Do you think it's good? Do you really? You don't think I should change her name? Jane sounds ordinary. What about Rebecca, but that has three syllables. What about the ending? I have done two. Which is the best do you think?"

Brendan's like a waterfall. He feeds his thoughts to me in fast and crashing sentences in a hurry to get his ideas out.

On the Friday, a grey early morning, the sky full of clouds weeping rain, I phone the number for the Artist's Studio, my voice shakes from anticipation. A man says in a loud confident voice with a foreign accent, 'Yes?' With a long 'S, 'Schram speaking.'

I have never heard someone say their surname first like that, well only in movies. It sounds very posh. I enquire about the studio.

'£60 a month. Gas, water, electricity included. It's first street off the bridge, Suffolk Street. It's in a building with five other studios, a potter, two painters, and two sculptures. What is it you want to use it for?

'I'm a painter.'

'It's a small studio but with a good light. Why not come round and see it? Say 7.00 tonight?'

'I will. Thank you very much"

He says 'bye' with a long 'ye'.

I'm in Suffolk Street five minutes early. I wait by the door on the corner of the road. Two minutes past seven a woman walks up briskly, breathing out puffs of air, introduces herself as Sally and says she is here to show me around. I've only known one Sally before, Sally Piddington, from secondary school, the first to wear a bra and the first to have sex and the only one around to tell me how to get pregnant if I wanted to. This Sally looks like an artist, one who likes colourful jumpers and scarves. Her rosy face peeps out from under her python of a green scarf and her hands are coated in mittens, one hand green, and the other red.

'Well, let's go inside and see the studio.'

My studio is about twelve times sixteen feet, white walls, and a grey painted concrete floor. There is a heater fixed onto a wall and two large windows facing west, with iron bar railings. It takes my breath away, the thought of owning all this space, the size of a Kingdom and being able to do what I want with it.

'Come on, why don't we give Katy a visit, meet one of the other artists.'

I step into a room a bit bigger than mine with plants everywhere, plants on the table, the floor, bromeliads, cactus, cheese plants, Yuccas, small, big, tiny, giant, and the smell of geraniums tucked near to the sink. The sink is as big as the hospital ones, industrial, this one is next to rows of jars, cloths, paintbrushes and tins. In the middle of the room is a woman sitting down in front of her easel, with a large ginger cat. She has grey hair in a ponytail and a face the colour of a potato crisp and wrinkles running from her eyes and her lips, which are full and dark.

'I'm Katy. So you're going to take the studio? It's a nice one, plenty of light. I hear you're a painter. What do you paint?'

'Fish mostly.'

'Love to see them.'

I look down at Katy's lap to the large ginger cat. 'Excuse me if I don't get up, it's just that I don't want to disturb Apricot.'

'I'd love a cat like yours and a studio so full of paintings and well, things.'

'I've been here a long time, fifteen years.'

Undoing my twiddling fingers I stretch to stroke the cat, it starts to purr, rumbling like a washing machine.

I leave the studios with my chin high. Knowing that I want to be something like Katy, though Katy is a little fat and with hands that have lines crisscrossing all over the place like a London bus map.

I arrive home, up the steps and through the door and all at

once I have to sit down. Everything rushes in on me. It flushes my face so I feel hot and sweaty. It means doing two jobs or extra hours at The Globe. I can't wait to tell Brendan. I picture it in my mind, my easel will go under the window, facing to the side to catch the light, pots and paints and turpentine stacked by the opposite wall. A settee, old and shabby, a tabby cat licking its paws and plants and canvasses and . . . Oh, my very own studio. Just like Katy's.

29

A Couple of Hours of Blissful Peace

The studio becomes the reason for the new explosion of activity. But, we don't speak of it often because Brendan worries about work, which fills up his mind and weighs him down like a yoke around his neck. Peeping kisses at the bus stop and waving goodbyes, are the only times we meet.

Sometimes my heart beats so loud it leaps out of me. I'm going so fast, flying from one job to another. As I flit from the late shift at The Globe to the even later shift of my second job at the Baba Kebabs, I walk the streets just after pubs close. Men tumble out like dozy sharks, falling asleep on their way home, the young ones looking for trouble. Even with my jeans on I feel vulnerable.

At the Baba Kebabs I stuff pita breads with salad and slices of meat, onions and sauces, and pass them to the outstretched hands in exchange for coins scrabbled for from pockets and purses. Once home I sink into our deep bed. Brendan's arms wrap around me, his furious other self, hidden.

*

The studio waits. Begging me to come in and give the white space colour and texture, fill it with rags and tubes. My easel stands there silent as a bony and bare skeleton. I have one commission to do, a black and white drawing from a photo of a couple at their wedding. I dream of painting, houses, rivers and people. And think of bringing the smells, textures and presence of fish, fruit and vegetables, to my studio, placing them on the rectangular wooden table, so I can draw them and later paint them in oils.

In my left-over hours I stare at the white walls, my legs curled under the chair I'm sitting on. I think it's antique, wooden arms, tapestry seat and the back has a tapestry panel surrounded by carved wood. I bought it at the second hand shop 'Doing the Rounds Again', down the road. With the warmth from the two-bar electric fire, another 'Doing the rounds Again' purchase, and the glare of the whiteness staring back at me I'm pushed me into a state of numbness. Some days I feel a tingle of happiness singing up my spine. I'm so pleased to have a space of my own, even if I have so little time to be in it.

The days are getting colder, autumn is here. The wind speaks in gushed howls, the sky, blue-grey, the rain spills on my cheeks. I start to wear a Mac over a jumper, my yellow, yellow as a canary, Mac, which marks the change over from summer to autumn. On one of these windy autumn days, biting through another creamy bar of chocolate, the second that month, putting energy and warmth into my bones, I hesitate in my footsteps. Do I see the same man I met in Hewley's, who gave me the magazine, *Art Now*? I can't remember his name.

'Hello. Yes it's me, Michael from the cafe. How are you?'

'I'm okay, I have got a studio.'

'Terrific, where?'

'Two minutes from here.'

'Oh, I know. Where Katy's is.'

'That's right, there is someone called Katy, always painting flowers. Her studio is full of them: plants, pots, and seedlings.'

'Well, I'm on my way to see her so if that's where you are going I'll come with you.'

Two weeks flutter by and Michael and I have become friends.

Michael doesn't talk much. It's me that goes on and on. Our favourite place to meet is Hewleys or Hemple Bar studios, which are for successful artists. You have to have a gallery and a long CV to be there. It's down Hemple Bar Street, just off the main road, ten minutes from The Globe and the parlour. I don't suppose Michael has ever been to the parlour. He is too innocent. He has the most interesting square jaw I have ever seen. When he says anything it's always to reassure me. He tells me, when I say I'm struggling to afford the studio, that it's okay to paint in the bathroom if that is all you have. Francis Bacon sometimes worked on his kitchen table. 'It's all an image. Lots of people have studios and call themselves artists and never put a foot inside them. They get filled up with furniture or they leave them bare.'

Michael does his work in his bedroom. Every night he pulls out from under his bed a folder full of blank sheets of paper. Under the bed further back are more folders full of drawings, paintings, and scrapbooks of newspaper cuttings. Cassettes line his bookcase. He loves listening to classical music, Berlioz to Wagner and Jazz music, Charlie Parker and Chuck Berry. Guilt creeps up on me as I think of all the paintings I could have done by now if only I could reach my studio more often. I remember how I had done a painting of Stuart in my bedroom in Dundrum. I hoped that was the last time I painted between a sink and a bed.

*

Sean, a friend of Michaels, a heavy man who paints like Van Gogh, lots of yellow and you can see and touch the brushstrokes, wants to know if I'm interested in working as a life model for Hemple Bar studios. I don't like the thought of being naked, people looking at me, but they are drawing me so that is different. Artists look at angles, shadows and shapes. There will be space around me and a place to change in. The only other things I'm really worried about—if it will be warm enough in the room, and how much they will pay me. Michael thinks it's a good idea. 'It will replace some of your hours at the restaurant and you will meet other artists.' I think about Professor Lucas's advice. *Taking your clothes off will bring your attention to your body.* I hesitate, but the thought of less hours work at The Globe persuade me.

Sean's studio is not so big, but it's difficult to tell because there are paintings everywhere. You can hardly see the white walls because of drawings and sketches, pastel and water-colours, fixed with brass drawing pins or stuck down with bits of sellotape. His canvases are huge compared to mine. I image one day he will be a great artist because his oil paintings are raging with emotion and energy. He paints landscapes and people. Michael says he is an exceptional painter.

It's a cold windy day. The sky is a sheet of bright blue. My clothes are piling up and falling down off the chair as the pile grows higher. I reach for a pink jumper and pull it out. All the other clothes tumble onto the floor. It's an effort to have to tidy them up and put them all in order. I fold them up one by one, like lining-up-soldiers, and put them into a drawer, squashing the last one. The dresses go on hangers. Since I only have three hangers they all have to share. Rich people have hangers in silk. Diana covers hers in bits and bobs from old clothes.

Into the outside world I go, the wind whips my cheeks. Now I have a new reason to put my best foot forward, on my way to Hemple Bar Studios. It's warm inside. There are twelve studios lined up as if in a pack of cards, separated by white, flimsy, walls, which stretch up to, but don't reach, the ceiling. A man called Henry shows me to studio number eight. 'This one is mine. It's the only one big enough to fit us all in.'

Being naked in the baking warm air feels strange. Wanting to cover myself up I fold my arms. Outside the handmade, velvet, crimson curtain—hanging on a rail, changing room, eight people walk up and down, steady steps, intense look, searching for the best view, the right angle, for some, this meant the easiest, not a lot of perspective. For others, views of the figure, like a row of hills, some steep, adventurous, others gentle, rolling. In the centre of the room, pale pink, I sit on a chair, my legs straight in front crossed at the ankles.

'No, no. We need some movement at first, quick poses, each lasting five minutes. You can take up any position and hold it. I'll tell you when five minutes is up.'

Finding a different position is like trying to find notes on a piano, when you have just begun to learn to play. My first position is easy, standing up with my arms loosely in front. I can't turn my head, but I try to see as much as possible, taking in the room. The people spin into a hive of activity as they start to scuffle into bags and boxes, bringing out paints and brushes. Soon the room fills with the familiar smell of turps. I don't look at them. I might catch their eyes and be embarrassed. It will be as if a rule has been broken. Instead I look at their easels or the white walls staccato with drawings of other life models. When it comes to my fourth pose, I try to be more inventive and twist my body into new shapes it has never been in before, yoga-like forms, peaceful to look at, but painful to hold even for a few minutes.

The final posture is sitting with my elbow on a table and my chin cupped into a hand. This posture is to last forty minutes. I look for a spot in front of me on the wall. I find it where a part of the paint has come away. I keep my eyes on it to help me stay still. It changes form as I stare, once it is a butterfly, then a spider. My arms and legs struggle to get away as if in a straight jacket, but they struggle unnoticed just tiny movements of muscles here and there. My elbow feels like a needle.

I can hear the scrape of pencils moving with great speed across the paper. It's as if I'm in a film, being watched, but not able to look at who is looking at me.

In the ten minute break, I put on my dressing gown. Stuart gave it to me. It's a mirage of silvery colours, blues, greens, reds, clouds and flowers, all the way from Hong Kong, silk sliding over my skin. I go around looking at people's sketches. One person has given me large legs, another, a fattish face. They are all different. Only one has me in it. It's Sean's. He has drawn my English, pear-shaped figure, my round face and my long neck. My eyes, although tired from looking at the spot, are restful. It has been a couple of hours of blissful peace.

30

A Flurry of Snowflakes
Melting on My Forehead

The snow comes and like a large sock, muffles us in white. Morning stings and nights chill. I wear so many clothes I am like a clotheshorse. As I have a small wardrobe I need to find somewhere else for my summer clothes. The pullovers blocking the door and the drawers, like heavy lorries, are difficult to wrestle with. Jeans with thick skins come pouring down from the locker above.

A woman who has to be up at freezing-five to look after horses advises me to put on several thin layers before the thick ones and a pair of tights on before socks to keep my toes warm. I'm a multilayered package for my journey to the studios.

Brendan dresses lightly, an extra pullover, a scarf and a bobble hat, thick socks, one pair and he is ready. Brendan is always on the move, he likes to keep warm that way. He would survive the Antarctic; he would be dancing and whistling away.

'Do you want a hug to keep you warm?'

'Yes. Yes, please. What are you going to do this morning?'

'Oh, off to the shops to sort out some things.'

'Is the concert going to happen?'

'Of course! What do you think I have been doing for the last three weeks?'

'Sorry, I have been busy with waitressing and life modeling.'

'I don't like you being a life model. Men looking at you.'

'It's not just men. Women draw me, too. In fact there are

more women than men.'

'I don't like it, it reminds me of when you worked in the parlour.'

'Don't be silly, it's nothing like that.'

'I'm not so sure . . .'

'So, you've a date fixed for the concert?'

'The 14th November.'

'Do you want any help?'

The 'No' comes quickly. The 'Thanks' is slower.

*

It has to be something to do with the gig. Brendan is on the go all day, marching from kitchen to sitting room, either with a cup of tea in hand, a pen or a phone, all day long, every day, until the evenings when Phillip, Reg and David come round to practice. They practice till three in the morning. We may as well have slept in separate beds. Breakfast, lunch and dinner turn into frenzied attacks on snacks, or piles of unwanted, cold leftovers.

Today I am life-modeling all day. Sean, the man who has made my body into hills and mountains, has almost *disappeared* me. Now, I am brushstrokes of colour: greens, blues, yellows, and violets sweeping across his canvas. While in other people's work, I have grown a foot, or finally been given all my fingers. On some I'm a criss-crossing of lines, measuring space.

Half four and it's time to unfold my creased and aching limbs, shake them and slip them into layers. I barely notice the cold outside on the way back.

As usual Brendan is tapping away on the electric typewriter which zings and clanks. It's a well used Remington. All the letters on the keys are shiny-smooth from use. Around the typewriter are bits of torn paper, recycled from Brendan's song writing notebooks, covered with messages, and telephone numbers. The table the typewriter sits on is a bit of hardboard on two trestles. On it are drawn doodles: hearts and horns, circles and squares, squares within squares and leering faces. There is hardly any room for the typewriter to breathe the table is so full of pens and pencils, tea stained mugs, and a pink covered diary.

'Are you working on a song?'

'No, I'm preparing more tickets to take to the printers.'

'Can I help?'

'Nope.'

'Cup of tea?'

'Yes please. Actually you could help with the poster. Could you do some sketches, an abstract or collage based on musical instruments, mainly guitars and drums. I've done the text. Then we can put it together and take it to the printers tomorrow.'

Sitting at the desk, for so long makes me feel like a life model again, still as a heron, one leg supported by the chair. Its eight o'clock and we haven't eaten. I wonder if I could stop for a while to make a sandwich.

An hour later and I hear the front door close, Brendan has gone out. The room feels empty without him. I carry on with the collage, tearing out images from Brendan's music magazine and sticking them down with copydex. I wonder if I can help distribute the posters, too.

I look at the clock on the wall, 10 o'clock and Brendan is still out, the work is finished. Hungry, but too tired to prepare something, I head for the sofa and stumble into it falling on to the soft cushions.

There are all different kinds of sofas. I don't know how people can put up with not very comfortable ones. In the big stores near us, there are a lot of uncomfortable sofas, they all come as part of three-piece suites, the chairs seem more welcoming and I think that is why they wear out and the sofa ends up in 'Doing the Rounds Again'. I tried all the ones they had at the time. Some I found too hard or not wide enough so your knees stick out at the end. The sofa, apart from the telly, must be the most important thing in the sitting room. My favourite sofas are old sofas. There are ones, which look like sleeping figures, arms and legs folding in, some pert and young. Some seem to hold you and some seem to throw you out. This sofa is a rusty-brown with four enormous cushions, with lying down room. You can sleep on it all night it's so comfy.

A dark outside, just the light of the moon peers through the windows. I sleep. When I wake up it's to Brendan calling softly.

'Wake up, sleepy.'

I can smell something very strong from the kitchen area, vinegar, chips, and fish in batter.

'I thought we needed something to eat. Thanks for the help.'

He kisses me not once but four times, a flurry of snowflakes melting on my forehead.

31

Particles of Dust Suspended in the Air

It comes with the short days. Like a disease. Over night a cloud, heavy and dark as lead, passes over my face. I can't lift my cheeks to smile, my eyelids, like flags at half mast, shroud my eyes. Nothing I can think of makes this happen. Though, yesterday, tiredness enveloped me. Diana calls it, "Winter Blues".

The things in our bedsit become like strangers to me, blurred into fuzzy, unrecognizable shapes. Brendan speaks, his voice startles me, 'I need you to have energy I need you to be beside me.'

'I am beside you, but I'm tired.'

'Why are you tired? You haven't done anything to be tired. It's me that is busy doing things. I have got to get the concert in order. I have a million things to do. Are you going to be okay tonight to do the tickets? I can't have you looking like this.'

I pick up my clothes one by one, sock by sock; moving like I'm in a slow motion film. In the spaces between my thoughts, I am lost. I push my arms into my green cardigan with the one button missing. Another offering from Diana, made from some spare wool she had. Brendan notices I have done the buttons up in the wrong order. I start again, but my feeble fingers fumble until I give up.

All through the day, Brendan darts around, but I couldn't win a race with a snail. There are three bands playing tonight, two local and a semi-famous band from London. Brendan's favourite band is U2. He has even stood in the room where they first began playing. It's his dream to have some success.

I put on a black dress made of cotton. As time passes my body moves quicker, but my saddened expression stays the same, like a forlorn clown's with a turned down mouth. I have had enough sleep, but vivid dreams disturbed me.

In Da's car we squash together, Brendan in the middle and Joseph the other side of me. It takes half an hour to get to the hall. In Brendan's head worries like little beads come out as questions: Will people come? Will the bands turn up on time? In Joseph's head happiness as he thinks about a woman called Rose. In my head I have a feeling as if I have lost something. I grip tight the box I'm holding. In it are the tickets, tap tapping on the lid.

At least I'm not going to have to move a lot. I can stay behind the desk, handing out tickets to greedy hands. And I hope the light in the room will not be too bright, not white electric light, because that will hurt my eyes. I check for my small sketchbook and pencils in my bag. Maybe, during the concert I can draw the people and the bands.

*

The room is massive to me. Wires are crossing wires on stage. Lights are tried, the beginnings of music beat out the silence and voices cry out the lyrics. One or two people come in through the door, but where is the queue? Where is the rush? I'm sitting with my tickets released from captivity, but no one wants them.

Brendan is in a nightmare, cups his hands over his head. All night we wait for people, but only twenty come and the bands play for them. The rain outside heaves a heavy curtain over the building, lightening breaks, but the roar and clash of the music continues. I'm surprised they play for only twenty

171

people, but they are professional and play to a bigger imaginary audience. The press is there too and takes photos. We are all there in our places except the people.

There doesn't seem to be a reason for the lack of support. Brendan has advertised in the papers, posters in shops, fliers through people's doors, in cafes, in pubs. Why, oh why, didn't people come, the remote venue or the weather? One moment we are all in agreement we have found the cause, the next we are back to asking, why?

The next day my black mood hangs over me like a sentry. Out I go, in the too bright sun, glistening and reflecting in yesterday's leftover puddles and with the car fumes condensed by the still, damp air catching in my throat. I pass a shop with grey blinds hiding what is behind. There is a small yellow poster stuck to the inside of the glass door. On it, it says, *Do you feel lonely, anxious, worried? Come and share your thoughts with us.— The Isis group.*

*

We all sit in an oval, the room is rectangular and a circle would have been difficult to make. There are eight of us and no therapist. I don't think much of a group without a therapist. Dorothy, a large woman with large breasts, round like footballs, wears a brown with orange and green flower top—swinging from the seventies—over a pair of jeans, asks us all to give our names. Three people before my turn, I grip the chair with my hands not knowing how to say 'Alice'. When I do it comes out a whisper.

The group finishes at 4.30 on the dot. I haven't spoken yet and soon it will be too late. I don't want to come away lost and feel forgotten or even cheated. With only five minutes to go I say in a quiet voice, 'I have come here because I can't seem to be happy.'

A hushed silence descends around me, heavy like a cloak of wool. They seem to want more, but I can't think of anything else to say. A person asks me where I come from.

'England.'

A woman in her forties with grey hair asks me how long I have been here. Numbers keep dancing in front of me but I can't remember how many months I have been in Ireland.

'I think you should go back home.'

'Try finding some professional help.'

'Come back next week, we are always here.'

They speak together offering different advice. No one sure of the real answer to my plight.

I can remember some of the people: there is Dorothy who has a drink problem, Theresa, who is so nervous she doesn't have any friends, Ellen who is going through a divorce and the mother of a kidnapped child, Debbie. I can't think of anything worse than that. It's her ex husband who took the baby back to the Ukraine where he came from. I have never seen a woman cry so much; her cheeks are bright red and it is as if her tears have drained the moisture from her straw-like hair as it hangs lifeless around her face. Even though she doesn't speak much her presence fills up the room. Theresa doesn't speak at all and Dorothy speaks the most, filling up and overlapping the silences.

Like a woolly pullover the group hugs me. I begin to talk about Brendan, the grey days, the dark days and the happy ones. They encourage me to see a professional and to leave Brendan. The thought of leaving Brendan gives me sharp pains in my stomach. But, I follow the other advice and find a therapist. He's called Mr. Tims. He has round glasses and makes me feel welcome. He wears perfume, just a little, but its scent brushes the room and all that is in it, which isn't much, a table, two chairs, a telephone and a clock, which is on the wall behind the chair I have to sit on, a waste bin and, a large, about three foot tall, cheese plant with brown tipped green leaves. The one window makes me think of the yellow room at the parlour with the tree branches moving from side to side.

I look at the long and thin Mr. Tims, who looks even longer because he sits very straight and upright, and compare him with the short plump, Professor Lucas. Will he be as good?

He has a confident smile. I like this, and I like his tie, patterned with flying ducks. He speaks in a soft, slow Dublin accent and says things like, *'Go on, I'm listening,'* every time I stop, until it's like my belt has been loosened and my waffling overflows the sessions. Both times we have gone on for as long as an hour, taking fifteen minutes longer than we should, which is strange to me as Professor Lucas's sessions last the exact twenty minutes. But, he is a famous professor and has to be in all different places.

My third appointment comes on a Wednesday. I'm talking on and on about Brendan when Mr. Tims stops me and says, 'You talk a lot about Brendan, but you don't talk about yourself. It's as if he was here in the room with us.'

We sit in silence because I can't think of what to say that isn't about Brendan.

'Why did you come to Ireland?'

'I wanted to be with Brendan and I had this dream that I could start my life again. But, I haven't done. Because, I am back needing help from a therapist. Though, one thing, at least I am not in hospital.'

Always before an appointment with Mr. Tims I'm nervous. I can't hide my grey, sad face buckling under worry. But, after each session I come out with the wind chasing my hair as if I'm on the moors of Yorkshire free and dancing. Until I reach home that is, and face Brendan. Then, I can't wait to return to Mr. Tims and have him release all my anxieties as if they were particles of dust suspended in the air.

32

My Roger Rabbit

'Alice, I have got some work. I'm going to organize activities for teenagers at the local youth centre. It's a six months long contract.'

'Oh, that's good news.'

'It means I can get some decent clothes, I need a new jacket.'

Does that mean that we can buy a new kettle, go to the cinema? I think to myself, but only ask, 'Where is it?'

'Welnooth. It's the new centre they have just opened.'

'You'll be eating at Ma's, then?'

I have only just put my two feet in the doorway and kick the door so it shuts with a bang. I'm still holding three plastic carrier bags, their handles eating through the palms of my sweaty hands. I try to untangle myself from them and get my little finger stuck in one handle, which spins round and my finger goes purple. I try to separate the conversation with Brendan, with what's happening to the plastic bags.

'I'll be staying over at Ma and Da's.'

'Can I stay with you?' I know the answer.

'No there's no need. I will be back for weekends.'

I manage to free my fingers from the handles. Deep red lines criss-cross over the flesh forming red puffy hills. I think of eating potato stew on my own and how am I going to cook everyday, I look around the room: the two chairs and the grand settee, the bright green colored wastepaper bin, the yellow blinds and the two pictures on the wall, one of Michael's, a self portrait, a collage done out of newspapers and one of my fish drawings and think how dark, empty and silent everything will seem when Brendan isn't there. A bright wintry sun streams through the windows, almost blinding me.

'Are you pleased?' I ask, not wanting to say that at all.

'Of course, I need the work and it will be easy being in Welnooth, I know half the people.'

'Then, I'm pleased too.' I lie.

*

Brendan always seems to have a football balancing on the end of his foot all weekend. He is in charge of the football team at the centre. He dances around the room, turning, hopping and stepping, the tame ball following. Ma's roasts and his job brought back the sparkle in his eyes after the let down of the concert.

I still meet Michael in Hewley's every Friday for a cup of tea. He gives me roses even though I tell him I don't love him that way. It's Michael who suggests animation.

'Let's go and see, My Roger Rabbit.'

'What's that?'

'It's a film done by Sullivan Bluths. I have two tickets for the first screening. I want you to see the wonderful world of animation.'

I have seen Bambi and The Snow Queen and liked them better than the cruder cartoons on the telly, like Scooby Doo whose mouths seem to open and shut like a stapler, not like the Disney cartoons, graceful and realistic.

There aren't many people at the big screening. We have seats near the front. The big screen hurts my eyes until I get used to it. The carpet dulls the sound of people walking in the aisles, trying to find their seat. A torch beam shows them the way. I don't think the audience will be the one for ice cream, as

176

there is an air of seriousness about. It's my first introduction to film people. They all wear long coats and dress in black. Michael could have been a filmmaker even in his beige suit. He has a look of boundless knowledge all contained between his large forehead and his flicked back, grey ponytail.

My Roger Rabbit's marvelous, very smooth action and uses real people together with the cartoon ones. I'm impressed and I buy a small Roger Rabbit, a white one dressed in red trousers. My Roger Rabbit's about five inches tall and specially made for putting on the fridge door. It's the first thing Brendan notices for days.

'Why didn't you tell me you were going to see, My Roger Rabbit? I would have liked to have seen it, too.'

'Sorry, but I thought you were too busy and Michael only had two tickets.'

I see the kitchen light glint on the golden liquid in Brendan's glass as I watch him cooking. His tipple of whiskey is now a regular habit. I breathe in the smell of onions frying and watch him slice up a tomato. It's his turn to cook. He always wears the apron Jan bought him on their first Christmas together. I dyed it pink. He says it puts him in the mood for cooking.

I put Roger Rabbit on the fridge door an hour ago and it has been two hours since I sat, tucked away in the dark cinema. Michael and I have had another chat after, in Hewley's. We discussed the film. Hewley's is like that, whenever you have something important or interesting to say, you say it there.

In my dreams cartoon characters begin to appear. They feel so real I could touch them and they have a surface, a kind of smooth velvety skin. When I wake up I half expect my bedroom to be full of leaping, wild-coloured characters. I tell Brendan about the dreams, but he says I'm sounding boring and that people's dreams are only interesting to themselves.

The morning is mean with light, and generous with snow,

a good inch lays on the ground. Cold creeps up my neck, I have forgotten my scarf. I have lots of scarves; a pile of snakes swirling in circles, half hanging off a chair. I have three pairs of tights on. I feel stolid as a snowman. My fingers reach for safety in my pockets. It's Thursday and Brendan has a day off. He has gone into town in the morning.

'Bye. See you in the café at twelve, right?'

I'm on my way, cartoon characters leaping through my mind. People are walking, heads down, or faces straight in front, but with a determination to arrive at work, or back home to some warm place. I think if they are unlucky, and the heating isn't working they will have to keep their coats on.

I'm the first to arrive, at 1.00, always on the dot, Brendan is never first. Steam beats the windows, people's breath make mists, the coffee machine revs up.

'Please can I have a hot chocolate?'

I drink my hot chocolate by twenty past and am now scratching at the wooden table anxious, but trying not to watch the clock. The clock has a big white face and simple black hands, with big numbers all the way round that seem to make the minutes stretch out longer. I count 100 in slow beats before looking at the clock. I haven't enough money to buy a second hot chocolate, but I could afford a tea, it will give me something to do. I line up back in the queue, leave my jacket slung over the chair to save my place. There is one person in front of me, a woman with long golden hair, plaited. She is curvaceous, could have been a character from a cartoon movie, there is something perfect about her. She is highly finished down to the rouge powder on her cheeks. She orders a peppermint tea, the strangest drink to have on a morning like this.

Tea on table, another ten minutes passes, I'm beginning to feel hot, not with the heat of the cafe, but boiled by anger. I can't do anything about it. I sit there, like a leashed dog. I have had enough of waiting for Brendan. He is over fifty minute's late, nothing unusual, but every time it affects me. The black hands moving round the clock face trigger the heat around my scarfless neck.

'Hello.'

'Where have you been? You are late. Why are you always late?'

'Calm down, I'm a little late. There was a queue at the bank. Don't get up I will get myself a tea.'

The heat around my neck melts away and my shoulders relax, my whole body sinks further into the chair.

'How are you?' He says and fumbles under the table for my hand. His eyes are brighter than normal and his smile bigger. 'Close your eyes.' And as if delivering a sweet and soft kiss, he passes something into my hands. It's a book. I can feel its rim, and shiny, cool, hard surface. It's about an inch thick. On the cover is a drawing of a brown, chunky, horse, repeated several times, but each time its legs positioned to show the different movements of a gallop. I read the title, 'Animation—The Basic Principles.' I flick through the pages, notice words like storyboard and cell painting, see pictures of flying birds and leaping frogs, in motion. I wish I could draw like that. Nice clear lines, no fudging, just like the characters in the film, My Roger Rabbit.

33

Fragile Diana

The page from the leaflet has grey smudges from my charcoal-black fingertips. I have been drawing today, now I have coal miner hands, except mine are soft. The wind blows the pages over and I try to return them, with my hands kept warm in fingerless orange gloves. It's freezing outside, the bus is late and I want to be home with Brendan. But, they have moved the porridge oats. They always have to move something so I can never find it. The aisles are flowing over with people. Arms reach out for bottles, boxes, packets and jars. This is the most popular time in the local supermarket, six o'clock, and people on the way back from work. I can see I'm going to be ages and there are five people in front of me all with trolleys stuffed full as a turkey and I only have a basket.

Still while waiting, I try to read my leaflet on animation, but the scuffling of feet, the pinging of the till machines, calling of the supervisor and the drum hum of people's voices all merge into one. I'm sweating and my heart is a cymbal clashing. Like a frightened, swerving and darting hare I make my way through, knocking elbows and rushing chariots, grabbing hands and clumsy feet, until I reach the entrance. The cold outside is a welcome, freezing, smack on my face.

The pub, The Moon, isn't too far away. Somewhere I can be in the dark, on a velvety seat hidden by wooden screens and can catch my breath. I panic like that in the big supermarkets sometimes. They are giant pressure cookers, with people bursting to get out and on their way home, but all the aisles and the bright lights are crushing inwards with only the two sliding doors at the front to set them free.

*

After a large, saccharin-sweet coke, bubbles popping in my throat, I lie back and close my eyes. Soon I will be home.

'Alice! What are you doing here?' calls out a surprised Brendan striding through the western style doors to my part of the pub

'Brendan, I'm so glad to see you, I had another attack in the supermarket. Hello Joseph.'

Joseph follows Brendan, a large shadow wearing a striped multi-coloured, woolen jacket, which I imagine was knitted by someone's mother, it sags and roams like rolling hills.

'Alice, you're so lucky to have a wonderful guy like Brendan to look after you with all your depressions and attacks.'

'Mine will be a pint of Guinness.' Brendan signals to Joseph. His breath already smells of beer. They speak, a stream of words pouring out, leave their excitement to catch the air and laughter spill. Their conversation continues for another two hours and walls me out. Well after the, 'last orders', bell rings, when the last inch of Guinness gulps down their throats and the landlord shouts, 'Closing time', Brendan and Joseph stand up stretch and turn to leave the pub, not looking back once to see if I'm still here!

The phone rings the morning after. I'm tired, the noise and the smoke of the pub still in my head clearing, but taking its time. Diana speaks in a high anxious voice, 'How would you like a visit from me?'

'Of course, that would be great. But are you okay?'

'. . . I'm thinking of Tuesday.'

'It's a bit soon, a bit cold at the moment.'

'Well, its cold everywhere. I feel like a change.'

The day Diana comes to Ireland missiles of rain sweep us forward and into our taxi, which seems a long way away, but in fact is only a few feet. Rain lands on our umbrella, heavy as stones, until we close the doors of the warm dry silver, lozenge-shaped Volvo, leaving the icy wet wind outside. I squeeze my hands inside my mittens. Diana has no gloves on. Her hands are blue, with chunky veins.

'You haven't any gloves on?'

'I think I left them on the kitchen table.'

This is unusual, Diana, like a Girl Guide, prepares for everything that might happen from wasp stings to heart attacks. She has a list of emergency phone numbers, three first aid kits, one for the car, one for the house and one spare. But, Diana is different today, thinner, fragile, and pale as a broken piece of porcelain.

'I'm sad after your father died. I'm quite lonely. I don't know what to do with myself, my mind is all a muddle and I keep forgetting things.'

Brendan sleeps at Ma's this night. I have never slept in the same bed with anyone else, but Brendan. It isn't a proper double, its two single mattresses strapped together, but somehow, either Brendan or me, make them move because in the morning they have risen up like a hill. I have my thickest nightdress on, my old hospital one, which I keep for winter nights and for nights when I'm alone. I sleep near the edge of the bed, eyes wide open and freeze as I can feel Diana's hand pass over me and rest on my waist. Her Nivea face-cream sends a familiar smell to my nose.

'Can I come closer?' She presses her warm body against me, my back turns to her, and I feel her curl into a ball.

She keeps her hand on me, but my body tenses and creeps

away in the night. In the morning, Diana has taken the sheets with her and I'm hanging off the other side of the bed, my hand touches the floor. Now I know why she slept in separate beds from Stuart. Like a whale, her body moves and rolls in the night and her feet kick out.

We share toast and strawberry jam for breakfast and have a pot of tea. Diana has her tweed skirt on and green polo neck jumper. Everyone in our family wears a polar neck jumper, Stuart wore them for golf, and Lee wore them until they stopped being in fashion and Diana wears the nylon ones that look like skin, all wrinkly. I talk a lot about Brendan and I talk about my new idea to become an animator.

'It costs £200. But I can get a loan from the Credit Union.'

'I'll pay.'

'I can manage.'

'I want to pay. What is the course called again?'

'Animation for beginners, you must go and see, My Roger Rabbit, it's wonderful.'

'I like science fiction movies, like Dr Who.'

Diana leaves Ireland with pink cheeks and my blue gloves to protect her hands, a woolen scarf and matching hat. She looks like an advert for a knitting magazine. Waving good-bye my hands cut through the cold air, like scissors, until the coach disappears around a corner, a large tank-like creature, winding through the narrow roads.

The course starts in January, but I have to enroll now in a school not far from the house with a grey playground, green litterbins and a car park surrounded by pine trees. In the hollow hall, tables are set out in a long line. On each is a card and written on it the subject. In this crowd I feel the hum of belonging, like-minded people jostling together making a crush thicker than the one in the Supermarket. But, all I can think of is 'My Roger Rabbit.'

Peering over shoulders and peeping between arms and elbows I see an, "A", and then an, "N", and as someone's body slips away I see the words "ANIMATION FOR BEGINNERS". The woman behind the desk has a white badge with her name pinned to her navy blue jumper. Mrs. Lint is in charge of signing up.

'You're lucky; there is only one place left.'

'Oh good, but I came here as quickly as I could.'

'People queue up for these classes, but, you're in.'

I sign the form and fill out details, tingling with excitement, which takes away the pain etched inside by my fears for fragile, knitted Diana.

34

Herald World

It's a clear day, the trees spiking the pale blue sky. I'm going to meet Michael in Hewleys. I have my tatty, marble-green portfolio with me, bought from the cheap market, which creeps into town on a Tuesday with stalls opening by seven in the morning and disappearing by four.

My portfolio is big enough to carry A2 size paper, but I only ever use it for A4 or A3. Michael is pleased to see me. He has blue trousers on today and a white shirt. Michael always looks smart. He orders toasted teacakes and tea for two. The butter melts right into the teacakes and the coffee from the machine smells sultry. The cafe is quiet except the chatter of a few voices.

It's impossible to open the portfolio fully, as it's much too big. I have to squash my hand in and edge out the storyboard, mounted on cardboard. I set it on the table moving everything else to the edges.

'My first storyboard: *Three ducks taking off*.'

'Flying for freedom,' says Michael,

Yes, if you like. I saw them on Doctor Tim's tie.'

I'm so excited telling Michael everything about the animation course, from storyboards and cell painting to Gina our auburn haired teacher with the very white teeth. My tea goes cold and I have only taken one small bite from my teacake.

'What does a cell painter do?'

'It's when you paint in a scene. It's like 'Painting by

Numbers.'

'Oh I see, adding the colours.'

'That's right. You use runny paint on transparent sheets of plastic.'

Michael begins to tell me about a place called, Herald World. He says it's an animation company in Blackrock. It sits right by the beach and near to the cliffs.

'They are looking for animators, contract work for a few months.'

Perhaps I could give up my jobs, I think to myself, squeezing my toes as I do when eager or frightened, but I don't think I'm good enough, though Michael says they will train me.

*

On walking back to the bus stop, my mind is like a film footage, whizzing through scene after scene: in hospital, pub, Brendan, Wicklow mountain, Dad dying, Mum crying, Da shouting, Ma cooking, Bernadette baking bread. By the time I reach home I'm bewildered. I tap the brass knocker on our white front door and hope Brendan will be in as I have forgotten my key.

I put my portfolio down in the porch near to the muddy wellys, damp shoes, and soggy umbrella. When had it rained, I wonder? Brendan says it tipped down for one hour or so when I had been in the cafe. I turn the corner into the room. There is Ma and Da sipping tea with a slice of bread and jam—Ma's homemade apricot, the sticky spoon balances on the jar.

'Wanted to see your apartment, love, jolly nice it is too.'

Thomas looks white as soap. I don't dare ask him if he is all right he looks so fragile.

'We have been discussing family things,' says Brendan.

'But, we're going now.'

Ma brushes the crumbs off her skirt and Brendan helps Da

up to his feet.

As soon as they are gone I look at Brendan

'Thomas has had a mild heart attack.'

'But, that's serious.

'He'll be okay.'

Not reassured about Thomas, but surging with adrenalin at the thought of becoming a cell painter I nip into the bedroom area and open up the wardrobe to see if there is anything I can wear for an interview. There is not, my wardrobe is full of miniskirts and crinkly old jeans, belts, scarves and my black velvet hat.

The next day is beautiful, frosty and crisp. Through the gleaming window I see a grey squirrel dart across the park, zipping up a tree. Today I'm going to buy some proper clothes for interviews. The high street is busy; men on tall ladders wearing fluorescent armbands, trailing the Christmas lights like tails as they struggle to put them up. The shops are full of Christmas trees; pretend presents, golden balls, silver tinsel and Father Christmases with long fluffy beards. I head for Hotshop, just off the main street. It has large silver snowflakes dangling from the ceiling along with special offer signs in silver writing on golden stars. The colour theme of the dispay is black and white jazzed up with colourful scarves and earrings, bracelets and socks. There is a white hooded fur top and black silk nightdress, black cotton jeans and short black denim skirt all in the window. I can't see anything I like.

'We don't want something too way out, but something with a bit of style, something modern?'

The assistant walks around whipping up an armful of clothes for me to try. I hate changing rooms. This one is awful, my stomach looks bigger than normal and I can see it from several directions because there are three mirrors. The light glowers at me, begging me to hurry up and leave.

'No, that's not okay.'

The tall assistant holds out a second skirt. I don't want to look up at a mirror, but I raise my eyes reluctantly, feeling hotter and hotter inside the narrow, tall changing room. But, the skirt doesn't look too bad with the white blouse.

'Not too short?'

'No, perfect, all you need now is a smart pair of shoes.'

It isn't long before I have an interview since Herald World needs people urgently. On Thursday, in the morning, I catch the early bus with a thrill of anticipation, which turns to excitement when I hear the seagulls calling.

Herald World is so close to the sea, I imagine having my lunch breaks on the beach. The bus stop is right outside too. I'm nervous in my new skirt, it's a bit short. I have black tights and shoes to go with it and wear blue oval shaped earrings. The reception is amazing. All along the walls are pictures of cartoon characters and in glass cabinets are awards. The receptionist has a smart lime green suit on with a lemon silk scarf. The waiting room is small with black leather seating, a black coffee table in the middle with a red rose in a slim, silver vase and film magazines on top of it.

A balding, short man comes through a door smiling with big teeth and large hands holding an important folder. He calls my name in a very quiet voice. His hand is cold as I shake it. Inside the meeting room more pictures of cartoon animals and cartoon people: shouting, roaring, smiling, confused and happy. They add colour to the bright, white walls. We sit at one end of the very long table and he tells me his name is Mr. Jordan.

'Let's see your portfolio, then,' He says. His voice holds a cheerful lilt, not off putting, like as if he's made his mind up already my work isn't good.

I open the grand bible-like first page and move aside. Turning the pages he reaches the life drawings. They had taken me hours to do—observing parts of the body, the angles, how many times the head fits in vertically, horizontally, the shadows emphasizing heaviness and depth. I couldn't have spent more time being objective so am very surprised when he says, 'You're a Fine Artist, and always will be. It'll be very difficult for you to draw like an animator, for that you need a different kind of training. But, your colour work is excellent.' He says he will start me off in the cell-painting department. Mr. Jordan, with his yellow fingers and big heavy wristwatch, is going to be my new boss.

Waiting half an hour, the interview has taken an hour, the bus trundles up and will take another half an hour to get me home. It's a swaying, leaning round the corners, double-decker bus. All the buses in Ireland are taller than ones in England, they give me slight vertigo, but all the same I go upstairs for the view. I snuggle into the seat. It's not soft, but offers a warm relief from the cold wintry wind that whips around the coast and around me. I stare out the window my breath makes steam. There are two boys laughing at the other end. Traveling when you have good news is a wonderful feeling, I'm on a high; so high I could touch a star. I'm going to be a cell painter.

*

I start work on my first day with the help of Caroline who is slender and tall, with very straight, ginger, shiny hair and a large mole on her right shoulder peeping out from under the strap of a red laced bra. Caroline shows me the book of all knowledge where we match the colours, numbers and drawings for every scene. The room is small and there are six of us, three contract workers and three permanent. I like pushing the different kaleidoscope of paints to the edges of the drawn lines. The paint is like liquid plastic and smells of chemicals, but it isn't a strong smell.

Three weeks later and life seems perfect as a pearl. My boss likes me very much and I like working for Herald World and even days with Brendan when his rage sours, seem to occur less and less. I sit on the beach, chilled to the bone, but loving it. There is not much colour around me, the sea looks dark and angry and its anger reflects in everything around: swaying leafless trees and grey swirling sky. I have a cushion to sit on—homemade by Diana. The cushion is a tapestry of cherries, strawberries and raspberries giving me thoughts of kinder seasons and how proud I am of what Diana creates. I think she has given that side of her to me, but I don't like working art with needles, I prefer to paint. I eat my sandwiches, spitting out bits of sand, the wind blows my hair across my face, and the salty smell rises up around me. I can taste the sea. Only when I remember Thomas do I think of how, without warning, life can become crushed and fragile.

*

Today after work, when I have painted a whole scene with hundreds of leaves, shades of orange, yellows, reds and earthy rich brown, all falling and floating off a large oak tree, I find Brendan sitting down at the table, his hands cover his face, his elbows rest on the table.

'What's the matter?'

You know what the matter is. It's the end of my contract and 'I'm out of a job.' I don't like the way he snaps, it breaks away from me the lovely things I did at work.

'Oh, I'm sorry, I had forgotten.'

'You've been too busy with your animation, painting and seeing Michael.'

'I don't see Michael that often.'

190

'We are going to have to live off your wages. It's better if you give me half. I don't want to be asking you all the time for money.'

'Of course I will support you, but I won't give you half.'

Brendan with his parasitic thoughts jumps up. Whiskey taints his breath as he bears down on me like a fire. His fingernails dig into my face. He curses like a demon and spits out, 'you stupid bitch, you'll give me all of it!'

All the nice things that fit in like patchwork: paid up bills, real cheese instead of processed, coffee, tea and cakes in the cafe, long conversations with Diana on the phone, presents for Brendan, the things that make life bearable, will disappear. My muscles tense into a bundle of knots. I have to sit down.

Later in the evening with the demon in Brendan stilled, it's a cold starry sky, the stars are blinking at us and one is moving, I never know the meaning of stars, the patterns they make. Neither does Brendan. We both stand and stare and look around for the moon. We are waiting for the queue of people in the grocer's to go down enough so we can squeeze in the tiny shop. Christian is serving. Christian owns the shop and is miserable to everyone. He never smiles and often doesn't even look at you, which is a shame because he has a nice round face and dark eyes and thick eyebrows. The customers he gets are because he has the only late night grocer's in our area. His eyes glint at me like daggers. He reminds me of Scrooge the way his greedy hands take peoples coins and notes, ping the till open and bury them. About to pay for the things in our basket, we discover we are short of one pound,

'I don't have a pound on me,' I tell Brendan.

'Run to the house, oh I'll run, I'm quicker, I'll go and take some out of the pot.'

'There isn't any in there.'

'What do you mean? There's got to be.'

191

'It went on eggs and milk.'

Christian sighs and signals to the next customer to come forwards. We keep the briquettes, we need to light the fire, but leave the potatoes behind. We leave the shop and walk home. I open a tin of sardines, which, when you are hungry and cold, taste delicious, but I'm dying for a piece of bread and jam, or a lump of cheese, I dare not think about chocolate, though I'm told that the sale of chocolate rises with unemployment. Well, it's cheaper than going to the cafe and a video is cheaper than the cinema, but we won't be able to afford those and wine will certainly be out of the question. Brendan is mad without his drink. He is very charming and polite to me until something upsets him, then he turns into a monster, bares all his teeth and gobbles me up with his anger. Now, when I walk into the room, I walk slowly, making no noise so I don't disturb him.

Four months pass like snow melting and my contract finishes, too. It's our last day at Herald World. There are six of us whose contracts are up. I clear my desk of all the personal objects: like a photograph of Diana and Stuart, a stress squeezer, a plastic zebra. Mr. Jordan thanks us and gives us all a bottle of Claret.

It's snowing on our last day and on the journey back, up the stairs of the red bus onto a floor wet with sodden shoe prints, I sink into the seat and stare out of the window. The snowflakes make a pattern on the glass enclosing me inside. The bus is empty and littered with cigarette ends, reminds me of a large public toilet.

It's eight and Brendan is in bed when I come home. For all the sleep he gets, fifteen or more hours, the look of unemployment never leaves Brendan. Dark grey circles his eyes and his face is pinched and white.

'Look I've got a bottle of Claret from work, it's a leaving present.'

'Can't they give you your job back?'

'It's good they gave us something, I wasn't expecting this.'

'I'll open it. You'll only break the cork.'

He unrolls from the duvet and his legs, pale and listless, slide off the bed like they don't want to do anything. In just his pants he walks over to the drawer in the kitchen. In his walk there is something he has to say. The cork pops out of the bottle and his next shock pops out of his mouth, 'Listen Alice, I can't stand Ireland anymore. It's too difficult to find work here. We have to go back to England. We can stay with your mother.'

My stomach feels tight and my breath shallow. I'm hoping to find more animation work now I have some experience. I know I don't want to leave Ireland.

'But, Diana might not want us.'

'She will if it means having you back home.'

Blindly I search for words. Finally I say, 'okay.' Then remember the flakes landing on the bus window and say, 'It's snowing outside. That means the animals are warmer.' But that wasn't in my thoughts. In them I wished with all my heart, they had kept me on at Herald World.

35

The Slit in the Door

'How much do you want for it?'

'£40.'

The small, eight inches by six, painting is of a trout's head, hanging down against my black velvet hat. I drew the fish in the morning and painted it in the evening and then gave it to Jenny, the next door cat, for supper. Marion, a student of the Animation Course has already bought two of my paintings and says she loves them.

'You're going to be famous one day. Make sure you have signed them.'

Marion's husband works on an oilrig. He is never at home. I wonder if she has ever had an affair. She would suit having flour over her hands and an apron would sit well on her motherly waist, but instead she wears pleated green skirts and carries a pen wherever she goes to finish off or start to write a letter to one of her sons or to her husband. She joins courses because she is lonely. The forty pounds she gives me is towards our ferry fare back to England.

'Are you really going? I shall miss you, but your Mother will be glad won't she? You'll come back and visit me and send me photos of your paintings.'

A pot of tea for one doesn't go far between two people even at Hewleys, where teapots are very big.

'You can get work in England.'

'I know. Diana sent me a page out of the *Haystart Times* full of jobs.'

I could feel Brendan gently move his legs to touch mine, his foot slides along my calf.

'She says she could have us for three months.'

I move my legs away and hold onto the hot cup of tea wishing time would stay still. Thoughts of England rush in like waves. Diana seems extra large in my mind, with her big soap-raw hands. Images float by of the animals we used to have, the goats, chickens, rabbits and a pig, dogs and cats, most of them buried under the apple trees now. In my mind, our house creeps in, large and dark and frightening, but I know my imagination plays tricks on me because I don't want to go home. I try to remember the comfort I find there when I do. But, still I list in my head the rooms. There are bad ones and the good ones.

Diana says in her letter we can have her bedroom and she will sleep in the spare bedroom. I'm relieved because my old bedroom is the bad-room list. The slit in the door, where Diana used to peep through, her worry for me making her oval eyes stare, like lasers, comes back to me and blots out the safety that used to hold me in there. It seemed at the time Diana knew all my thoughts, but didn't know how to help me. Her pain increased the depression, which came black as shadows, as did the beast of the house, which lived in the bathroom, a pair of pale blue scales—the forecaster of the day, a happy, sad, melancholic, foggy grey or a hungry day where my hollow stomach felt twice as big as my head. Last time I visited, the scales had gone. I wonder if thrown out, as rust had etched into the metal around the edge and the cork platform for standing on had fragmented or maybe, remembering and worried, Diana had hidden them until I left. The kitchen in those dark days was hell, Diana nervous and stiff as a dictator, Stuart a machine gun gunning us down if we got in

Diana's way.

Memories stand up like fighters, for a moment trampling over a frail, fragile Diana and over the grave of clumsy, forgetful Stuart, taking me back to before, when French Fancies ran havoc over our lives and no-one knew what to do about it.

Standing in front of the mirror the next morning after a day of no arguing with Brendan, I look at myself and see two big eyes with very dark rings below them. They are so dark, like as if charcoal drew them there, instead of the late night packing. The one time I concentrate is after midnight, my mind stops racing and I make some decisions: to throw away socks with holes in them or keep them for a rainy day to mend, which shoes to take. Did I need that many sketchbooks?

Brendan doesn't have much to pack. He still has that trait— ready to go in an instant. I put all my things in boxes taken from the supermarket. There are always a lot on Monday morning with the arrival of new stuff for the shop. The transport van picks them up for England the day before we catch the ferry. Ma, Shaun, Barrie, Owen and Moira come to say goodbye, but Thomas is in hospital again.

On that day there is an extra special sky, a glistening sky with the light rimming the clouds and the roads gleaming. The sea sparkles. I'm happy now that all the boxes are on their way and all my fish paintings in them. Recently I have painted lots of fish, tiny fish all squashed together in plastic bags, which make them look like submarines, so many tiny pinhead fish,

'There's no space to breathe in your new paintings.' says Michael.

Michael is probably the person I will miss most. We say goodbye in Hewleys. He buys me my last pot of tea and toasted teacake, promises to send recorded tapes telling me all about Ireland and what he is doing. For a goodbye present he gives me a drip painting of Charlie Parker.

*

One week in Haystart and it's as if a part of me has been numbed. I can no longer feel Ireland's presence. Haystart remains the grim little town of old, but still I have my favourite features: the power station standing there proud with all three towers, their waists shaped like an hour glass. They tint the night sky a rosy orange and the noise they make sounds like singing ships. The church and the cemetery where now I go to visit Stuart, instead of him coming to visit me in his just dusted, oil and water checked, car. And, the old part of Haystart where there are still houses with thatched roofs spilling over their perfect white walls, adorned with flowers climbing, trailing and hanging from every corner.

Sometimes a memory of Ireland trickles through, but my pinhead fish are back, filling every moment, not an inch of space on the canvas spared. I finish the paintings in one sitting and use up all the colours on a quick smaller one. Paint smears my clothes. Tubes of oil lie, like strange animals, colour dripping from their noses. It's because of all this mess, I paint in the shed, attacking and ravaging canvases one moment, caressing and touching lightly the next. Cleaning my hands and arms is a ritual, scrubbing with turpentine and soap until the water turns clear again.

Diana tells us over meals what is on her mind. On Tuesday lunchtime she cooks shepherds pie, and places the large dish in the middle of the table. There is enough for eight people. She then asks us all to turn our knives pointing inwards as I had forgotten to lay the table properly. After a prayer barely whispered, forks and knives shuffle the pie and peas. Until Diana's voice interrupts, 'You can stay here for three months, and bed by ten thirty, as I have got to get up in the morning.'

She repeats this everyday.

We both look down, one month has already passed.

'And what are you going to do tomorrow?' She says, looking at Brendan.

'Oh, don't you worry, I'll keep myself busy.'

'And what do you mean by that?'

'Any help needed around the house?'

'No thank you.'

'Sure enough, I have an appointment with the job centre tomorrow.'

'Good.'

'And you Madame, what about you?'

'I'm cleaning with the firm again. Diana you're smoking too much.'

'I know, it's because I'm stressed. I've got too much going on and now I've got you two to look after.'

Brendan excuses himself and Diana grabs my wrist and whispers,

'I don't mind you being here, love, but I don't like him at all. When you are out he does nothing. He sits all day and eats and eats and eats. I don't trust him. He comes from Ireland. And if you can find a job cleaning why can't he find work. I'm very worried. I can't sleep at night.'

The argument blankets my mind. I remember the noise it makes in my head. Usually there is at least four feet between Diana and me when we argue, with a table or a chair in between us, but this time there is nothing. It's like being in front of the angry sea hurling its waves at me and spitting. Diana's finger points at me like a lance. When we argue I wish I could turn it into a magic wand and disappear Diana away with it. It starts with the battered fish. I can't stand fish in batter and I'm sure Diana remembers.

'You're punishing me for being here.'

'I'm not putting up with your food fads anymore. You can eat what you're given. I'm not having it. And I want Brendan out. All he does is sit here and watch the television. Yes, he's very charming, but I don't trust him.'

'Well, I go with him.'

'I don't want you to go. You can stay here as I'm happy to support you.'

'I can't, you don't understand.'

'I don't need to understand and I've decided right now I want him out.'

Diana always wears a lot of face powder, but I'm sure she is bright red underneath it all.

*

My boxes come in a white van one month later. Diana is very distressed when she sees them.

'I'm not having those boxes in here. I don't know what's in them.'

It's a freezing winter day, icicles on the window sills. I buy a newspaper. In the small adverts are rooms to let. I circle three. When Diana is in the bath and Brendan sleeps I phone them. The third sounds promising, a bedroom, kitchen and living room £200 a month, to share the house with landlady.

The landlady who we visit on a cold Friday, tells us her name is Janice and she is Polish. She is quite short and hunches her back. Everywhere she goes she carries a stick and points at things.

'You'll help me a little won't you, with the washing.' She points her stick at the light on the ceiling. 'And I need someone to put in the light bulbs.'

Already we feel we are living there. We give Janice the deposit. She counts the money with hands covered in moles and large veins.

Diana is very bad in the head. It's just after her birthday. Everyone's birthday in the family is remembered except often Diana's. Today there is a cake covered in flakes of dark intense chocolate, her favourite and a card of a drawing I made of Bobby, but a tension is in the air, icy tight under a vice waiting to break. This birthday is hushed. A present is waiting on the table, but all the same she is bad in the head. I understand, times like this are difficult for her without Stuart.

'I'm going to do away with myself one of these days . . . I'm going somewhere and not coming back.'

'You can't do that, that's not fair.'

'When you go to Darlington, I'll be here on my own again coping as usual. You don't realize.'

'Diana, it's not very far.'

'Diana gives me a hug and I stiffen. There is something odd about Diana's hugs. They're all different types of hugs: penguin hugs, bear hugs, light hugs that barely whisper. This hug is like hardboard. But then, so is mine. We are two hardboard hugs together. The taxi is waiting with Brendan and our bags. I squeeze Diana's hand before finally moving out with Brendan. Diana blows me kisses until we can't see each other because of the cherry trees and I feel her love for me stretching out to hold me back. I can touch her fear, like when she used to look through the slit in the door.

36

The Voice Whispers

Blood, dried and dark, faces me. With rubber gloves on, grey in colour, not bright pink like the ones I wear at home, I start to clean the black, waterproof-covered bed. The water stirs, mixes to a red slime. I wipe and rinse and wipe and rinse, change the water, one more wash and the bed is, pristine. I spray it with disinfectant, not pine or lemon, but the distinct, hospital-smelly one. A light bulb flickers. I hear a scream and another bed wheels past, a nurse in white pushing it along, her steps striding. I see the patient, her stomach like the rising sun.

Spick and span the room is finished. I shove my mop, broom, dustpan and brush, clothes and disinfectants into the bright red, plastic box fitted onto the trolley and return, wheels squeaking, to my shady, small waiting-room. Here I wait for the next call. Bossy as a captain, light number twelve flashes, off I go again. Wheeling past an open door I peer in thinking it's the right room, I'm in such a hurry. A voice calls out from over the other side of a vast mound of tummy,

'Come in if you want, I don't mind.'

The doctor smiles, but looking at the patients gaping wide legs, I mind. Embarrassed, I rush my trolley onto the next room, number twelve, calm and empty. Through the motions I go, but somehow, blood has stained the light bulb and I have an awful time getting it off.

This is John Hopkins Maternity Unit, and it is always busy. I clean there on a Monday and Tuesday. On Wednesday I clean at Fairfield Hospital, sometimes called an asylum, the oldest left in England. Its walls and floors show its age, crusted with dried, yellow paint and spotted with bare patches, as though war-time or before, had been the last time it saw a lick of paint. A very cheerful supervisor called Phil shows me what to do.

'Don't clean the toilet, that's my job. You mop the kitchen floor.'

The patients in Fairfield hospital are sometimes as old as a hundred, brought in by their relatives, but often not fetched home again. There is nothing in their eyes, like someone emptied out all of their feelings, looking into them is like looking into space. One day I peep around the curtains drawn around the bed of a patient called Judith. Judith looks asleep. The bones of her hollow cheeks are very pronounced. Blue, tiny, veined lines run along the surface of her pale and creased, like fine tissue-paper, skin. I see a beauty I hadn't seen before, a peace settled like a butterfly over her face. In quiet movements I start my duties. A nurse comes, pokes her head through and snaps, 'Come away please. Sweep over there, on Unit two.'

'I haven't finished sweeping under Judith's bed.'

'Doesn't matter, Judith died not long ago. We're waiting for the doctor.'

Broom trembling in hands, I take it to the next, now empty bed.

Frimley's ward is the violent ward. A nurse in a blue, round-necked jumper, one of the care-workers, escorts me to the kitchen and locks me in. The kitchen looks like all the other kitchens, yellow walls and stainless steel sinks. I can see the patients through the kitchen window. They look in their 30-50's. They don't look violent. They sit around, relaxed, playing cards, jigsaw puzzles, reading and chatting. They can move in and out if they want to, a key hasn't locked them in like me. Perhaps it's a punishment for being with a Judith who has died in her bed.

I itch to thread the lines of their faces together with a pencil. My A4 sketch book fills with people from the hospital. I rush home carrying the memories with me, hurling them down before the images slip away. I draw Danny, Jill, Jeremy, all with long drawn out faces pounding with fear, sometimes sadness, their eyes as if separate, float in their sockets, their smell seeps, pungent, or sweet, sickly, deathly into the pages. Sometimes I use biro and etch their faces deep into the paper. There are times I feel sad when drawing them, but often light, as if taking them from my mind to the paper lifts a weight from my shoulders.

Cleaning jobs are the easiest to find. Even Brendan ends up cleaning with me at Fairfield hospital. Sometimes we sleep over in their staff accommodation if doing late shifts. We meet men from Portugal who immigrated. They live and work in the hospital all the time.

'Phil, can I have my own ward now, I have been here two months?'

'Well that's new, someone who wants more responsibility.'

'I don't mind doing bits of everyone else's wards, but I would be happier to have my own to take care of.'

'I'll speak to Annie.'

Annie is the Head Care Assistant. She has a large build and always looks frightened as if something bad is going to happen any minute. Her husband has a good job, I think, because it can't be Annie's wages that pay for her Barbour jacket and Passat estate car. Annie grants my request and Frilford ward becomes my own.

That afternoon Brendan and I are put on the evening shift.

'Alice, can't you ask to change shifts? We are seeing too much of each other.'

'We don't speak when we're working.'

'Yes we do, we argue.'

It's eight o'clock and I can hear the soft, low call of an owl. On late shifts you clean whichever area needs doing. Tonight I have to Hoover the great big carpet in the meeting room, maroon and faded in places. I hate doing it because it has ruts and the Hoover often trips up. Brendan's assigned to emptying bins. He is wearing a large pair of bright orange gloves and his blue overalls. It's dark outside and if Brendan's not here I'm sure I would hear ghosts, I always do when I'm on my own, with the drinks machine, chairs and the sea of carpet.

I pause to catch my breath, hoovering is hard work, we stop for a break, stand by the doorway. Brendan takes his gloves off to hold a plastic cup of tea, which he finishes, scrunches up and throws into his sack. After a tense silence, I speak, 'We're lucky to have this job.'

'What do you mean? It's a shit job.'

'It's in the countryside and the money is not that bad.'

'It pays a pittance. I've got to get another job.'

'You're good at your job and you get on with people. The patients love you.'

'I don't want to spend the rest of my life cooped up here cleaning.'

I can smell the fire of whiskey on his breath as he speaks. His skin looks sticky with sweat. I'm very close to him, and conscious he doesn't like me in my cleaning clothes. *'They make you look dowdy and twice your age.'*

'It takes time to settle into a new job and new part of the country.' I say, hoping to lift his mood.

'They hate the Irish here.'

'They don't hate you, they think you are great.'

Brendan turns. His breath exhales the alcohol fumes over my face. His eyes flare, his face turns puce and the veins on his neck bulge an angry blue. I flinch, but he doesn't slap me, instead his hands close around my throat and he shakes me like

204

an animal. My body judders. I can't breathe, or cry out. He thrusts me away as if I am nothing. I crumple, my legs don't hold me. I crash down hitting my head on the door. Brendan slips away, like a vampire, into the shadows and the vast room takes on a hollow emptiness. A burning pain grips my throat. My neck feels bruised. I can't stand up, it's as if my body is frozen to the floor. Then into the space around me comes a snarled, *'Why can't you just shut it, little Miss Perfect?'* It's from inside my head—the voice whispers.

37

Cold and Lost

On the journey back to Darlington the train stops at every station. The seats are empty, just Brendan and myself. The conductor comes by and I'm relieved someone else is on the train with us. Brendan's mood has changed and he now looks sad. At least he has some feeling about what he did to me.

Forty minutes later and we are at our house having forgotten our keys. Tap tapping on the white door, Janice with hair in rollers, answers. The hallway is so narrow we have to shuffle behind her until we reach our living room. Janice, who seems to shrink every time I see her, is wearing a grass-green, woolen jumper and has a necklace of pink beads. She follows us into the living room.

'I don't want the furniture moving.'

'Which furniture?' I ask. My throat still hurts,

'You know which.'

'We haven't moved anything.'

'You have moved the wardrobe two inches. I don't want the furniture moving again.'

That night I sleep as far away from Brendan as possible, in the big double bed, still feeling his grip on my neck. Only a noise distracts me. I creep out of the room into the hallway and switch on the light. The cupboard under the stairs is open. The plastic tube from the Hoover lay across the hall.

'Brendan, come quickly, I think someone's in the house.' I whisper my first words to him, since leaving the hospital.

Brendan shuffles on his slippers and comes out of the bedroom tying the string on his pyjamas and rubbing his eyes.

'Are you sure it's not Janice?'

'I hadn't thought of that. I saw the cupboard door open.'

'The light's on in the sitting room. Janice, is that you?'

Brendan walks in front of me. Janice is bending down. She seems to be doing something on the floor. Her beautiful nightdress strikes me, white with tiny blue flowers and a fluffy pink dressing gown with lion cuffs.

'What are you doing?'

'There are bugs in the carpet. I'm sweeping them up.'

*

There is snow and snow, snow so white you can hardly look at it and blue snow and snow with a hint of lemon as the sun unfolds its dewy eyes. This snow seems to glint of all the colours of the rainbow. I begin to build a snowman shaping handfuls of snow into a lump for a trunk, for the head I roll the sticky and crunchy snow into a ball. It smells cold and reminds me of the deep freezer at Diana's house. I taste it. It tastes the same as the water from the tap except it's colder.

The sky, heavy with snow clouds opens up and snow bursts out in frothy flurries. Janice comes out of the house carrying a plastic, light blue washing basket choked with clothing.

'Will you help me put them on the line?'"

'But, it's snowing.'

'The snow cleanses them.'

'Oh.'

I wish I could see things how Janice sees them, just for a second.

The cold freezes my heart as I remember the moment I felt Brendan's hands around my throat. *Things couldn't get worse* I think to myself

'Your brother rang, said to ring him as soon as possible.' Brendan says his voice anxious and uncertain. 'There is a problem with Diana.'

'When was the phone call?'

'This morning, before I left.'

Lee tells me the facts over the phone in a solemn voice. 'Diana walked out into the snow in her nightdress, down the street, like she was sleep-walking. A neighbour couldn't persuade her to go back in so she called an ambulance.'

'But why did she do that, is she all right, where is she now?'

'She doesn't know. She thought someone called her . . . She said she thought it was Stuart, she said, he was cold and needed her with him. They say she's not well, stressed and still in the throes of grief, that she needs to rest . . . They couldn't keep her in the hospital and couldn't send her home to be alone, so they've sent her to a rest home. I'll let you know when I have more news. When we can visit, that sort of thing . . .'

'Are you okay?'

'Yes-ish.'

Diana, cold and lost is all I can think about for the rest of the day. But Diana normally hates going out at night. What made her leave the house that time? Was she really looking for Stuart? Perhaps she had been on her way to the cemetery to be close to him? She goes everyday to see the grave and sits there for hours, talking, so the neighbours tell me. Perhaps she felt extra lonely that day. Diana's different now not the Diana I know, strong as steel, impenetrable, but a vulnerable Diana.

38

I Wonder Whether I could Leave You

Brendan slams the door shut. The walls in the room echo his shouts and accusations. I rub my shoulder, brushing off the pain from knocking it on the door as I looked around for my coat. The rain taps on the window like voices urging me to get out. I creep past the bedroom knowing Brendan is in there. He might try to stop me, to lock me in. I don't want another terrible row tonight.

Outside safe in the dark, dressed in my nightgown under my coat, I start to walk, shoulders hunch as if to protect me from everything, the rain, Brendan, my thoughts about Diana. Brendan's voice follows me, serpent like, twisting my thoughts, but the faster I walk the more distance I put between us and the better I feel, though my breasts are sore and my stomach feels swollen. I walk round in a circle. A roar of thunder lurches forward, followed by a zigzag of lightening and I stand for a few minutes listening and watching, oblivious to the rain soaking me. Is this how Diana felt? Detached, unfeeling? I decide to go back. Devine Road is like a mountain to climb. Every morning I find new targets on it to help me to get to the top. *'I'll pause for a breather when I get to Mrs. Beans.'* But this night driven by the cold I reach the top without stopping. I creep back into the house and tip toe into the living room.

The next day as if laughing at the storm the sun comes out strong and dazzles the wet pavements. Sleep marks line my face, my hair is still damp, I slept at an awkward angle on the couch, so my back aches and I can hardly turn my neck to see the clock.

It's twelve. Brendan drapes over the bed like a large cloth. His whiskey breath hangs in the air. His snores flap his lips when exhaled. I pull his shoes off and put an orange woolen blanket over him, a present from Ma to keep us warm in winter. We have several blankets all great for snuggling under while watching a film.

With my stomach still swollen and feeling sick I go to see Doctor Kay. The test comes out negative. I remember Millie, she had been a black mare at a stud I worked in. The vet said she had a phantom pregnancy. I remember her stomach swollen for weeks. I wonder if I have a phantom pregnancy like Millie. I'm sad I'm not pregnant.

'If I could take contraception I would, instead I have to rely on you. I don't trust women. I know women who have deliberately got pregnant to trap their husbands. Look at Joe and Andrew. Andrew never wanted a child. Look at them now, they're going through hell.'

'Yes but, you want children don't you?'

'I had this out already with Jan. I'm not ready for children?'

'But it might be too late, by the time you want some it may be too late for me.'

'I can't think that far ahead.'

Hearing his fading words I feel a mixture of relief and disappointment.

My stomach feels less swollen later and I begin to relax, the air between us is not so like an iron rod, Brendan even talks about his brothers coming to England to visit us. We both settle down to watch Dr Who. Last night's storms of anger and rain seem part of a dream. By seven o'clock my head falls onto Brendan's lap, his arm lies over me, his head tilted, but in secret I have my eyes open, my mind yo yo's.

How much more can I take? I'm losing weight, lots of weight. I can't say how much.

I mustn't check it. It's bad for me to know.

The phone rings—a bulldozer through the evening. It's the night manager of the rest home. It's an old 16th Century building in a few acres of ground. It used to be a convent. As you enter a little wooden gate, to the left are hens with feathered feet. They look as if they are wearing socks. Pecking and clucking, they form beautiful, gold and black shapes on the green grass. Entering the building is like entering a very busy church which works as smoothly as the parts of a watch. Always it seems there is someone cleaning, swishing a mop over the beautiful wooden floor and giggly young care-assistants running upstairs with armfuls of linen. A middle aged lady who greets everyone with a slight bend as if pushed by the wind mans a reception desk to the right.

Diana's room is small and very basic, with a bed, a bedside table with a small lamp, a small desk and a wardrobe. To wash she has to use the shared bathroom down the corridor.

'Your Mother's fine.' The manager says. 'She should be able to leave by the end of the week. She has been very busy here, helping with the dusting and the polishing. We can't stop her!'

'Is she taking her medication?'

'No, she won't have that, so she's not sleeping as well as she might do.'

'But, she's eating okay?'

'Very much so.'

'Is she there? Can I speak with her? Diana, is that you?'

'Yes love.'

'Are you ok?'

'Yes, I'm fine now. Just a nasty depression, after Stuart died.'

'When are you coming home?'

'Oh, I'll be home on Thursday.' She said sounding very

211

clear. 'I'm fine now I have stopped taking those awful tablets they gave me.'

I try to work out how long ago since Stuart died, but my mind can't stay with a single thought.

*

Back home like a dawning of a new spring season, Diana's life continues, not a trace of the few previous weeks showed, not an extra line on her face. She comments on the list of telephone numbers she has for me. Look, there are six on this page. You have taken up all the space for the "A's". When will you stop moving about, love, and why are you moving again?"

'It's Janice, too difficult living with her, she's always accusing us of breaking things or moving the furniture and she is obsessed with bugs.'

'Well I hope this is the last time for a while.'

*

So do I, but before we move the discovery of a dead body in the next door house to our new house almost puts us off.

'Body Found in Attic, In Wise Hill Street.' Headlines in all of the local newspapers next to the name of the man charged for the murder—Wilfred Hunt. Toby the landlord thinks the next-door neighbour is gay.

'They shouldn't be allowed out,' he says.

Brendan and I look at each other; a dead body and a homophobic landlord. An interesting start to a new life in Wise Hill Street.

Janice hangs onto our deposit. 'You damaged the Hoover,' she says. I wonder if she needs help, for the last time, to bring in some washing. 'No your hands are unclean.'

Our new landlord wears a pair of thick black rimmed glasses on his nose and looks down at the floor or at my feet, so when he looks up at me moving inch by inch like a snail, I feel he is taking in every part of my body. His head nods as he makes this journey with his eyes.

The smell of the new house is different. Toby uses copious amounts of oil. Everything is fried. It doesn't give him spots, but probably gives him his plump rosy, shiny cheeks.

There is a wooden staircase leading up to the first floor and our bedroom, which looks across the street. It has all white walls and a double bed in the far end. My easel is the first thing to put up. Luckily Brendan doesn't mind the smell of turpentine. Up goes my painting of a spawning trout, painted from a video while I had it on pause. It's the nearest I can get to painting things alive when it's too cold to go out and Brendan has banned me from bringing fish inside.

After about a week Brendan begins to sing again: in the bathroom, and the kitchen, wherever he goes he sings songs about us being together, or being apart or losing each other. I stand half way up the stairs listening.

'You're not really going to leave?' I ask confused.

'It's just a song.' he answers,

'You won't leave, promise.'

But then, a sly voice slips through me leaving its trace, *I wonder whether I could leave you.*

39

The Blue Jumper

Something wakes me up, it's only six o'clock. Still dark, but not the black dark of winter as spring is gathering momentum and I can hear the birds singing. A weight bears me down. Brendan's heavy limp arm lies across my breast. I push it away in gentle movements so as not to disturb him. He rolls over and grunts. I slip on my rose, velvet, open-toe slippers and tiptoe down the stairs. Toby's snores rumble around the landing. I think most people snore. Stuart snored, Diana snores and Brendan snores, and I snore.

My toes push through and clench the lush, thick carpet pile. The house has lots of other little luxuries: the Swiss coffee maker, a tumble dryer, a twenty one inch TV screen and a splash pool in the garden. Toby's parents come to see him one day, both sit on the edge of the floral settee.

'We try to look after Toby as best as we can. We bought this house for him as an investment as well as a home. We're very happy to have you two here. Toby needs friends.'

'But, Toby is fifty,' I say to Brendan after they have gone. 'Yes, but he's not all there is he?'

*

The first cup of tea is the best. I sit there sipping the hot and sweet liquid. I can still hear the early birds singing to a back ground of the wind rustling, a gate scraping, a car passing, but

I can't see anything out of the window. Now I have switched on the light inside, it is very black outside. We are one of those houses where no one bothers to close the curtains downstairs, but now, unnerved by others seeing me and me not seeing them, I feel as if a ghost could walk through the window, so I whip the blinds shut and at once feel comforted.

Brendan and Toby come downstairs at 8.30ish. Toby in his blue flannel dressing gown and Brendan already dressed in his white trousers and grey jumper. Toby is an awful lot shorter than Brendan and wears thick black glasses. Brendan's glasses are gold and round. I wear glasses, but only for reading.

I remember Brendan has one of his interviews coming up.

'What is the job you are going for?'

'I've told you once, Psychiatric nurse. It's not a lot of money.'

The Brendan the world sees would be good at this, but my mind screams, *'But, that's someone who cares about people, who couldn't hit and hurt others.'* I make no sign of my thoughts, but say, 'It'll be interesting.'

'I'll get training.'

'You're great at making people laugh.'

I remember how watching Brendan when he told jokes made me burst at the seams with laughter, but that was a long time ago.

'I know how to be with someone who is down, or if they're feeling high . . .Haven't you got an interview soon?'

'Yes, next week, but it's only for another cleaning job.'

*

There are sales everywhere today. Shops with giant red posters shouting "SALE 50%" gobbling up the window space, you can't see much of what they are offering. The high street is brimming with people, knocking elbows, hurrying through, darting here and there hoping to find a gap. I shuffle, chin right up making me taller, though I can't see more than bobbing heads. I can make out Debenham's at last, and I only want a pair of socks. I pass a man with fingerless gloves putting hot roasted chestnuts in small paper bags, if I hadn't been in such a hurry I would have bought some. Their delicious, nutty smell teases me all the way to Debenham's front doors.

On the way to the socks section I pass men's clothing and look at the jumpers. I love wearing men's jumpers, so big and comforting. A round neck, thick-wool one, catches my eye. Its Brendan's favourite blue and it's the right size; I can see it on him. It's a long time since I bought a present. It's perfect for his interview, and I'll never see another one like it again and perhaps it will give me a week's peace. The queue to the cash desk is long. Queues everywhere are today, I have to wait twenty minutes for a coffee and can't face waiting for my socks, but glad I have bought the jumper.

'Here's a present for you.'

'I don't want presents.'

'Why?'

'I haven't got you anything.'

'I thought you might like it.'

Brendan tries it on and it makes his eyes bluer and his hair blonder. He looks delicious in it. I give him a hug and he squeezes me and whispers thanks in my ear.

'It's expensive. I have never had such a good quality jumper.'

*

The same day as Brendan's interview the hospital phones me up and asks me if I can come to my interview tomorrow. I don't think there is a problem. I know they will offer me work. The hospitals are short of cleaners.

216

Woodgreen hospital is up a long, hilly road. My interview is with a man called Mr. Read. He is very handsome and young and wears a tidy, grey suit with a white shirt and a blue-grey tie.

Mr. Read brushes his finger along the edge of the cupboard. 'See this?' He holds his finger up. 'This is what we don't want to see.'

His dust covered finger wavers around ten inches away from my nose.

'Detail is important, look for corners, they collect dirt. Always check the top of cupboards. Remember this is a hospital. Everything clean, please.'

I have made it to the top in cleaning hospitals. It's a much smaller hospital and I'm a permanent member of staff, not a contract worker. I'm pleased somebody wants me. Cleaning dust from a well-cleaned ward isn't too difficult. I don't have to serve food or do the toilets, just Hoover, mop, polish and dust.

*

A month goes by. Everyday I clean the same ward, the same bedside lockers. I dust under the fruit, the books, the pens and pillboxes, cigarettes and sweets. When a new patient comes they come with different things: one person likes spy novels, another has a collection of earrings.

Teatime is a break from dust hunting. I always have a plastic cup of hot chocolate from the machine. The ward is very quiet. Mostly, people come there after their operation. My mop becomes a third arm, I use it so much, and dusters become extensions of my hands. My nostrils breathe in the smell of disinfectant.

Places I don't clean include the stairs, and the coffee machine area. There is a cupboard I never touch, big as a wardrobe, too high for me to reach the top. Inside are two broken Hoovers and some blankets.

One day after my hot chocolate, after a morning of dusting, but not wanting to, I stand motionless like a robot about to expire. I open the cupboard door. No one is about so I climb in and close the door behind me. The inside dark comforts me. I'm not frightened like I am of the outside dark. Forest smells filter out from the untreated inner sides and door—sawn, rich wood, bleeding resins and tall uncut pines. I slow my breathing to absorb them and rest my head on my knees. Thoughts wind a slow path through me. I sit up knowing I can't stay in this cupboard all afternoon.

I have got to get another job, but what? Like the switch of a light it occurs to me I can't take cleaning anymore. But, what use is a degree in art? Besides I don't even have time to paint nowadays. Oh, why do I always end up cleaning? But then, a degree is a degree. It might not be too late.

After work, on the way home, I go to Derby's newsagent and buy a *Guardian*. I can't wait till I get home so stop in the middle of the street and try to open the job pages. But, out fall leaflets and it's a scramble getting them back again. The wind prevents me from opening the paper so I try folding it. A gush blows it backwards and people begin to show their annoyance at me for standing in the middle of the pavement. A cafe is nearby. I tuck the paper under my arm and enter. A warm buff of air sweeps over my face. I order a coffee. It's still difficult opening out the paper on the round table. A man in the corner is reading a pink, *Financial Times* and he seems to manage. I reach the job page and read a few headings.

'Gallery assistant—Graphic designer—Arts coordinator.' I put the paper down for a minute. The warmth of the café seeps out the last of the cold of the wind. The excitement of the newspaper and the possibilities it holds out to me bring on a sleepy feeling. I close my eyes. When I wake up I find half the paper has slipped under the table and outside, street lights glare through the dusk. Its six o'clock. Only just light when I left for work, then dark in the cupboard and now a dimness to walk home in, the day has passed without me.

It's been a week since I discovered the cupboard. I go there every day. Sometimes I finish polishing early, but as it is, I can't leave the building until five so I stay in the cupboard daydreaming about all the different jobs I could do. On Tuesday at 11.45, Mrs. Dine calls me into her office. Mrs. Dine is the Senior Manager.

'We have to let you go. Miss Picking has complained of your slowness and disappearances.'

I take out my clothes from the grey locker, leaving it bare as a ghost for the next person and take a short cut through the park. I'm sad, but relieved. I had begun to be friends with a patient called Liz and I will miss Ben, one of the workers. But, I'm glad to say goodbye to my mop and rubber gloves. I don't normally whistle because I can't whistle very well, but today I start to whistle the old classic, 'Summer time'.

In the distance I see Brendan. Just before I open my mouth to call his name a woman with long auburn hair and a green coat runs up to him. He turns around, looks surprised and pleased gives her a hug. They kiss the biggest kiss I'd ever seen and I shrink to the size of a pocket. I let people walk in front of me and I walk backwards to hide myself amongst them. Brendan, with his arms holding the woman, remains in my sight. My wobbly stomach and loose limbed body, small and of no worth, boils into a furnace as I realize he is wearing his present from me, the blue jumper.

40

S for Samaritans

Tendrils of jealousy torment my body, I search for something comforting, a shoulder to lean or perhaps a reassuring voice, but my mind lands on food and I let my feet find a familiar way home back from the park. I know I shouldn't let them go this way, but don't resist.

I'm in Moron's late-night grocers. At first I think it's a mirage until I move closer and can hear sweet tunes crying out to me. My body sways forward. My mind says, *'No'*, but the French Fancies win when I only came in to buy an apple. With slow movements as if I can then change my mind I take one box at a time, one then two and my heart melts and the pile gets higher. *STOP! Three's enough and I'm not nicking them!*

It's a long time since French Fancies corrupted my body. Three boxes of six add up to twenty-four, which I consume like a demon on wings, hiding in the doorway of a closed shop. Not a second passes between swallowing each one almost whole. Their scent possesses me. The fleeting taste of the sponge interior melts the sadness inside me. All the time a voice is running through my thin body, howling like the wind.

Why are you doing this to yourself? You've done so well, you're stupid. It's a shame. But, you can stop. Stop now!

MacDonald's is the nearest place with a loo. It's a place where I could sneak in unnoticed by the queues of hungry, impatient people.

Frightened by the harsh tapping—someone has the nerve

to knock on the toilet door, I call out; 'Wait!' With my stomach emptied of the offending cakes I walk a lonely path, cowering, humiliated and tearful. Disgust at my action hangs like a heavy cloud over me. *How could I do it again?* My body heaves like a ship and lands in shudders. I feel cold, exposed and ill.

In the clarity of daylight I remember why. I remember that kiss. Brendan hadn't even looked around to see if I was there. What if I had auburn hair, would he kiss me like that? The scene replayed inside me like something out of a movie. How dare he wear the blue pullover! My anger rises like a hunting shark out of the sea.

*

Through my hazy sobs I hear a knock on the door. It's Toby, with hair like straw, which he rarely seems to wash. I have only seen it wet once. If I were his mother I would have to wash it for him. He isn't embarrassed about my sobs and peers over his spectacles, which are hanging half way down, he pushes them up with a finger and I can see his chubby, greasy, spotty nose.

'What's wrong?'

His voice is kind and I feel rotten for thinking him stupid and unable to wash his own hair. I daren't tell him Brendan has been kissing an auburn haired woman, nor that I have binged on French Fancies and puked in MacDonald's or how alone and faint I feel, in case he becomes even more friendly and sits down on the bed beside me.

'I have had a bad day, that's all.' I say, blowing my nose and trying to look less red and tearful. But, Toby creeps over and sits right next to me his thick thigh against mine, his steamy breath filling up his glasses. On a bus I wouldn't have minded, but in our small bedroom and, what would Brendan think if he walked in? Toby puts his arm around me, it just makes me

221

cry some more. For a second I think I can hear the front door close and I have, because Brendan yells up the stairs, 'I'm home, honey,' as if he is acting in a film. I can feel the sarcasm in Brendan's voice, there is no hope I decide, but I drag my sleeve over my damp eyes and make a real effort to look normal. I push myself up and Toby slips out of the room. As I go downstairs I feel sticky and sweaty and swollen and my thoughts become blacker and denser. Perhaps he can hear them, they go like this: *Is it my hair you hate, no it's my stomach, it's too big and my nose is too fat, if I looked like her slim with pale skin would you like me then?*

Brendan sings away, frying bacon. His bread already spread lies on the board next to him. He doesn't notice that I'm keeping at a distance of at least two feet from him. He hasn't even bothered to say hello, he wouldn't have seen my distorted face, as he's in a bubble all of his own

I have an appointment with the hairdresser at three, which I almost cancel. Do I really want people to see my face all blubbery? Perhaps I'll tell Anne. Anne has started to do my hair every six weeks. The result is it looks shinier and like the models on the adverts. I have less money for coffees and teas, but Anne makes up for that, she has a sparkle in her eyes and gleaming dark brown hair. Anne always makes me feel better.

'How are you, chuck?' she asks.

'Not very well today, Anne.' I try to stop the curtain of tears from falling,

'I'll get you a cup of tea. Donna make Alice a cuppa will you, for me? Now, tell me all about it. But, first what do you want, the usual?"

'Yes please, but as little taken off as possible.'

'Now tell us all about it. Donna, can you see to Mrs. Heindman, please?'

'I saw Brendan kissing an auburn haired woman.'

222

Anne stops brushing, holding the brush in mid-air, 'Are you sure it was Brendan?'

'I am, at least I think I am. I'm so confused and tired. It was in the park I was so happy and I had to come across that!'

'How far were you? It couldn't have been a mistake? But, you know Alice I have had my doubts about Brendan. Donna, Mrs. Heindman wants to settle up. Now, how much do you want off?'

'Not much, yes that's okay. I'm trying to grow it long.'

'Yes I know, but we don't want to keep the split hairs, do we? It's looking so nice now. Donna's going to wash your hair so I'll be back later.'

Donna has kind, large hands and rosy as a robin's breast, plump cheeks. I could let my head fall softly into her hands, though when it goes too far I have difficulty sitting up again. Donna massages my hair with her fingers, moving about the foamy sea, oozing out my tears and sending them away. *What if I have made a mistake, what if it had been a different man, another with a jumper like the one I bought Brendan?*

'Back over here,' signals Donna.

My hair wet and shiny like a silvery eel drapes over my shoulders.

'Well if you're not sure I wouldn't say anything, just watch. See if he wears a different perfume or has lipstick on his clothes. Is he unusually happy? Asks Anne.

'But, I don't want all this!'

'You could always ask him.'

Stepping outside the hairdresser's is a bit like stepping into a fridge. It is a chilly day, some of winter, stubborn and reluctant to leave hangs around. The wind blows my new hair against my cheeks wafting the smells of the hairdresser's into my nose: The shampoo they used and the fixative they sprayed.

When I arrive home delicious aromas of burnt toast greet

me. Brendan says the reason I like burnt toast is because I lack minerals. I like normal toast, too. It depends on the bread. Doorstep bread is excellent if you have a grill, but we have a toaster, which can only fit Mother's Pride medium sliced and thin sliced.

Brendan is humming and I can see a golden aura of happiness around him. The telephone rings Brendan leaps two to three stairs at a time yelling, 'I'll take it in the bedroom.'

My hand creeps towards the telephone and I pick it up, 'Yes?'

'It's Alison from the unit. Can I speak to Brendan please?'

'Hi, I'm here on the other line, you can put the phone down now, Alice.' His voice is firm.

'Yes, but don't be long I need to make another phone call.'

The phone to Brendan is like a drip. A permanent supply of conversation especially with his Ma and Da, but now also, with his new female friends. They all work at the unit. A herd of mermaids wearing gold bracelets and anklets on their ankles, all with perfect teeth and lovely lips, laughing, and Brendan, his blond hair and my blue jumper melting in.

I wonder if one of them has auburn hair. I don't know what colour hair Alison has. But, they were on the telephone for over an hour—Brendan and a witch! It suddenly occurs to me that I might be the witch with my long brown hair and spine-like, poisonous thoughts. Perhaps Brendan is innocent.

My new hair covers me like a skin and I feel an ounce of confidence—a shield of armor holding me together. I can stand up to Brendan and ask whom Alison is.

'You know who she is, she works at the unit.'

'Does she have auburn hair?'

'What? No she has blonde.'

'Where are you going?'

'I have to make another phone call.'

'But, you are on the phone all the time now. As soon you as you come in you go upstairs and talk for hours. Are you seeing someone, you look so happy recently?'

'Don't be ridiculous, they are people I work with.'

'Aren't there any male nurses?'

My hair stays shiny for four days and for four days my confidence bubbles up, but as soon as it becomes lanky as if it has anything to do with my hair, my confidence falls. It is on the fourth day I see Brendan with another woman. A woman with long hair, brown and wavy with a black and white blouse, square shoulders and large thighs which squash together.

I turn the corner to Rudolph Street, a little way away from Wise Hill Street and I stop because in front of me about fifty feet away I can see them. They are laughing out loud, their bodies move in unison, bumping against one another. I step backwards and turn the corner again. There is only a hedge to lean onto. What I need is something strong a lamppost, or a gate, so I can go straight home carrying my wobbly legs.

The nights are opening up, it is light until seven. New smells arrive in the air. It is more humid. I don't need scarves, but I need an umbrella, put my mittens away and get out my cardigans.

This day seems to stretch longer. I reach the house when it is still light. After what I have seen, somebody might well have given me an apple with a maggot in to eat I want to spit the whole thing out and forget about it.

'You're getting on my nerves. Her name's Jessica and I work with her.

Brendan lies like a maze, tricks you into thinking you have found the way out.

'Well, why do you have to spend all night on the phone to them if you work with them all day?'

'What do you mean by, them?'

The argument rolls on like coils of a snake. My hair feels like I imagine the skin of a snake to feel, even though they say it feels like velvet, I think it must feel slimy like my hair, it's time to wash it.

Brendan often comes in late to find me bug-eyed in bed with a cup of tea.

'Why aren't you asleep? It's late.'

'I can't sleep until you have come home. I worry.'

Thursday night and Brendan hasn't come home. It is two in the morning. The mermaids float across my eyes teasing me. That's where he is, but with which one? I am in the middle of the maze, the walls get higher and higher, I don't think I will ever find a clearing where I have a view, let alone come to the end.

If he hasn't come home by four I will leave the house, go for a walk, but I dare not leave my bed. The hands on the clock grow and grow and the numbers glow in the dark. My eyes are pin-pricked with fear. I hold my breath. I hate being alone waiting. My feelings start to sink well below the surface of the sea near to the bottom. For a second I think of the razor blades in the bathroom. If only I didn't have to worry anymore? But, what if he has had an accident, why can't he phone me?

Four o'clock arrives and shouts at me like a Sergeant Major. I get out of bed and walk down the stairs into the sitting room, switching on a light; there under the telephone table are the beaming yellow pages. I wonder if anyone is on duty to help me at four o'clock in the morning as I look under S for the Samaritans

41

A Drunken Stranger

The maze starts to disappear as the man from the Samaritans' soft voice brings my noisy thoughts still and quiet. I tell him all about my day and before that, right to the beginning. Feeling sorry he has to listen, but remembering he's probably used to it. The most difficult of all is telling him about what I did in Macdonald's after eating twenty-four cakes. I didn't mention that twenty-four to me is nothing, that seventy-two or more is or was my usual.

'Well, don't worry about it. You can't expect a habit you've had for years to disappear after a few months. Start again tomorrow. Imagine if you are dieting and one day you eat six mars bars, you've broken your diet for one day, not for the rest of your life.'

I can't believe he's talking about dieting to me, but his analogy works and I half smile down the phone.

Exhausted after the conversation, but relieved I don't have to go on eating French Fancies because the demons have gone away I tread up the stairs to bed. It's time to sleep, but one hour later I hear the pad padding of feet on the stairs, Brendan has come home.

The following days open with a bitter taste. I walk around the house shoulders hunched like an elderly woman. Brendan waltzes around triumphant. Then, I see a glow in the dark. It comes in the form of a crumpled newspaper I find on a crowded bus full of people with tired faces, some swaying as they stand hanging onto a rail. In the contents page I see, 'Jobs section' my mind radiates waves circling and confusing until my body is jerked forward as the bus screeches to a halt,

'Mind that person, will you!'

Someone shouts as the bus driver just misses a pedestrian crossing the road.

It is eleven in the morning and I am heading for my midday shift at the hospital. A different hospital called Woodward's, I'm back on the agency again, not a fully fledged hospital cleaner with a permanent job. I manage to straighten out the pages of the paper—*The Guardian Weekly*. I pass the pages of articles: The wars, the murders, football, cricket and one happy story, 'Triplets survive miracle birth'. The Media and Creative Section comes like glitter, opening up shiny new opportunities. There is a page especially for Media and Design: Creative Writer needed, Artistic Director, Technical Illustrator. Then, I see it. A small add to the left-hand side of the left page. The words all squashed in a tiny box, *Computer Artist—Person needed for adds and charts for Publications Company, will be part of a small dedicated team. Full training provided,* blazes away in front of my eyes.

Off the bus down Wise Hill Street, a thrush with a fat chest singing, the sun startles the sky with its brightness. Today is a blue day, only a small scattering of clouds and the fresh smell of spring hinting of summer. Then, I'm on my way home again, thoughts and hopes still swimming together in my head. The house is empty, that bare emptiness you wish you could fill immediately. I switch on the radio, take off my coat and put the kettle on. I go straight to the paper, just as Brendan comes in and goes straight to the phone.

I'm seething inside. Angry at him, angry at me and not knowing how to change things I leave things as they are and seethe some more. If only I could get a proper job.

The next day there is a difference. Brendan comes in drunk.
'Lend me some money.'
'What do you want it for?'
'I don't have to tell you, just give it to me when I want it.'
'No.'

The sting comes as a shock. My head jolts to one side. I see his hand raised again and an ugly hate in his face, but I stand straight and strong. The second slap forces tears of humiliation to tumble down my hot cheeks. Brendan stares at me. His face slackened by the drink, slobber in the corner of his mouth. He doesn't know me. He cannot see Alice, his lover or Alice, the artist or Alice the cleaner, he sees a barrier to his life and one he wants to crush. His hand strikes one more vicious blow, before he picks up my bag and helps himself from my purse and leaves.

Anger surges through me. I pick up the teapot full of tea and hurl it through the air. It smashes against the wall. Tea runs a path to the floor leaving brown stains peppered with tiny tea-leaves. I get up and fetch a bowl of water and a cloth.

*

I have to sort out my old portfolio. Some of my early stuff mixed in with the animated drawings and others I scrabbled together from life drawing classes can stay, but my paintings of fish, there are an awful lot, which are my proper paintings, I take to a place which prints beautiful, colour copies of things. They make some large prints of my best ones, my trout head and mackerel. When I have these altogether I go out and buy myself a big, black, shiny portfolio to keep them in.

My interview is very quick, with a man in his forties and a thick, hanging moustache. I know they say you should never trust men with moustaches, but this one seems kind and is very impressed with the painting of the mackerel and says I draw well. They say it is difficult to find an artist who will work on the computer. It doesn't matter that I have only done cleaning work for a long time and he is interested to hear about the animation work. He tells me I will have full training. There is one condition; I must drive a car to see the clients. It is ten years since I passed my test, for which my instructor told me to blink more often so I looked normal. I passed the third time, but have never driven since. I tell the secretary, Julia who has perfect nails, not wedge shaped like mine and a bob with not a hair out of place. Julia tells my boss Stephen who smiles and says I can borrow his BMW until I buy my own. I don't want to buy one of my own, but they insist. The BMW is my favourite car ever. It is gold and has teak wood paneling.

My first client is a big company in a bleak industrial zone on the outskirts of Slough, which is famous for its chocolate factories. My nose wrinkles in delight as the smell invades the car park. I try to open the car door, but I can't. Everything in the car works by pressing a button. I press them all. Music blares, windows swish down, wipers flash backwards and forwards, water sprays on to the glass, sun roof slides back, and then, there is a click and the door opens. I remember which one did the trick and press all the others to put things back to normal. The car stands in peaceful, innocent stillness as if it hadn't done a mad dance to loud music.

Brendan says he envies me the car. He asks for driving lessons, but I refuse because it is my boss's car. I decide one day to surprise Diana and take her for a drive. We go to Henford Hill, a little hill with a clump of trees. It is a beautiful breezy day, Diana is so happy to see me in my navy suit and gold BMW.

After a while comes my red Peugeot, which costs me £3,000, most of it from Hartley's Bank. It is smaller and a lot less posh than the BMW, but it is shiny and new and smells of vinyl inside, but above all, it is mine, unlike Brendan who is becoming like a drunken stranger.

42

Charlie

Wrapped in the comfort of my pink dressing-gown, bought from Hilary's, a secondhand clothes shop, a shop like a dungeon with one dim light bulb, mountains of clothes sliding off one another, and sitting amidst it all, on a stool, is Bridget. 'Can I help you?' She says in her faint as the light bulb voice. I always come out with something, something I don't usually need, though this time I did need it and I love the feel of its soft, brushed cotton on my skin.

I squeeze my hot water bottle against my tummy. Lime green curtains are still closed. It is 10.30 in the morning. A swish of the door brings in a cool draught and Brendan strides through. 'Get up will you. It's late.' His rough, morning voice, grates. He yawns and stretches his arms towards the ceiling.

'I'm too comfortable.'

'Here's a letter for you.'

Through the air sails the white A5 envelope, landing next to the sofa. The sliding sound of the curtains opening further pierces my tranquility.

The letter is post marked, London. Excited—the only post for two weeks, I tear it open. The writing seems familiar and as my eyes focus from out of bleary sleep I recognize it. It is Peter's scribble joined up, like skipping rope writing. *Dear Alice*

I hope you are well and painting. The other day I saw a scholarship for young artists, offered in the Andvil Arts Centre, Italy. I thought immediately of you. I think you have a good chance. Why

*not apply? I can give you a good reference. I have enclosed the details
and an application form. Let me know soonish.*
  Peter

If anyone else had suggested I applied for a scholarship I
would have hidden, but Peter suggested it and he knows my
work.

I'll ask 'Quick Print' to photo ten pictures. They are the—
just down the road—specialists of wedding photography. I'm
sure they will do my paintings. I choose pink shrimps with
their beady black eyes, silvery mackerel, glistening in all
colours—rainbow trout, tiny pinhead fish and some life
drawings of Vanessa and her robust figure, done in charcoal
and chalk.

When finished I put them all in an A4 envelope taking care
to seal it, and then, send it down the stern looking mouth of
the bright red, standing tall, like a policeman, post box.

*

That same week, for the first time, Brendan brings a woman to
the house.

Matilda makes me look like a turnip. She has a delicate
nose and sea-green eyes. Looks like a model out of Kay's
Catalogue Clothing for Women. A perfect figure slipped into a
costume of all black, I wonder if she has black moods as well.
The only relief from the black, long and slender nails, painted
pink.

'Alice, meet Matilda. We work in the same unit. We're going
out to Jenny's Nightclub. Want to come with us?'

Tongue tied, unable to say, yes or no, I think of other
evenings, when Brendan is out without me when panic rises,
walls close in, fearful thoughts attack and all I can see or think
about are cakes. With relief at not having to face that struggle,

I say, yes.

Brendan is wearing a black shirt. He never wears black. I have my beige, woolen skirt and matching cardigan, which Diana bought me as a treat, from C&A's. I don't think it is right for a nightclub, but I don't know what to wear anymore.

Spring has a chilly nip in the air. It's eleven o'clock, we set off in the dark. Our footsteps rapid to shake off the cold, the passing traffic smoking warm unpleasant fumes and we begin to run to catch our bus.

Brendan sits beside me and Matilda opposite, but they may as well be together, I'm invisible, they talk. Brendan keeps his hand on my knee, poor me, a pathetic old dog.

There is a queue for Jenny's Place, full of colour: People in glitter dresses, fishnet tights, high shoes on wedges, like cheese made of cork and tight sexy trousers. Some have leggings in luminous colours, bright pinks and lime greens. Matilda blends well with them, but I wonder if they will let me in, in my plain woolen outfit, but we shuffle by the two men, burly, boxers with large muscles in their necks, guarding the door.

Jenny's is thick with people and smoke. A swirling mass picked out by the coloured lights, like fish in a fog. The music booms and I watch the dancers. Some let their wild arms and legs move independent from their bodies. Others move in tiny steps, they keep repeating. I wonder they don't get bored. A flashy man in white trousers twists and dives. I watch them, sipping my gin, until my head feels hazy, separating from my torso and drifting upwards.

Matilda and Brendan talk. I try to stand. My limbs unfold and feel okay. I walk towards the space on the outside of the dance floor and join the shoal of people. My feet don't know what to do. I copy the woman in front, trying to find the rhythm. After a few tries the hum of the music enters me, my feet no longer feel encased in concrete and my octopus arms twist and turn. Memories of my holiday with Derek and the clubs, the dancing, and the freedom jog me along in a mist of pleasure.

Looking at the floor, I notice another pair of feet moving in my space. I look up and see a kind, young, boyish face, with a mop of curly hair. Nervous, I dance on. My space gets smaller and smaller. The curly haired person's smile encourages me and I find my stalk legs loosening even more and my feet following until the beat gets easier and I'm dancing as if on a springy mattress. All the bad feelings, the guilt which appears from nowhere, the jealousy when I see Brendan with one of his nurse friends and the anxiety about nothing, vibrates out of me. Then, the music changes, the dance floor begins to empty, people form couples and the beat slows.

'I'm Charlie, would you like to dance?'

Charlie looks very relaxed, arms dangling beside him, not like mine with my hands trying to comfort each other.

'I'd love to, but my boyfriend wouldn't like it. He's over there in the corner, he'd see me.'

'Not next to the woman in black?'

'Yes, that's Matilda.'

'But, he has his arm around her and they're almost . . . kissing?' His eyes open wide.

I shrug my shoulders. 'It's like that.' A black hole opens up in my stomach and tiredness creeps into my bones and into my soul.

Like bumper cars we jolt our way across the dance floor to the corner. Brendan looks up and straightens himself. 'Brendan, this is Charlie, Charlie Brendan.'

Brendan, his arm hooked around Matilda has a smile on his face. A smile which says, *I have been drinking*. Matilda, still as a doll, awkward in her silence, reminds me of me!

Charlie put his arm around my shoulders. It feels like a

235

safety belt and the gap between Brendan and me widens. My drinks change from gin to vodka, fog blurs thoughts as they try to speak. Squashed onto the bench a silence keeps us together, taut as a line of wire, until 3.o'clock when the room is flooded with light revealing squinting eyes, painted faces and a floor leaking with spilled drinks.

'Let's get a cab,' Says Matilda.

Like being in a cubicle, though we are all in a taxi, we sit close together. Me with Charlie opposite Matilda and Brendan, very odd, but I quite like it. Brendan's face falls forward and stays there as though hung by a noose, his head bobbing to the movements of the taxi as he sleeps. Matilda looks out of the window until her stop at Clifford Street. Charlie's stop is next.

'I've got to go now, but here is my number. You can ring me anytime. I'm going back home to Scotland on Saturday. Take care.' His lips brush my cheek leaving an imprint of pleasure.

A sharp pang runs through me. I'm on my own again. But, then I think of Charlie.

43

I Think I'm Going to be Crazy about You

Charlie stays in my mind like the trails of a favourite scent. The memory of the night leaves me tall, straight and beautiful, or, at least feeling attractive to someone.

I turf out bundles of clothes, retrieving a crush of mini skirts I used to wear for Brendan. Out struggles the skirt I wore for my interview at Herald World, unleashing itself from the tight pack of clothing. I slip it on and tuck in a white cotton blouse. Picking up my bag, light footed, I swing open the front door and drive off to work.

'You're looking smart, Alice. Mr. Burke is coming this afternoon for his demonstration.'

Like super glue my eyes fix onto the screen where I will work on the mysteries of a new software package, finding out its treasures and its downfalls before presenting it to Mr. Burke.

Two hours flash by. My eyes begin to flicker and my mind drifts.

I must phone Charlie. No, he's too young and I have too many problems it wouldn't be fair. Just to talk to him . . . but he lives in Scotland.

My hand hovers over the phone, but returns to the keyboard. I remember Diana's words, 'You're doing very well at your new job, but you don't look well. I can tell something's wrong.'

She can't have seen the bruise on my arm. Didn't I cover it up when I last saw her? Yes.

The days are longer and, feeling like sketching, I drive along the High Road until I arrive at a pub, The Feathers. I love this pub, a collection of ties hang from the walls like giant tickets. Beautiful colours and pictures adorn them, one with horses galloping across, another with Mickey Mouse, and yet another with a poor fox running, probably away from hounds.

Nestling myself into a dark corner with a little square table and a good view of people, I begin to draw hands. Hands holding glasses, propping up chins, shaking salt over heaps of chips, confident hands, timid, large and gnarled—rooted in their branches or flying, kite-hands.

After about an hour another pair of hands came into sight, very close to me. They're on the table next to mine, rolling up a cigarette. Lovely job! I begin to draw them.

Like a burst of sunshine comes the hat on his head. How can I not draw that, too? Wide brimmed, made of straw it throws shadows over his striking features, though I prefer older, wrinkly people to draw. His jaw makes a sweeping line from large neck to chin. Everything about him is like satin, so perfect. His hat makes a wholesome round shape around his face. Not many people if any in Darlington would wear a hat and not one with such a wide brim, except the teenagers wearing baseball caps, which stick out like duck beaks.

'Hey, can I see?' He leans towards me with hopeful, clear grey eyes.

'Oh, sorry, I hope you don't mind. I was just sketching your hands.'

I push the sketchbook two inches his way, not too far as I'm not sure I want him to see. My attempt at drawing his long lean hands feels all wrong, out of proportion and like I'd never drawn hands before.

'Hey, that's good! You've got style!'

'Thanks. So have you, I mean with your hat.'

'My name's Tom.'

'Alice.'

'Nice to meet you, Alice.'

A pause fits in before a torrent of sentences rush onto each other, colliding all the way.

'Do you live here?'

'About ten minutes away. And you?'

'Just around the corner.' The pupils in his eyes are becoming enormous. They seem to take up the space of the pub.

'Do you come here often?' *Oh, God that sounded corny* . . .

'Every night, same time, after work.'

'What do you do?'

'I work on a building site in Dowley, I'm a student working in my holidays.'

'You look like a student, with your straw hat.'

Our conversation claims two hours carrying us away on a magic carpet, which never once touches on my past. I relax into my words, not like with Brendan. I'm frightened of saying the wrong thing to him.

'Do you have a boyfriend?'

'Yes.'

'Is there something wrong? You look sad, after being so happy.'

'It's just that he drinks a lot and spends most of the time on the phone talking to other women.' My outburst surprised me.

His face hardens, focuses on my arm. I had accidentally pushed up my sleeve, forgetting the bruise.

'Why do you stay with him?'

'I don't know anymore.'

'Perhaps you should leave him . . . I'll speak to my landlord, Ken. He has a spare room if you ever need one.'

My eyes, growing larger, snatch up the space between us.

'Oh, don't worry. It'll pass. It's just when he drinks.'

'No worries.' He puts his hand on my arm, for a second.

Tears flicker until I squeeze them away.

'I have to go now. Here's my number. Call me anytime.'

*

'It's the Ireland versus England match on Friday night. I'm inviting Catherine and Matilda over. Why don't you invite someone?' Brendan says, passing by, holding a mug of tea. My eyes look down at the carpet. I try to hide my astonishment, why is he asking me?

Tom's face appears in my mind for the hundredth time that day, teasing me. *I'll invite Tom. I can cook an enormous cauliflower cheese.* The smell starts to dance in my nostrils.

The nearest phone box is the pillar-box red one on the corner. Two of its windows have been smashed and it smells of urine and fags and encloses you like you've stepped into a greenhouse. But, I daren't risk using the house phone because I know the way I talk to Tom will infuriate Brendan. I can't help myself. My voice sings out like fairy lights would if they could.

From outside the phone box, comes rain tapping on the window, plunging into our conversation. I can smell the water. It seeps under the door and through the broken windows it spit spots on my legs. As I talk to Tom our enthusiasm grows and we talk fast and loud.

Friday and the baked potatoes, their skins crisp and dark, bring the smell of warm winter fires into the house. An excited Toby wrings his hands, stepping from one foot to the other. There will be the football and all these new people to meet. Just as there is a knock on the door Toby pounces on the doorknob and I wonder if it will be Catherine or Matilda and if Tom will come. Of course he will come.

'Alice, its Tom for you.'

'Hello, yes it's me again. How are you?' His large frame squashes the doorway.

Even though he is six feet tall and bear-like, he is light as meringue. I've never met anyone so cheerful. I didn't know cheerfulness like this could exist except in movies. Brendan laughs a lot when he's with other people, but is cauldron-black when with me. Now his face grows like a big red cyst, eyes getting bigger and harder as Tom steps in to the slightly humid hallway.

'You said you were inviting someone, but what's this?' Brendan says in a rough voice while Tom waits, holding his bottle of wine. Ignoring Brendan, striding past him out of the kitchen, I take the bottle of wine from Tom. It's cold to touch and comes with a sophisticated label 'Jacob's Creek'. I never know what drink to serve people and always ask them if they want to drink ours first, which is in a box, from Tesco's and is red. I'm glad I bought a large packet of peanuts to eat as they will have to wait for the cauliflower cheese.

The cauliflower cheese turns out perfect. There's no Catherine, just me, Toby, Tom, Matilda and Brendan. We have treacle pudding bought from Tesco's, and custard, which I make for dessert. Tom especially likes the cauliflower cheese, Brendan likes the treacle pudding, and Toby likes everything. I have drunk a bit too much too care.

The conversation over dinner seems sparse and spiky like cacti in a desert.

'Its starting.' says Brendan.

Moving into the sitting room we take over the mushroom beanbags and stretch ourselves over the chairs. Matilda and Brendan share the settee, sitting legs and hands touching. Humiliation begins to creep into my reddening cheeks until I catch Tom smiling and winking at me as if he knows my thoughts.

Football matches are boring, but I like watching people running and even though they are small because they are on TV, you still get a feeling of space and freedom. I feel sorry for the goalkeeper who seems to have nothing to do. Brendan sits there mouth open, hands clasped between knees, looking on in wonder and apprehension. Toby still seems to be looking at his feet though looks up occasionally and Tom is thoughtful, leaning on his hand. He's wearing a dark green T-shirt and a different pair of combat trousers, darker green, but lighter material. I can't imagine being with him. I'm with Brendan—resigned to my prison.

Stuart was in the army and he never wore combat trousers, only brown trousers with perfect creases down the middle of each leg. Combat trousers have lots of pockets you can put things in. From one of his pockets Tom slips out a tiny packet and a small tin. He rolls himself a cigarette.

'Does anyone want one?'

'I'll have a puff.' I cough and my eyes begin to water.

Bored I get up and go to the table, pick up the empty cauliflower dish and build a pile of dishes on top until I have only a finger left free to open the kitchen door with. I make the water extra hot and soapy, plunging my hands into it, reddening them. The plates float fish-like until weighed down by more plates.

I feel the presence of someone coming into the room, it isn't Brendan, there's no squeak of his trainers on the linoleum kitchen floor, it isn't Toby because he shuffles and this person is quiet as a shadow.

'Do you want a hand with the dishes?' enquires Tom.

'Yes please, but don't you want to watch TV?'

'No, never been one for football.'

Tom looks around for the tea-towel which as usual can never

be found, so I get a new one which comes all the way from Devon and has a picture of a cow's head on it in a background of green. It reminds me of the Devonshire cream teas I used to have with Diana and Stuart on holiday. It's one of the things Diana gave me, but she only gave me one, I would have liked more tea towels and less bathmats as we have four of those and only one bathroom, whereas we are always short of tea towels.

In a red hot silence, afraid of dropping something in front of Tom, I listen to the soothing clinking of the dishes in the water. Tom wipes the dishes dry while I wash them until they are squeaky-clean. Our arms brush, our elbows bump,

A mug slips from my soapy hands, crashing on the tiles, breaking its handle. We both make to pick it up. Our fingers touch as we reach out for it. I feel a rush of prickles light up my spine.

A roar breaks into the moment, 'Ireland! Ireland!'

Ireland must have won the match. But, as the bells ring loud and clear, a tingling feeling rushes through my body as Tom's beaming eyes mirror mine saying: *I think I'm going to be crazy about you*

44

The Spare Room

Brendan or Brenny as Matilda calls him, cries, 'Bye, see you tomorrow.' His words spill out, sentences fold into one another, his empty vodka bottle by his side, 'Ireland, Ireland!'

Heaving himself up from the sofa he staggers forward to an apprehensive Matilda. Toby is in bed, sleeping and snoring and snug, Tom on his bike going home.

Cushions everywhere, beer cans, and plates still leftover. The house has become a large dustbin. Collecting cups is the first thing to do, one by one as I feel pretty tipsy and tired myself. But a smile rolls out from cheek to cheek as I think of Tom.

I stretch tall to itch the sleepiness out of my bones. Just as I'm relaxing, I feel a hideous weight thrust into my back, I gasp, shocked, an enormous shaft of pain shoots across. By the force of this I tumble forward, head to toe in different directions, landing on my chin and breast across the sofa, body following.

I struggle to a position where I can turn my head and there in front of me with a plank of wood is Brendan with a smear smile over his face. He sways under the weight of alcohol.

'Tom, so that's who you're dolled up for?'

He throws the wood aside and stares at me with iron eyes, I look away catching the beer stained carpet, feeling nausea and in pain. I can hear the door bang as he leaves the room.

I try to sit up, but for a few minutes my body lies limp. Inch by inch I move until I am behind the large sofa, safe in case Brendan comes back. I don't want to anyone to see me and upstairs seems too far away.

*

Uncomfortable, I doze, unable to move. I wait for the morning and Brendan to go to work. The door closing wakes me up. I touch my face and pass my hand over the crinkly pattern left by the carpet.

'Bye, Toby.'

'Bye, Brendan. Alice going with you?'

'Nope.'

I hear the noise of a bike down the garden path. The big black racer, the bike Brendan left for me before going to America, the bike I had an accident on, but is now fixed and once again Brendan's.

From out of the sofa I come and try to stand up. Its okay, I can stand up straight, I ache a lot, though and can feel something moist. Blood is coming from a small wound on my hips. Perhaps the plank had a nail in it. I recognised it from the day before. Toby had taken down an old shelf.

Nine o'clock chimes on Toby's Grandfather clock. Longing for fresh air, I reach out for my jacket, putting my hand in its deep pocket. I feel a piece of paper—Tom's address. Toms face appears like a mirage.

*

I stand on the bottom step of 40, Cherwell Road feeling very short. I stretch up and knock. There's not a sound. Impatient, I wait. Knock. Lean my ear to the door. Nothing.

'Hi! Coming in for some lunch?'

I gasp in surprise. A large Tom comes up from the street, walking in front of me, opens the door with a twist of the key, and enters. My hands are trembling. Is he really pleased to see me again? It's a windy day, the wind carrying the scent of newly cut grass.

'How would you like to share an omelette with me? Hey, you look a bit frightened. Something up? Come and sit down.'

'I'm okay, just need a glass of water.'

'You don't look okay. Do you want to talk about it?'

'Not just yet, thanks. Just like to sit still for a while.'

'Sure, take your time.'

'In fact, I'd like to talk about anything, but my problems.'

'I'll show you round the house and after I'll cook an omelette which you have no obligation to eat.'

*

The house is like a building site with paintbrushes everywhere and the smell of gloss paint. But Tom says Ken the landlord likes aikido and not DIY, that's why the house is never finished. He practises in the living room. I'm used to fitted-carpets, not floorboards, but it all seems exciting.

In the kitchen is a chunky woman with lank, black hair clutching the sides of her face. She puts fish fingers in a frying pan, covers them in lots of oil, and heats them. I have never fried food before—far too many calories—but am sure you heat the oil first. I don't think she is well in the head, like me, but I wouldn't do that with fish fingers.

Tom sits crossed legged in the middle of his room surrounded by books and clothes. Books I long to pick up and explore. I used to love reading, but with Brendon it seems so out of reach. There is only one shelf in the room and that's full of all sorts of objects I can't make out. I'm smiling as I half expect an animal to crawl out from somewhere and wouldn't mind if it did and because the bedroom seems so friendly.

Most of his clothes are khaki coloured. I wander if he has ever wanted to be in the army, but no, he says, he is against war and would refuse to go. He has weak lungs so they probably won't let him. I can't imagine Tom with weak lungs since he looks so fit and handsome. I'm glad to be a woman.

He surprises me by bringing out a pack of colourful, large cards. I know of brightly dressed women at fairs with some like them, but they don't fit the image I have of khaki, combat-trouser wearing, Tom. He offers me a reading. The cards are beautiful, rich with colours, figures, and shapes. A card with cups and swords reminds me of a medieval castle.

'Oh no! Not a skeleton!' I cry.

His lemon meringue laugh appears, making me want to cry out once more, just to hear it again.

'That's a good thing. It means transformation.'

I wonder if he is going to tell me I'll meet a handsome man and run away with him, but he tells me all about things I already know. Waiting to hear something new, my eyes begin to stray until Tom exclaims, 'Watch out, your health is at risk, physical and mental.'

'Both!'

'Yes, but don't take me too seriously, I'm learning. On the other hand you came in looking rough. You look much better now. And you're sitting up straight. Is it your back which is hurting?'

'Yes, my lower back.'

Putting his hand there he massages it, with light, patient movements. I wince where it hurts, but his soft touch relaxes me.

'I'd see a doctor.'

Panic returns for a second as I think of what a doctor might say, and how I'd explain.

The bedroom feels warmer and I have pins and needles.

My blue suede miniskirt stops me from sitting cross legged so I sit on my knees with my ankles tearing away at the crimson, worn carpet, dying to move.

'Do you ever wear long dresses?'

'No, but my mother sent me a long green dress through the post, it's nice with pale green elephants on. Bit hippy.'

'Have to take you shopping.'

Is he joking, I wonder.

'Brendan will want to know where I am.' A dark, starry sky outside and the thought of a big black taxi ready to take me home comes into my mind, just as Tom touches my knee, 'Do you want to stay the night? I can sleep on the couch.'

The warm room invites me to stay. Seconds of staring at the bookcase squashed with books, and books on top of books, with thick dictionaries and skinny novels haunting the shelves, feels like minutes. I wish I had been somewhere long enough to collect so many books. A cosy bean bag in the corner, cushions up against the walls and a mattress lying against one side of the room. My back begins to hurt again and I could just lie down and go to sleep.

'I had better not. It's just that . . .' The words run out like a speeding car, 'I'll get into trouble.'

I begin to stand up, my aching back making me twinge. 'It's Brendan, isn't it? You know you can stay here if you need to.'

'I'd better go home.'

'I'll get you a taxi. You be careful now.' It's as though he is sending me away to some land inhabited by man eating plants. On the way out is an even taller man, Ken, who speaks with soft words, 'Alice, You know you're welcome anytime. You can have the spare room.'

45

Pecking Like Crows

I step into the porch taking my black, leather biker-jacket, I nicked in 1985. The last thing I ever stole. Guilt creeps over me as I put it on, but it is my favourite jacket, with silver studs and big shoulders, which make me feel important.

My 10.45 coach is late and the pale sky starts spitting rain. There is a tiny patch of blue, I don't think the rain will last, it is very light. I stay under the cover of the bus stop, worrying my mascara will run, though often I rub my eyes and look like a panda.

The bus stop is outside a famous Pizza place called, The Hippo Pizza Palace, which serves mainly students: intellectual, sporty, carefree, worried, and, in-love, students. All served with gigantic baked pizzas swelling with toppings. I can smell the dough cooking and the cheese melting. It isn't that far from lunchtime.

The coach driver is a man, black with a wide smile and shiny white teeth with bright crimson gums.

'A day-return ticket to London, please.'

'Okay, love.'

I don't mind a handsome man calling me love.

Today is the day I'm going to see Professor Lucas to ask him for help. My yellow-brick road is the grey M40. Professor Lucas only listens and never gives answers, but today I hope he will.

I fall asleep on the rocking, rolling coach, until the bus

driver calls out, 'London Paddington.' People stand up, reach for their bags and coats from the shelves above squashing me and leaning on me, I feel like pushing them away. I wait until all have gone before stretching my legs and letting out a huge sigh, remembering again where I am and why.

It is over three years since I have been to Blackheath Road. The building work has almost been finished, but there is still the noise of a road digger, which makes the thoughts in my head jump up and down. The steps to the hospital seem steeper this time. There is the old brass doorknocker shaped like a hand. I always feel I am touching a real one.

'Come in,' cries a deep familiar voice.

I open the wide wooden door and a hand thrusts forwards and shakes mine, his strong definite movements sending rivers of hope through me.

But the room starts to tumble. My thoughts, gathered together on the way here, sway in silence alongside the swaying lamp,'

'Here, sit down.'

The invite comes just in time as my mind goes black my bottom finds the cool seat and the room turns the right way up.

For a moment, besides his breathing and my heart beating, the room is in silence.

'What has been happening, Alice?'

'It's difficult to . . .' I hide behind my large white hanky, another of Diana's bargains.

'He tried to strangle me . . .' Words screeched not spoken. 'And yesterday he hit me with a plank of wood.'

I stare at my handkerchief now a tight ball in my fist shaped hands.

'This is Brendan?'

'Yes,' gasping for air.

'I see.' His bushy eyebrows lift and a frown appears along his wide forehead. I can feel his eyes warming the space I am in.

The next few words cut like diamonds. 'I have to advise you to leave Brendan.' But, to my surprise they are just what I want to hear.

'If he is being violent, he won't stop. You are at risk of further abuse if you stay with this man. For your own safety, it is best not to tell him, just go quietly. If you still love him it will be difficult.'

'I wanted to talk to you about something else.'

'Yes . . .'

'I have met someone, a nice man.'

Tears start to spill, the large handkerchief dots with moisture. 'And what is his name?'

'Tom.'

'Well, this relationship will continue, if it has a future, for now concentrate on leaving Brendan.

A rare moment—Professor Lucas telling me which path I should take.

*

The door slams shut, no good-byes anymore, just the sound of the bike peddling down the drive. It takes forty minutes for Brendan to cycle to work. Today he leaves his sandwiches. With fear nestled in my throat I call him on his work number. Matilda answers. My heart chills and my voice trembles.

'Is Brendan there?'

'Yes, Alice,' comes her firm confident voice.

'Brendan, you've forgotten your sandwiches.'

'I'll get something from the canteen.'

Good he's at work and he won't be coming home.

251

First of all the pullovers. It's spring and I don't need all of them. Pushing as many into a rucksack as I can, red, black, grey, blue, all in and off to 40, Cherwell Avenue. Ken is waiting.

'Difficult?'

'No, no, I have left Brendan my green jumper, he loves it so much.'

Little things go first, rubbers, pencils, notebooks, socks, forming a trail all the way to 40, Cherwell Avenue. Until there are some very big things left like my easel and the rest of my paintings.

I wish Brendan would notice something. I'm sad, relieved, and disappointed, all at once. The room seems less like a home, without my things. Brendan never has much, enough to fill a suitcase, always thinking that one day he might get up and go somewhere.

I'm not going to take the television or the Hoover, which are mine, but Brendan will need them. In spite of all the floorboards in Ken's house he has a Hoover.

Tom rubs his large hands together, impatient to help out to carry things, but most of all wanting to be at the house with me in case Brendan appears. One day Tom did come, I held my body stiff and alert. Afraid Brendan might come back at anytime!

'That's why I'm here, to protect you. But don't worry, its okay I saw him in the City Centre. I said hello, but he was in a hurry. If I didn't know you I would think he was a perfectly normal guy.'

'Well, he's not.'

*

The carpeted stairs of the house are steep, but I leap down two by two.

'You're looking good. Not for me though, of course not! I'm going to be late tonight.'

Since when has he ever bothered to tell me that! Thank goodness he doesn't ask me what's in my bulging bag.

'Nothing unusual,' I answer back.

'What?'

'That you're going to be late.' My cheekiness shines.

Days clutch each other as I prepare to leave. Most of my things have gone from the bedroom.

'Have you tidied up?'

'Yes. I've thrown away a lot of things.'

I look around the house. It seems to be whispering to me. *Time for you to go.*

*

A giant Tom will be waiting, a thin Ken and the frying fish-fingers, girl. I have somewhere to go to.

'By the way,' Brendan boomed in my ears. My sister is coming to stay for the weekend.'

'This weekend!'

'I haven't seen you to tell you. Where have you been lately? You're hardly ever here. Can you pick her up from the airport, with me, Friday night?'

'Yes, of course. Brendan . . .'

'What?'

'I have something to tell you.'

'I don't have time to listen, not now.'

'Later, then . . .' My heart lifts a beat with relief.

*

Out of the dark, dense night, the fourth day of Moira's stay, comes a shuddering shout,

'No!' Brendan's nightmare. He shouted it so loud I think it must wake everyone, but no one runs into our room.

I switch on the red, pleated bedside lamp. Brendan's breathing weighs heavy in the air. He is a few inches away from me. A long time has passed since we have curled up in each other's arms. I can smell his salt sweat.

'Are you okay, Brendan? Wake up.'

'A nightmare . . . An awful nightmare, I had a dream that the walls of this house were falling in, the bricks tumbling down, dust everywhere and objects crashing down. I had a terrible feeling of losing a part of me. I just checked my legs to see if they are still here, that I am all here. It must be something else I have lost. It was a frightening nightmare.'

'Perhaps you are losing something.'

He glimpses sideways, his face so far away in fear, looks at me with glazed eyes, a beast ready for slaughter.

I lie in the silence. After a deep breath, 'Brendan, there is something I have to tell you. I'm leaving.'

The silence almost becomes stagnant before Brendan utters, 'It's Tom isn't it?'

'No Brendan. It's me. I just have to go.'

I felt a hand, the hand of the Brendan I first met, melting into mine, and his warm soft voce, that I hadn't heard for what seemed like years.

'Sorry. It's me isn't it?'

'No. I want to leave.' Tears spread across my cheeks, my breathing seems to cease.

'You won't survive on your own. I know you. Don't go.'

'I have to. I have to go. I can drive us all to the airport and I won't be coming back home after.'

'You're things disappearing. I thought something was strange. You haven't been talking to someone. Somebody's told you to do this?' His voice is still gentle.

'No, Brendan. Nobody.'

On the way back from the airport I want to drive so fast, Brendan will stick to the side of the car. That way he can't touch me, hate me, or love me. I reach 100 mph and frighten myself. My tears sit in the corner of my eyes pecking like crows.

46

Buttons in a Distant Universe

The bedroom has a dusty, 'nobody's here' feel to it. Not even the sneeze of a ghost. Downstairs my things long to be put into place. A chest of draws, four shelves and a wardrobe wait, mouths open. Ken said I could put my pictures behind the settee. "Not on the walls. I like my walls bare and white."

The view from the room looks out over a street lined with tall elegant lampposts. Rows of gardens, some with neat privet hedges and others spilling out onto the pavement with grass filling cracks and runaway footballs.

From out of my shoulder bag, the clock chatters the time away, nudging me to reflect on how long it is since I last saw Brendan. One week on Tuesday. Already my mind feels uncluttered, like an empty wastepaper basket.

My fingers begin to crave for a pencil, a 6B, soft and dark. *But, please not fish again*! I feel like drawing something different. I remember an art tutor in my past, Mathew Taunton, saying, 'Try to keep to the same subject, because you keep on changing! Go out to the market today and draw. Choose one sketch you like, paint whatever it is and don't stop.' But that was five years ago. If only Mathew could see my collection of fish pictures now. Fish in bags, on stalls, at the markets, tiny, multi-couloured, silver, mouths turned down, eyes moist and staring, pretty prawns with black beady eyes and lobsters with spiky pincers.

'Alice!'

Interrupted from wondering thoughts, I turn my head, my neck creaks giving it the jab of a hot poker.

'Yes?'

'Brendan on the phone, do you want me to say you're not here?'

What does he want? I left all the CD's and kept only one set of photos.

A pearl soft voiced Brendan comes down the tunnel, into the room. 'Hello, Alice. I've been worried about you. How are you?'

'I'm okay. I can't talk to you, Brendan. I have to go.'

'No wait! Oh, Alice I miss you.'

'Stop, Brendan.'

'I'm wearing your favourite cap the one you always used to wear.'

'It's no good.'

'Can I see you?'

Gripping the phone, I sit down, waiting for the trembling waves to subside. Tom's arm snakes around my waist and his chin rests on my head. With numb lips I say, 'No, I can't meet you, Brendan.'

.

*

Soothed by the pinkness of the room's walls, I rummage in the deep, dark pocket of my bag. I find a pen, but putting words on the page isn't easy and my hands still shake.

The dull sound of the phone downstairs reaches the bedroom door and I sigh. *Not for me this time . . .*

'Alice! It's for you again. It's Matilda.'

Her voice comes down the phone etched in acid, scratching and pleading. 'Alice, I'm so sorry to phone you.'

'What's wrong? You sound upset'

'I need help.'

'Speak slowly, take a deep breath.'

'It's Brendan. Alice, he's gone crazy.'

'He is crazy!'

'He's drinking too much.'

'Not beating you up, I hope.'

'Yes. I don't know what I've done.'

'Nothing, you've done nothing.'

'Alice, I've moved in with him. He couldn't bear to be alone after you moved out.'

'You've got no choice. You have to leave him.' I say, solemn, reading from the tomb-like book in my mind.

That evening, lying on the settee, head resting on Tom's shoulder, rain persevering on the window panes, Brendan and Matilda become tiny as buttons, in a distant universe.

47

A Rude Parrot

'I want to paint like Van Gogh, fill the world with colour!' Tom moves back, out of the way of my gesturing hands.

'Whoa! Hey, you've got some ambition.'

'Yes and you're a bit of a dark horse. Tell me about your family.'

'Right then, not much to say, Dad's a very brave fireman who unfortunately likes his drink too much and spending money. My big sis, Sandra is a nurse. Always pissing me off because she thinks she's right, but I love her. And there's Mumbo who you'll meet very soon. She's not frightening. And, like you I dream. I dream of becoming a monk.'

'What and have your lovely golden hair shaven off!'

'You haven't told me that much about yourself—apart from wanting to be a second Van Gogh.'

'I'm tired all of a sudden'

'You've got that sad look on your face again.'

'I could do with some sleep.'

The hospital and the parlour—giants in my mind—stay secrets, in little grey boxes.

One day Tom comes into my room looking flushed.

'I've got an opportunity to go to Romania to help in an orphanage for three months.'

Guilt spread-eagled across his face. Tom had seen the advert in a local newspaper for a fit healthy person.

'I applied months ago, before we met, but had given up

hope as I hadn't heard from them.'

'I thought you wanted to be a monk?'

'Sorry, I know this might be a bit of a shock.'

The news of his voyage acts like a golden key to my grey boxes. Unlocked, the truth pours out. The wick burns right down on the fat, white, church candle and my mouth dries from talking, making my voice hoarse.

'I knew food was a problem for you, but I didn't realize it was that much of a problem! So next time my biscuits disappear, I'll know where they've gone.'

'I don't do it anymore. I have to tell you one other thing. I worked in a parlour, the sort that pleases men.'

'What. That sort!'

'Yes. What are you thinking? That I'm dirty or cheap?'

I glance up for a second expecting to see a look of disgust on Tom's face, but his cheeks seemed to have become paler and his open wide in concern.

'No. Not at all, just that it can be dangerous and well, if you were ill.'

Tom lowers his head, deep in thought, then stretches his arms, locks his fingers until they click. Changing the subject, he asks,

'Where did you get those nice ankleboots from?'

'Oh!' I exclaim, my cheeks flushing.

'Oh a client gave me them instead of money. But all that happened in Ireland,' I add quickly.

'So you have stopped?'

'Yes, of course.'

'Well, they're nice boots. I'm not going to ask you how much they cost!'

*

Three months seems like a jungle of bewildering days away from Tom. Would I splinter in two?

A leaping salmon appears in my dreams. Doors open and shut, the wind blows sea waves over me. One evening before going to bed, I clear out my black box of collages and there it is shimmering like a jewel, made from paper and watercolours, a picture of the leaping salmon I had painted at Peter's Studio.

'Here, I want to give you this. I pass over the six inch by eight inch painting to Tom's large hand. He studies it for a few minutes.

'Hey, this is stunning and I can fit it in my rucksack. I'll take it with me! It's beautiful, love.'

His kiss tastes sweet and his breath smells of oranges.

'I am coming back you know and you are coming to see me in Bucharest, aren't you?'

'Tom's a kind person, he won't let you down,' says, Elaine, Tom's mother. She takes a size XXXL, reminds me of a giant panda on two tiny feet and has red, chubby hands, which are clever with the needle, especially good at repairing Tom's trousers.

I stray away, frightened, from her Sunday dinners, which come with huge portions. Tom's stepfather, Joe, who is a stick insect, has a beard, which moves a lot when he talks and bright, bird-like eyes. Joe is the only other person who can't finish Elaine's roasts. When it comes to her homemade apple pie nothing will make me eat it, with all its custard filling up the bowl until it is a pond. But, I know I offend her because Tom mentions it to me. 'Can't you eat a little bit?'

Discovering Elaine's apple pie is like finding treasure in a forest. I ask for a tiny dollop and a spoonful of custard. 'Really, not much, I can't eat much.' Finishing it in seconds I wish I had the same size pile as everyone else.

The apple pie opens a flood gate. From our local pizzeria we buy glaring pizzas in equally large white boxes, and Tom

261

piggybacks, tipsy me to the off license. Under the laughter of chocolate and the begging wine, time breathes light notes, even after plunging onto the scales one day and discovering I have put on five pounds.

Visiting Diana, her triangular face and long slim neck perk up when she sees Tom.

'Dance with me.' She always asks him.

'Think your mum fancies me.'

I laugh, happy and secure. I tell Diana about my weight gain, 'I can't see any lumps,' I say

'No, none to see, you look beautiful. But, you're not pretty enough for Tom. He'll wander,' chirps Diana, like a rude parrot.

48

The Painter

It is a dry, dusty day. The earth is cracked and trails of ants cross the path. Ken's garden is very small, just big enough for two white, metal chairs, a table and pots of geraniums and nasturtiums. I begin to water the plants, when glancing at my watch I see it is five forty. I put on my shoes and start to make my way slowly to the newsagents, heart thumping in anticipation of meeting Tom on the way back from work.

In the distance there is a large man, the sun is in my eyes, but I can see it is Tom from his walk, a slight swing, leaning to the left. Closer he comes until I am in his arms.

'You always seem to be going to the shop at the same time as I'm on my way. I am coming home you know.'

But, still I daren't believe him.

'Done anything nice today?'

'I'm trying to find something other than fish to paint, or at least paint fish in a different way.'

In a corner of the local library, on the last shelf below the section for thriller movies is a part kept for documentaries. My quicksilver eyes spot the video 'Twelve Chefs Cook Fish' Intrigued by the cluster of chefs in white hats, I take it to the desk to be stamped before burying it in my bag.

Putting the video on pause, I draw with bold lines and heavy shading. Chef's in their white uniforms, some with blue and white checked trousers and chattering hats, hovering over plates of fish.

'I've found something interesting to draw,' I yell out to Tom who is preparing stuffed potatoes, the smell of melting cheddar cheese filling the air.

Next day I phone up the Elizabeth restaurant,

'I'm wondering if I can draw the chef while he works?'

'Chef speaking, sure, but seven in the morning, after nine it gets too busy.'

I get up at six o'clock. It's a soothing part of the day the best time to be awake. The streets are quiet, the sound of one or two cars rumble as they start up and only early morning cleaners, on their way to clean offices, before the doors open. The builders come to the transport café for breakfast. I walk to Queen's Street. The bus service doesn't start until seven. Carrying an A4 sketchbook, pencils, sharpener and some bread in a green canvas bag, the bread is excellent for rubbing our pencil marks. I have lost my rubber.

'Sit up there, next to a sink.'

I soon peer down from the high edge at Terry's shiny hairless head. My legs dangle off the side. I feel age six.

Terry has a round stomach, a white apron and white trousers, both stained. His huge body leans over the table, arms moving in a chopping motion. Vegetables slaughtered into tiny pieces, stolid thick thighs keep him upright. His white hat disappears and reappears like a giant butterfly.

With all the objects: spoons different shapes and sizes, knives, two enormous sinks and a large chef, I feel squashed in the kitchen which is like a ship's cabin, swaying to and fro to the movements of Terry's heavy steel toe capped shoes.

He moves to a large pan, smelling of chocolate, teasing my nostrils. For a second, devil-faced French fancies float by, but they are nothing more than phantoms.

My hands glide again, with the movements of Terry, the pencil following the curve of a pan. I use a 6b to capture the intensity of stirring with the arm of a big wooden spoon and the denseness of the chocolate. Enraptured by the day I forget to accidentally bump into Tom on his way home.

On a humid morning the sun filters light through my curtains. I sit on my bed daydreaming of painting Terry stirring his chocolate fondant, amongst a display of spoons, spatulas, frying pans, colanders or even better flinging myself against Tom's big soft body. Funny, disconnected fantasies disturbed by the sound of the postman's van stopping and the rustle of envelopes through the box. I run down the stairs and take the long envelope, white as a dove, post marked, 'London'. Inside on a sheet of paper: *'We are pleased to offer you the Andvil Scholarship for painting . . . Andvil Arts Centre, Italy.'* The words warm my skin like rays of the sun. My breath seizes with inspiration. I launch myself into a drawing. And, later, Tom gives me a hug. Brendan would have been bright, lurid green with jealousy.

The month of June is here and I see the first butterfly of the year on the next door neighbour's buddleia, which hangs over our garden. It is a Peacock. My favourite butterfly is the Brimstone, which is very yellow, and also the Orange Tip, which is white with orange on the tips of its wings. But, I like the Peacock, too, because of its markings and its big peacock-feather eyes.

'You can have my room when I'm gone. I'll put all my things into the attic. It's a nice room.'

It is. It has a big bay window with a large ledge to put plants on.

'But where will you go when you come back?'

'You'll have to make room.' He whispers, tickling my ears.

But then, I find my painting scholarship begins on August 22nd, which means I will have to leave one week before Tom leaves for Bucharest. So we will leave the rooms as they are. The house will be empty, just Ken. Emily has gone into hospital, after setting the kitchen on fire with burning fish fingers and seeing the secret police again.

There are three dates circled on the calendar, one in yellow—the date I leave for Italy and the green one is the date Tom leaves. The third date on the month of November in red is for the date we are going to meet in Bucharest.

I jot all the dates down in my small, orange, velvet diary and put that in my rucksack, which I have to sit on to close, but the zips are very sturdy. I just about get it all in. I don't have to worry about my art materials, I receive them when I reach the centre.

The big black taxi is waiting. Tom helps me with my rucksack.

'Coach station, please.'

I give Tom a hug, wrapping my arms around him as far as they can reach. I only come up to his hairy chest, which is where I snuggle my head. I'm sad, but not too sad because I know it isn't for the last time.

*

Up and up into the hills, along the sidewinder roads, holding onto the seat, feeling a little dizzy; Italy rings loud in my ears. I murmur the words 'Casole d'Elsa' as they pass on the white road sign.

Arriving at the Arts Centre, a converted monastery with a prominent tower, I'm in a pocketful of happiness.

Digby, who is eighty, with an ancient face as brown as parchment, is my semi-famous professor. He shows in a London Gallery, walks everywhere with a wooden cane, stays near the castle and is afraid of falling. Digby is partially blind, but in a good light he can see my paintings.

'More contrast,' he says. 'Limit your colour.' Every word from Digby puts a spell over me.

Most days after lessons I climb up the stone, narrow steps to the top of the tower—forty steps with paints, easel and a large canvas. The view meets my gaze leaving me stunned. Cyprus trees form lines along golden fields dotted with roaming haystacks, looking like small cottages. A streaming blue sky and a burning midday sun, too bright to look at, though I try to take a glimpse, my eyelids like shutters. I'm like a wild animal as the light glares at me begging me to paint before it changes position. I brush, slap, scrape using bold colours, cobalt blue and lemon yellows, hints of cadmium red, dark viridian greens. After three hours, not satisfied, incensed by my attempts I hurl a bottle of turps at the painting and watch the colours streak and blur. Trees and fields melt into the sky. With a cloth and sponge I begin working into the paint, broad blocks of tone, simplifying the shapes I see. The new forms give my eye a rest and I stand back content. I gulp down water and let the heat shimmer through me, feeling every ray, soaking up the intensity. Three hours later in 44°C I remember my hat, which I put on, with its chin strap, so even the wind can't blow it away.

I love the heat, the air, my bedroom with its cool stone floor and simple white, cotton covered bed and Barabel the very large, black cat who sits in the corner of the court yard, under an olive tree, in a brick-red, clay pot and sleeps on my bed at night and eats chicken from my hands. I like being with the students with their easels and sun hats and sitting under a, stretching on blue, sky, even when a surprise, rolling thunderstorm pelts us with furious rain.

But, best of all, in my stomach lie a warm nugget, hugging me. It's Tom. Sometimes I imagine he's with me, his laughter floating to me over a beer. I imagine us meeting at an airport, on the way to Bucharest. The feeling of deep certainty, in him, and in my life coats me with an aura of gold.

A gentle breeze brings back my thoughts to the canvas, to the paint spirits dancing over the surface. As I pick up a stained, worn, filbert brush, every thought and feeling I have works through to my hands and fingers, into every brushstroke and I know I have found my passion again, to paint.

ACKNOWLEDGEMENT

My thanks go to the following, all of whom have contributed advice and insightful comments and kept me focused during the writing of this book: Jean Gill, Penny Napthine, the late and much missed Maureen Ploughman and Pat Thornton, Alan Diffey, Helen Ganly, Pierre Nicchini, my family for being there when I needed them and to Mary Wood, for her energy, and enthusiasm in carrying out a creative writing edit. For the final polish and edit, the cover, and for publishing *From Under the Bed* I am very grateful to the fantastic team at ROMAN Books.

JASON HINOJOSA

THE LAST LAWSONS

'A wonderfully subtle novel . . . this terse, deceptively simply told story is a moving study of how trauma can unwittingly be passed on through generations.' *The Bookseller*

'an impressionistic narrative . . . powerful' *Publishers Weekly*

Only one person knew that Ed Lawson used to watch his sister Mary Anne in the shower. But it is only in the more recent past when Althea, Ed's daughter, meets her Aunt Mary Anne at her father's funeral, that she starts to understand and reconcile her own resentment with a growing understanding of her parents' motivations, desires, and failures. Told in three distinct parts by the defeated Ed Lawson, his manic wife Josephine, and their bitter but earnest daughter Althea, this compelling tale of violence, sexual shame, and personal failure recounts the dreadful secrets of a broken family. In order to be healed, Ed, Josephine, and Althea must each tell their unique stories, and each of them must seek, acknowledge, and eventually accept "the fearful truth" about their pained and haunted lives together.

Jason Hinojosa taught literature and creative writing at schools in Florida and Hong Kong. He published a number of short stories and won two literary awards. *The Last Lawsons* is his debut novel.

Hardcover | £16.99 | $25.95
ISBN 978-93-80905-30-3
Available at your nearest bookstore

DAVID JAMES

DESCENDANTS OF EVIL

'An encouraging debut' *Library Journal*

Autumn, 1884. 10 Downing Street, London. Roger Evesham, a young Oxford graduate is unexpectedly summoned by Prime Minister Gladstone to investigate a gunpowder-plot that could have shaken the very root of Queen Victoria's government. During that time Roger has been suffering from an incurable emotional pain as his fiancé Amelia has abandoned him for Charles, Roger's friend. Roger accepts Gladstone's offer believing that it might help him to erase his emotional ache. As the investigation progresses Roger finds himself in the place of his late father who too, during his long service to government, was engaged in a similar case of gunpowder-smuggling that ended with the smuggler's suicidal death before he could be questioned by the police. But are these two affairs connected? Or does this descend from a forgotten past? As Roger continuously tries to save himself from the murderous attempts on him, he suddenly discovers that the clue to this mystery is connected to none other than a man whom Roger knows very well.

David James was born and brought up in Wales. He currently lives in Carmarthenshire with his wife. *Descendants of Evil* is his debut novel.

Paperback | 228pp | £8.99 | $13.95
ISBN 978-93-80905-24-2
Available at your nearest bookstore

www.roman-books.co.uk

MINI NAIR

THE FOURTH PASSENGER

'An inspirational story and a terrific read' *Publishers Weekly*

'A feel-good read' *The Bookseller*

'A lovely novel . . . affecting and inspiring' **Sashi Tharoor**

Set in Mumbai during the Hindu-Muslim conflict of the early 1990s, *The Fourth Passenger* is the story of four women raised with traditional Indian values, whose partnership give them the temerity to stand up against the religious extremism. Having reached their thirties and disillusioned with their lives and husbands, their decision to open an urban food stand is mingled with their memories of a distant past when two of them loved the same man. But, in order to establish their fledgling business, they must contend with individual temperament, extortionists, ruthless competitors, and most importantly, the prevailing religious intolerance.

Mini Nair has had two of her books published in India. A postgraduate in chemistry, Mini Nair lives with her family and twin daughters in Mumbai where she was also born and brought up. *The Fourth Passenger* is her first novel.

Paperback | 260pp | £8.99 | $13.95
ISBN 978-93-80905-25-9
Available at your nearest bookstore

www.roman-books.co.uk